I0819791

Tartarus and the Labyrinth

By Jonathan Gatsby

Published: Jonathan D. Dunham

Cover Designer: Ricky Gunawan

Editor: Nicole Smith Nieto

Formatted by: Brenda Wright – Formatting Done Wright

Chapter One

On the day appointed for the Sons of God to make a report, Lucifer as he had done so many times in the past, showed up with his brothers to present himself before God their Father. The Sons of God were a sect of angels that God created to specifically be his sons. The angels had thousands of different assignments, but the Sons of God were the elite and had the most power.

The Sons of God were ruling angels that were spread throughout the Universe. Man always assumed that they were the center of God's attention, just like they assumed for so long that they were the center of the Universe. God had so many other creations throughout the Universe, and rather than focus on all of them, God appointed his sons to rule over each of his creations. They were to bring daily reports of how his creations were doing.

Every Galaxy had at least one to three planets with life on them. God allowed his angels to rule over the planets and galaxies, and very rarely did God ever interfere. As on Earth, the creations on each planet formed religions and made their planet the focus of God's attention. Earth however was special. Lucifer led the first and only revolt in Heaven, and was cast down to Earth along with a third of the angels that fought with him against the Creator.

Over time, many of the angels became weary of following Lucifer, such as Rah, Ouranus, Odin and their families. They divided themselves into different realms over the Earth. Leaving the realm of Earth in Chaos with Odin ruling one part, Rah ruling another part, Ouranus ruling part and finally Lucifer ruling the last section. God the Father was displeased with how things were falling apart on Earth, and decided to destroy it. But another angel who was a Son of God, and also was a part of God, loved the planet earth and the humans that were on it. In Christianity this angel is known as Jesus.

He had watched them for a long time, and even aided the humans in secret when the ruling angels neglected them. As God was getting ready to destroy the world, that son sacrificed himself in human form. Suffering as a human in humility and pain. The realm still would belong to Lucifer, Rah, Ouranus and Odin. But anyone who accepted God's only son to be born in human form could escape the punishment that would befall Lucifer and all that were under his rule.

Many of the Sons of God were very aware of the results of the first tournament, where the demigods beat Lucifer's most ferocious beast. Some snickered while others shook their heads at their former brother who fought against their Father in not one, but in two wars. Lucifer noticed his brothers watching him, and Lucifer being Lucifer, decided to Taunt them. He lifted his head high and walked as if he were the greatest soldier in the world, down the middle aisle to present his plan for the next tournament to his Father the Creator.

To taunt his brothers even more, Lucifer resumed his former form that he had while he was among them. Lucifer had blonde hair. His body was muscular and made out of every instrument to exist in all of the Universe. Lucifer's face in his former form was a handsome face. The Father told his Prophets, that he inspired to write his word into the bible, that Lucifer was the most beautiful angel. One could not even describe his looks because it was so complex yet perfect. Pipes protruded from his robes and as the music began to play. Lucifer began to bob his head up and down to the upbeat music. Lucifer then began to dance the entire way to the music he was playing. Just as he was about to reach the peak of his song, a foot stuck out and tripped him.

The other Sons of God all began laughing as Lucifer tumbled a few feet forward. Lucifer jumped to his feet in embarrassment, he quickly looked around to find the culprit.

“Stupid bieathdie,” Lucifer cursed in a language not known to man.

“Language”, Michael said laughing.

“Yeah that was so funny”, Lucifer angrily replied.

“It really was”, Michael chuckled. “Look even the Father is laughing.”

Lucifer looked at all of his brothers, and the Father laughing. "We will see who is laughing once this next tournament is over!” He yelled “Hahahahaha!” Lucifer psychotically laughed. Lucifer’s face clearly caught between embarrassment and anger, as his eyes twitched and his face turned red, with his top teeth biting his lower lip.

Michael and the other angels laughed even harder.

“Michael, Lucifer!” The Creator called out to his two sons, ”come before me and tell me what the next trial is.”

Lucifer and Michael walked together down the aisle towards their father, The Creator. Michael wondered if he was going to get in trouble for tripping his brother.

“I don’t see the need to go over the details,” Lucifer stated to their Father. “You knowing all things already know the plan and I’m sure have already prepped the remaining Demigods for it.”

“I actually would like for you to remove any design you have on this battle, and to un-foresee this battle. Let the Demigods and my sons make their own destiny in this battle.”

“I see you still lack understanding.” The Father said to Lucifer. “Me knowing what is going to happen ahead of time is not the same as me interfering. Their paths are designed by their choices, part of them having free will.”

"Can I know what the battle is this time," Michael asked. "Since I'm the Demigod's Guardian." Michael had cut Lucifer off as he was getting ready to begin a pointless argument.

"My sons against your Demigods," Lucifer replied smiling, "in the Labyrinth. Whoever can make it through the Labyrinth first and alive wins."

Michael showed no emotion as he heard the news. "Okay. Well what are the rules so I can inform them." Michael said more irritable than he had intended to.

Jesus, who had been sitting on the right hand of The Father stood up. "The rules will not be all that Lucifer wants. Yes, the monsters will be allowed to attack. Except I will send a spirit to cause the monsters to attack both teams rather than just the Demigods. It has come to my intention you have already blackmailed all of the beast into attacking only the Demigods. So, to keep it fair I will cause a spirit to force them to attack both sides."

Lucifer lowered his eyes under the mighty gaze of Jesus. The situation with Jesus was complicated. He was a Son of God but wasn't at the same time, because he was God. God was three entities at the same time, 1... The Father. 2... The Son or Jesus 3... The Holy Spirit. The best way to describe it is this, you take one glass of water and pour part of it into an ice tray then you pour another part into a pot and leave the remaining water in the glass. It is all the same water, from the same glass, but the water in the cup remains liquid, The Father. The water in the ice tray becomes solid, The Son, and the water heated in the pot becomes vapor, The Holy Spirit.

"The tunnels will have light during the day and will be dark at night, as it is on the surface. The Demigods and your sons will be allowed to leave the maze at night and sleep instead of having to stay awake twenty-four hours around the clock for however long they might be down there. The light will slowly set as it does here on earth. If they make it to an exit before the light sets then they will be able to rest but if they don't anyone caught in the maze at night is in for a long night. Arachnid has agreed not to let her babies hunt because nobody could beat billions of spiders in a cave. However, Arachnid herself will hunt at night and at night only."

"Next," Jesus said as Lucifer opened his mouth to speak. "The goal will go far past making it out of the Labyrinth alive. The contenders will have to enter Tartarus and escape from the other side past the tormentors."

"I can agree to these rules," Lucifer said, thinking deeply in his head about if the new rules were an advantage to his sons or the Demigods.

"Neither." Jesus spoke knowing Lucifer's thoughts. "The battle is fair, and either side has a fair chance to win."

"Okay, well then I assume Michael will get those turds ready the best he can and I will get my sons ready. How much time do we have before this tournament takes place?"

"We want to give the Demigods a little bit of a break after that last tournament. So, seven months from now. Which will be more than enough time for you to train your sons," Jesus answered Lucifer.

Michael snickered which did not go unnoticed by Lucifer.

"Laugh all you want. We will see in the end who will win."

Michael and Lucifer were always arguing. Gabriel was actually relieved that this time they kept themselves better behaved. Lucifer and Michael had to go back to their places as the other Sons of God presented themselves and gave their reports for the parts of the Universe that they were rulers of.

The throne room literally has no description. It was there but it wasn't. It was made out of gold, diamonds, rubies and many gems from systems far from earth. There was no ground to stand on and no walls. Yet it was a building of sorts with rooms.

Time didn't exist when the angels gave their reports because times with God and his creations differed by thousands of years. God would freeze time while the angels gave their reports and would unfreeze it after the angels all went back to their kingdoms.

"The rules are not all the way we want them, but the tournament is set." Lucifer's voice echoed throughout the halls of Olympus startling Zeus who was dozing off on his throne.

"What are you going on about?" Zeus asked Lucifer.

"Jesus changed the rules. Our plan to persuade all of the monsters to attack just the Demigods won't work. The monsters will attack everyone and he will make sure of it."

"What are the new rules?" Zeus asked, curious to know if Jesus was cheating for the Demigod's.

"Well, they can now leave the maze at night. Arachnid can only attack at night. The beast will attack everyone, and the tunnels will mimic the sky on earth, light during the day and darkness during the night." Lucifer gave the shortened version of the rules.

"I see." Zeus replied.

"Also, the end of the race is not the middle of the Labyrinth, but they have to enter into Tartarus and escape past the tormentors. Then out of the only exit, which is guarded by Tartarus himself."

"I have seen your sons doing their little magic tricks. Not much for going against these Demigods." Zeus said to Lucifer after a moment's pause.

"Those magic tricks are just to please the humans. They both can do far greater things, but don't in fear of being rejected by men. They don't even know that I am their dad."

"That doesn't surprise me, you being a deadbeat dad," Zeus responded grinning.

"Yeah, well I can't say you were much of a dad yourself. At least my sons didn't fight against me." Lucifer said laughing.

Zeus' smile faded, "yeah, well that will all come to an end soon enough."

"Are we still allowed to train them?"

"Yes, we are allowed to still train them."

Chapter Two

Chris Blaine looked down while floating ten feet above the ground, suspended in air, with no strings attached to him.

The crowd was cheering in a frantic state, yelling, "CHRIS-BLAINE! CHRIS- BLAINE!" Over and over again.

Slowly Chris Blaine descended back towards the ground. Once on the ground Chris bowed and collected money from the audience in a cheap performer's hat. Chris was dressed in the traditional magician's tuxedo with the top hat. His hair was a dark color and he was no taller than five feet eight inches. He had a scar below his left eye that he was born with. His eyes were strange for a human. They were emerald green almost as if they glowed in broad daylight or at night when light touched them.

Chris was performing not far from Central Park near a poor neighborhood. Chris did not need to go where the people were to draw a crowd. Wherever he was, the crowd came. Chris had begun to do his shows in the poorer neighborhoods and would donate the money earned to their communities. He made his cost of living finances by stealing small amounts of cash from the insides of Armored trucks while they were stopped.

Placing his thumb and pointer finger to his lips, Chris whistled for a cab. And within seconds a cab was pulling over to pick up Chris from the sidewalk. That was the good thing about New York, there were always cabs nearby. Chris got into the cab in a hurry as the paparazzi tried to ambush him for photos and videos. The cab drove quickly down the street away from the paparazzi.

"So where are we headed?" The cab driver asked as he turned his head to look and see who was in his back seat.

"Whoa, holy crap man, you're.... You're Chris Blaine!!!"

"The one and only," Chris replied while smiling and taking a bow while sitting down

"Really big fan. Wow, my friends are not going to believe this!" The cab driver said in his Indonesian accent. The cab driver was an Indonesian in his late thirties.

"Well you could always take a photo of us on your phone." Chris said to the man, thinking of ways to help him prove to his friends that he really did drive him around.

"Okay!" The cab driver said pulling out a Nokia phone. The one that had the bright light on top of it that came out in the early 2,000'. "So, tell me Mr. Blaine, how do I work the camera on this?"

"Umm. . . I actually don't believe those phones have cameras on them." Chris honestly replied.

"What I can do if you want," Chris continued, "is I can take a photo of us both and tag you in it on social media."

"Ooh this is very exciting!" The cab driver responded.

At the first red light, Chris took off his seatbelt and positioned himself to take the picture. He leaned against the back of the front seats, with his face facing the rear window. The cab driver turned in his seat so that his face showed towards the camera as well. Chris got the picture just as the light turned green.

"Okay, so what is your twitter account name so I can tag you?" Chris nicely asked the cab driver

"No Twitter", the driver responded.

"Do you have Facebook? Snapchat? Instagram?"

"No, I do not." The driver responded looking back at Chris smiling.

Chris fake smiled back. "Okay well I just posted it." Chris said. Intent on keeping his word, Chris posted the photo to his Instagram account but with no titles.

"Thank you, very kindly sir," the cab driver said as he continued to drive. "Sir, I forgot in my excitement, you never told me where we are going?"

"Just drop me off at Central Park," Chris Blaine replied to the driver.

"Very good sir, this I can do for you. No charge."

"Well, thank you." Chris said smiling.

The whole ride to Central Park the cab driver kept looking in the rearview mirror and smiling every time Chris looked up. In no time the cab pulled alongside the curve for Central Park.

"My friends are going to be so flipping jealous!" The cab driver said as Chris stepped out of the cab.

"Well I hope you have a great night." Chris said slowly walking away from the cab.

Chris walked through the park as he always did at night before teleporting to his studio apartment in the Bronx. His home was junky and was in a bad neighborhood, yet that made Chris feel at home. Chris turned the T.V on using the remote. Flipped down to his internet and cut his Netflix on. Chris had a habit of watching old shows from the nineties they were his favorite. Chris currently was halfway through the first season of Cheers.

Just as the show's theme song was ending, the phone began to ring.

"Hello?" Chris answered his phone.

"Hey honey, it's your mom. How was your day? How was your show?"

"It was excellent, as always. I left with the crowds swarming me."

"Oh, I always knew that you would be special. I've told you so many times in the past!"

"I know Mom," Chris interrupted. "You made a bargain with Lucifer after my brother Darrin died from heart failure and that night you had a dream that you and Lucifer had relations. When you woke up you were pregnant with me."

"That is the first half of the story," Chris' mom said in a shaky voice.

"What do you mean?" Chris asked sensing something was wrong.

"Part of the deal was that if he ever needed you, you would have to do whatever mission or battle he needed you for." Chris' mom started crying on the phone.

"Mom what's wrong?" Chris asked, becoming very concerned. He had never heard his mom cry before

His mom tried to tell him what was wrong twice, but burst into tears each time.

"Do I need to catch a flight over there?" Chris asked.

"Yes, please come," His mom said sniffling and still crying softly. Chris could tell she was trying to fight crying but it kept forcing itself out.

"Okay, I am on the next flight out." Chris said without any hesitation in his voice. He was very close with his mom and hearing her this upset had him on edge.

Chris went on his phone and got on the site cheapflights.com and made a reservation for a 1:00 AM flight out. Although he could technically teleport to his mom, he still did everything he could to lead a normal life. He quickly packed his bags and headed to the airport. As Chris waited in the first-class line, he scanned the airport around him. There were a few cute girls he noticed, which he glanced back at them a few times. They didn't seem to know who he was.

There were too many kids running around and security was walking back and forth through the ticket purchasing area. The airport seemed very busy for such an early hour in the morning.

"Next!" The ticket agent yelled.

Chris stepped forward. "Hello I reserved a ticket on the 1:00 AM flight out. My name is Christopher Blain."

The ticket agent began typing it seemed a thousand words per second. "Here it is. I have you on the 1:00 AM flight out. Will you be checking in any bags?" The ticket agent asked Chris while keeping her eyes glued to the computer.

"Just this one." Chris said as he lifted his bag, and put it on a conveyor belt that was in between the two ticket agent's desks.

"Okay", the ticket agent said as she checked to make sure Chris had filled out all of the contact information on the bag's sticker in case it got lost.

"Everything seems to be good. Here is your ticket and your flight will be out of gate number B12 in forty-five minutes. Enjoy your flight and Unity Airlines thanks you for flying Unity Airways, the best way to fly." She recited the airline's slogan back to him.

Chris next went and stood in line to go through the metal detectors and security checkpoints. The line was too long. By the time Chris had passed through the checkpoints and had his belt and shoes back on, he had to jog to the mini train that took you to the various gates. He stood holding the top pole as the mini train lurched forward and began picking up speed.

Chris looked at the map. His gate was near the third stop. Once Chis was off of the mini train, he continued jogging towards his gate down a very long hallway. Chris managed to reach his gate just as they were about to close the door.

"Hold up! I am on this flight." Chris yelled, running and holding his ticket. The Flight attendant held the door open waiting for Chris. Chris handed her his ticket once he had reached the door. "Whew!! I was scared that I was going to miss my flight for a second", Chris continued as he wiped a few drops of sweat that had begun to form across his forehead.

"First class I see." The flight attendant said, scanning the ticket. "Oh my God!" The flight attendant yelled. "You are that famous magician that can levitate and hold his breath underwater for three days and stuff!!! Wow, wait till the others hear you are on this flight!"

Chris smiled and waited for her to finish admiring him. She walked Chris down the ramp to the plane, praising all the great tricks he was able to do. Chris took his seat in first class once fully on the plane. There was a T.V, an iPad on the counter top to Chris' right side, headphones, and the usual stuff that came with first class. Chris' favorite thing about first class was that he didn't have to use his data, because they had free Wi-Fi for first class passengers. Chris had not had a chance to sleep since his show the night prior so he took this opportunity and slept the entire flight. Chris even slept through the beverages which rarely happened since it was his favorite part of the flight.

"Sir", the flight attendant said, trying to wake Chris. "Sir we are here and the plane is un-boarding."

Chris reluctantly yawned as he stretched and opened his eyes.

Okay," Chris replied to the flight attendant as he slowly rose to his feet, maintaining one eye open while keeping his other eye closed hoping at least one eye could finish sleeping. Chris exited the plane onto the ramp that led into the airport. Once inside of the airport building, Chris headed to the mini train that would take him to the area leading to baggage claim where he patiently waited to pick up the one bag that he had brought with him. The baggage strip circled around three times before Chris spotted his bag.

Chris slowly walked with his bag as he focused on the airport signs to navigate his way to where he could hail a cab. After asking for directions twice and walking for what seemed like forever, Chris was outside and a cab was pulling over to take him to his next destination. Chris casually looked out of the window of his cab as the cab driver drove him to his mother's house. It had been a long time since Chris had been to Baltimore. It was as beautiful as ever. All of the bright lights were shining in the darkness. It was 4:00AM and the streets were still crowded as if it were 11:00PM. Chris watched the beauty of downtown and its crowded streets disappear behind him as the cab began to pass more common parts. Trash began to appear everywhere on the street and the smell of homelessness, cows, and sewer began to fill Chris' nose all at once.

Chris watched as three very large men chased a much smaller guy down the street with baseball bats. For some reason that excited Chris. It almost fueled him.

Chris lived on the extreme with his magic shows. Everything he did was life threatening. It was like he kept setting up dates with death and death kept standing him up. The other reason Chris didn't mind neighborhoods like the ones he was passing through, was when he was twelve he had his hat on backwards in a neighborhood where your hat was supposed to be tilted upward towards the sky and slightly to the left, in no time gang members from the neighborhood were chasing him and shooting at him with their guns.

No matter how many bullets they fired, the bullets just bounced right off of Chris and did no damage. Chris ran as they were shooting at him. It wasn't until he got home that he realized no harm had been done to him. It was then that his mom first told him about who she believed his dad was.

The cab pulled over in front of the address Chris had given him, 555 Nonya lane. Chris' mom came rushing out of the house.

"Chris, Dear, I would have come and picked you up from the airport."

"Oh, no mom it is okay. I didn't want to bother you."

"It wouldn't have been a bother sweetie," Chris' mom said, hugging him.

"Are you okay?" Chris asked his mom. Chris stared at his mom with a sadness in his eyes that even a puppy could not imitate. Something was terribly wrong and Chris wanted to help, but he didn't even know what happened yet. "You were distraught on the phone and said there is another part to the story that you never told me."

"Let's talk inside." Chris' mom said as she carefully surveyed her surroundings, slowly looking in all directions, as if somebody was watching them and eavesdropping on every word.

"Okay", Chris agreed as he paid the cab driver.

As they entered the house Chris helped his mom onto the couch. She was an elderly woman in her seventies, while Chris was in his early thirties.

"Okay so here it is", Chris' mom began. "Anytime a bargain is made there are two sides to the bargain. My side of the bargain was I would be able to have a son in whom I could give all the love in the world to. Lucifer's side of the bargain was that he could use you for any mission or battle that he would require of you."

"Wait. What?" Chris asked, not quite sure what he had just heard.

"It was selfish of me to make that bargain, but all I wanted was a son. I didn't think that Lucifer would actually need you for any mission. I am so sorry." Chris' mom said through sobs as tear after tear fell down her cheeks.

"It's going to be okay, but I'm still not sure what exactly is going on?" Chris honestly replied.

"He is going to take you from me!" Chris' mom cried and shouted at the same time. Her emotional appearance was that of one of those people on the streets screaming that the end is coming. She was hysterical. Chris hated seeing his mom like this, but didn't know how to comfort her because he had never before seen her this way.

"I'll just tell him no." Chris firmly stated hoping to calm his mother.

"You don't understand", Chris' mom cut him off. "It is not a choice. If you say no, he kills us both along with your son that you had in palm beach with that Hooter's waitress."

"Wait. He would kill Chris Jr? He has nothing to do with this!" Chris said infuriated. "Why would he kill you or my son if I say no?" None of this was making any sense to him.

"I'm so sorry my son but that is just how he works. He also will torture you in attempt to get you to say yes. I promise you his tortures will make you wish you were dead. He will break you."

"I understand." Chris solemnly responded as he pondered possible solutions to get out of whatever the Devil needed him to do. "So, what exactly does he want me to do?" Chris finally asked after a long moment of silence.

"I don't know. He just whispered to me that it was time for me to uphold my end of the bargain before he disappeared. I never even got to see him this time."

"Try not to worry yourself too much mother. I do have powers beyond the average magician. trust me, I will be fine. I'm going to go upstairs and put my things in my old room and get some sleep. I haven't slept since my last show, except for on the flight which was only a few measly hours." Chris said getting to his feet. "I will complete this mission whatever it is and come back to you." Chris put on a brave face just as a soldier would in the early B.C wars. No matter how skilled of a fighter they were, and no matter how many songs they sang, or pep talks they gave themselves the night before battle, no matter how many times a soldier said it would be an honor to die this way, none of them wanted to die. The mere sight of great armies in front of them made the legs of soldiers' quake. You could only hope to be placed in the far back of your army so that by the time you had to defend yourself against your first warrior the battle would already be nearly over, and there would be far less chances of you being swarmed by four to five soldiers at once.

Chris' brave front partially fooled his mother but not his heart. He was a scared little boy again hiding beneath his covers from the monster that he thought was under his bed. As he made his way up the bantered stairs. the floorboards loudly creaked beneath his feet. Death seemed to be calling his name over and over again. Chris made it to his bedroom and decided to try and focus on something else as he opened the door.

His bed was neatly made. His computer was still plugged into the wall using up tons of electricity even though he hadn't been there in over eleven years. Not that he had not seen his mom in eleven years, because he saw his mother at least several times per year. Chris just had not been to her house in Baltimore to see her because he was extremely busy on the road doing his performances around the world. Normally he would just purchase a ticket for his mom to come and visit him. Chris pondered hard on what was about to happen. He was partly scared but once he started remembering all of the powers he had he became excited. This was going to be the thrill of his life.

At first, he was bothered by being forced to do this for his supposed father in whom he had never personally met. He felt like a pet or slave in the fact that he had zero choice in the matter. But now that he was relaxed in his room, he began thinking about all that he could do with his powers. Chris had visited a Satanist church when he was a child. What he learned there made him laugh. They actually believed that Satan and Lucifer were two different beings and were waiting for the one true child of Satan to be born of a virgin. Chris ended up being kicked out of their church for laughing.

Chris closed his eyes and slowly drifted off to sleep. When Chris opened his eyes, he was in some sort of underground cavern. A beast emerged out of nowhere having a snake's head but a spider's body. The spider snake quickly scurried up the wall and across the ceiling to get to Chris. Chris turned and ran but the spider snake was too fast. In no time its fury body was on top of him. Chris doubled himself to confuse the beast.

As the snake's head struck out at both Chris', the real Chris and his double rolled in opposite directions. The spider snake monster debated on which Chris to attack. Its hesitation was enough time for Chris to double himself again into four. All four of the Chris' that were now surrounding the spider snake shot fire from their hands cooking the beast. The spider snake reared in anger before it lunged at the real Chris who was standing directly in front of it, no more than seven feet away. But Chris disappeared into the shadow of the wall causing the spider snake to miss and nearly slide into the wall that just seconds ago had been directly behind Chris. The spider snake retreated a few feet trying to figure out what happened and to escape the other three Chris' who were still burning it with flames from their hands.

The three doubles of Chris shot more fire from their hands at the snake as the real Chris remained hidden in the shadows, out of danger's way. The spider continuously attacked the fake Chris' in vain. Within minutes the spider snake was dead from being burnt to a crisp.

"Very good my son." A figure said appearing between the three Chris'. The man was tall with white skin and brown hair. He had a blackened scar under his left eye.

"I'm guessing you are Lucifer?" Chris asked, appearing alongside the other three Chris's. He kept the other three Chris's there because he did not feel it was safe to reveal the real him just yet. Not until he could be sure that the figure in front of him wouldn't attack.

"That would be correct", Lucifer said waving away the fake Chris's leaving just the two of them in the room.

"How did you do that?" Chris asked Lucifer. The fire of confidence that had been in Chris's eyes burnt out immediately. Any plans that he had made to fight back against Lucifer were now gone. Lucifer without any effort or strain showed Chris that his powers were useless against his. It was as if Chris had been given a race car to race against a jet across the world. While a race car is fast, it stands no chance against a jet traveling across the world.

"It was rather simple if you must know, but to more important matters. I see you know how to enter the shadows but you also have the ability to jump realms here on earth. There are four realms on this planet, the shadow realm which you jumped into to escape Francis."

"Francis?" Chris asked smirking at the name of the spider snake.

"Yes Francis", Lucifer replied. There are two more realms, the realm of dreams, and the realm we are in now. The realm of reality. Your illusion of doubling yourself is a good one, but you have not yet reached your full potential in your powers dealing with illusion. Every night when you fall asleep, I will enter into your mind and train you for the mission you have ahead of you."

"And what mission is that exactly?" Asked Chris, his eyes bolstering with concern.

"It is an important mission. You and your brother will be in a race through the Labyrinth, ba—"

"My brother? Will Darrin be with me?" Chris asked with excitement showing on his face.

"No." Lucifer replied. "Your real brother. Born from me, David Angel."

"Wait, he is my brother?" Chris asked, confused as ever. David angel was Chris' only competition in the world of magicians.

"Now as I was saying", Lucifer continued," from the Labyrinth the two of you will have to enter into Tartarus and escape through the only way out. Which is guarded by Tartarus himself, if you can get past the tormentors."

"What happens if we don't make it past the tormentors?"

"You will be killed by them. And you souls will belong to the tormentors, and they will torment you day and night."

"I don't like those odds," Chris said, no longer excited about the mission.

"It is not optional. The only thing that is optional is whether I train you for the tournament or just let you go into it unprepared. Whether you choose to do it or not, you will be summoned to the entrance of the Labyrinth in exactly seven months. Once inside of the Labyrinth the only option is to go forward."

"I have to prep your brother tomorrow and after he has his one on one with Francis, I will begin training you both together."

"Okay." Chris said, exasperated about the race through the Labyrinth and Tartarus. He now wished he was normal and had no powers. Is this the price you pay for being a demigod Chris thought to himself. Having powers was awesome but not when it put your life in harm's way.

"Be encouraged", Lucifer said to his son. "You will do fine. I believe you have what it takes. If not, you will by the time I finish with you." With those words Lucifer disappeared.

Chapter Three

John and Jasmine had both dropped out of High school. There was no point in going anymore knowing that they were going to be forced to do seven tournaments and could be killed in any of them. For John he rather enjoyed not being in school, but Jasmine on the other hand found a way to get her high school diploma online.

"Good Afternoon." Michael said to John and Jasmine as he broadly smiled at them.

Jasmine acknowledged Michael but was not happy to see him so soon.

"Wow, talk about no rest time", John said out loud.

"Calm down." Michael replied to John." You guys have seven months before the next trial. I just came to give you the details." Michael was a bit disappointed in the Demigods not being as happy to see him as he was them.

"This tournament is more of a death race. You will be competing against Lucifer's two sons, David Angel, and Chris Blain."

"Wait, those are Lucifer's sons?" Jasmine asked in shock.

"Who are they?" John asked, having no clue who they were.

"Those famous magicians that hold their breath underwater for days and do other crazy things."

"Oh, yeah, I have heard of those guys."

"Well, you two have to race them. The first part of the race takes place in the Labyrinth. The second part through Tartarus. You have to make it past the tormentors and the Angel Tartarus, which is impossible enough by itself."

"So, what you are saying is nobody is going to live through this one?"

"No, just like the last time, once the entire opposing team is dead the tournament is over and whoever is still alive is declared the Victor. So, you just need to stay alive long enough for the other team to die."

"We don't actually have to get through Tartarus, just live longer than the other team?" John questioned Gabriel wanting to make sure he was understanding everything correctly.

"That is correct." Michael replied. "Now for the Labyrinth. There is beast down there and they all can attack you at any time except for Arachnid. She can only attack you at night."

"That doesn't sound any better." Jasmine stated. Feeling it would be better if they did not have to fight any beasts at all. In the last tournament against only four beasts, two of their friends died. She could only imagine what would happen this time, especially since Arachnid was in this tournament.

"Well, it will sound much better in a second," Michael continued. "The Labyrinth will be changed into the weather on earth. Meaning, if it's raining on land it will be raining down there and if it's snowing, it will be snowing. When it's day on earth the tunnels will be lighted as if the sun is lighting them. As night approaches the light will slowly begin fading away just like a sunset above ground."

"As the light begins to fade you need to get to an exit and you will be able to rest outside of the Labyrinth, safe from any attacks. But if you don't make it to an exit, you will be stuck in the Labyrinth fighting off beasts all night. And if Arachnid finds you, it is not going to be good for you guys."

"I hear you." Jasmine responded in a faint voice remembering her Vision of John being killed by Arachnid, and remembering the book's detail of Arachnid facing their Ancestors. Arachnid was near impossible to beat. Without Marcus they couldn't do the same thing their ancestors did. Which was to kill Arachnid by electrocuting her with water and electricity. They would have to devise a completely new plan with zero guarantee that it would work.

"So, I have a question, is the Labyrinth the same thing as the Catacombs?" Jasmine asked.

"A very intelligent question", Michael responded. "And the answer is no and yes. The catacombs were made by European slaves enslaved to religious priests. They were an imitation of the Labyrinth but nowhere close to its actual design or danger. The Catacomb caves never change. They are always the same design. While the Labyrinth on the other hand changes every night."

"Well how are we supposed to race to the end if the maze is always changing?"

"It is possible." Michael answered John's question. "To win this test it will not require bronze nor speed, but more brains. Remember this, the battle is not given to the swift nor to the strong but unto the wise."

"That's nice." John said sarcastically. "But more importantly, do any of the Labyrinth changes put you in the same layer as Arachnid? Is she allowed to attack you if you wander into her layer? And are there any entrances or exits, located in her layer?"

"No to the second part. Her layer is far away from any places that you need to be, but if you do happen to enter her layer on accident you are fair game. All of the spiders are going to remain around her layer. So, if you start seeing spiders, run as fast as you can out of there. If you can get out of her section before she can get to you, she cannot touch you and if she tries, I will intercede."

"Awesome." John responded smiling for the first time that day since seeing Michael. "That is very comforting and I mean that. That was my biggest trepidation was Arachnid." John looked over at Jasmine to see if she noticed the college word that he used. Jasmine did and she gave John a smile and a high five.

"And rightly so", Michael said. "But those are the rules. I see you guys practicing your powers every day, so I want to train you in other areas. More mental and thinking training. To give you a break however. I will start in a month. As long as you keep practicing getting stronger and stronger in your powers, I see no need to cut your break short."

"That Sounds like a plan to me." John and Jasmine said together.

"Okay" Michael replied. "See you guy's in a month." With that he disappeared from sight.

"Well I guess we can relax for a bit." John said to Jasmine smiling, but seeing the look on Jasmine's face John knew she didn't agree.

"Jasmine if Michael is giving us another month to relax, we should take it. What?" John asked, throwing his hands up in the air in desperation. John didn't want to do anymore training or studying, but knew that was exactly what Jasmine had in mind.

"We are going straight to the library to study. We need to know everything about the Labyrinth, everything about Arachnid. We need to find out about what beasts are known to be down there. And we need to research what kind of torches were used by the priests in the Catacombs because those torches would last them all night.

"Why am I not surprised you have already read up on this?" John said laughing.

Jasmine laughed mockingly in a sarcastic but flirtatious way, biting her lip, and smiling at John. They began to walk down the street towards the library. A few guys cat called at Jasmine from their vehicle as they slowly drove at the same pace Jasmine and John were walking, causing John to raise his eyebrows. But against his urge to turn around and use his powers on the guys, he kept walking. It irritated John that guys were so disrespectful to try and holler at a girl obviously walking with her boyfriend. One swoosh of John's hand and their car would go flying in the wind. But they weren't worth paying attention to.

“I’m impressed you are getting better at not reacting so much.” Jasmine praised John for his ability to demonstrate immense self-control.

“I know,” john replied smiling back.

“Anyways bighead,” Jasmine said laughing.

“Any spare change?” A homeless man asked as they passed him. John had a five-dollar bill on him and handed it to the man and Jasmine gave the three dollars she had as well. They still had the unlimited credit card so they didn’t really need money. Jasmine’s dad still gave them both an allowance each week for doing household chores, it made him feel like things were still normal. John was at their house so much that Jasmine’s dad considered him a resident.

“Aye big homie, you got a Black’n Mild?” A kid asked who had went to school with John and Jasmine before they dropped out.

“No.” John replied as he and Jasmine kept walking.

“I don’t like that guy”, Jasmine said while holding on to John’s arm and leaning against him as they walked.

“He is alright.” John said.” He only acts the way he does and is in a gang because his older brothers forced him to be in their gang. Where he lives, if you aren’t in a gang, you are a victim waiting to happen. You have to remember Chicago is a rough city in certain places, and before we had our powers we were just regular young adults trying to graduate high school. Well, at least you were. I was just there to study you”, John said laughing and jokingly hitting Jasmine softly in the arm.

“But what I don’t understand is, why don’t his parents just move? “

“I don’t think they can afford to, and it isn’t that simple. They would have to move to Antarctica, or to an even more foreign place like Alaska or space because the gang he is in, if they find out where his family is, they would send contracted killers after them.”

"I don't like that", Jasmine said, as her thinking face came on. "Also, I don't see why we can't use our powers to help people like them? I mean, I don't recall a rule saying we could only use our powers during the tournament. I mean they are our powers, so really we could do what we want with them."

"You can't save the world." Michael said appearing behind them. "Not with powers anyways. As long as there is a need for money, and people that need money, corruption, violence, and greed will always exist. If you take out that gang, another one will rise in its place." Michael finished.

"Well we aren't talking about saving the world just our friends." John said to Michael after seeing Jasmine look at the ground in defeat.

"If you take that gang out, a more violent gang will rise, and your friend back there will be murdered by them five years from now. Your mom and your dad, will be captured by the government while you are in the Labyrinth. They will be examined to see if your super powers came from them, and murdered. Is that what you want?"

"No", John answered Michael joining Jasmine in defeat.

"Okay," Michael said. "I know you guys have the best intentions, but sometimes you just have to let life play itself out because changing things will only make them worse in most cases."

John nodded his head to show that he understood, Jasmine did the same. They entered the library and headed to the back to sit in one of the cozy chairs. The library had six private study rooms. If you walked into it and went straight, the rooms would be on your left-hand side. It had over forty computers for people with library cards and guest to use. To the far back where John and Jasmine were, they had seven cozy chairs that lived up to their name. They were very comfortable and one could really just fall asleep in them while trying to study unintentionally. As you walked into the library to the right there was a children's section, that was its own section. There were walls separating it from the rest of the library with a very large four car garage size opening for children and their parents to enter in and browse the children's books, or play with the toys. Jasmine pulled out her laptop, and connected to the library's WI-FI.

Labyrinth. Jasmine typed on her laptop. The movie about the Labyrinth and a few fictional books appeared, but nothing that dealt with real monsters or beasts. With the Catacombs, many things popped up. Apparently, many people who entered the catacombs never came out. There were many entrances and exits throughout London. Some were known to everyone. There was actually a circuit of people who used a certain part of the Catacomb to get from business to business. They entered the catacombs through one bar and would travel through them until they exited out of another. These small parts of the tunnel were lit by electricity but beyond this very small circuit, most never ventured. The ones that did were never heard from again. One couple supposedly made it all the way through the catacombs to the center of the earth and exited it in a park. Their lie was revealed when the city sent a team in there to check it out, it was just a regular exit in the Catacombs, so they had not actually gone all the way to the center of the earth as they had claimed.

"Well we know that the Catacombs are not the same as the Labyrinth, but they are designed after it. And that most likely demons in there are killing the people." John said as they watched a video, found on a camera in the catacombs. The man saw something, dropped his camera, and began running and screaming then disappeared from sight, and was never found."

"Agreed." Jasmine said. "And because they are so different, I doubt we can learn anything from the catacombs either", Jasmine finished.

"Well let's go home." John suggested as his stomach growled. "We need to practice making our powers stronger and eat."

Jasmine looked at John with a sideways glance, "yeah I know why you want to go home. You could care less about practicing your powers, you just want food."

"As George Washington stated, I cannot lie."

"Yeah, yeah, yeah.... I'm sure he lied just like you have before."

"And when have I lied to you?" John asked, waiting for Jasmine's answer.

"Well I wouldn't lie to my girlfriend either, if she could read my thoughts."

"Yeah but we have an agreement, and you are not allowed to read my thoughts."

"I try not to," Jasmine said. "But back to my point, I never said to me, I just said you have lied before, as has Washington."

"If we are being literal", John began.

"We are", Jasmine cut John off.

John looked at Jasmine trying to smile through his irritation at her always trying to point out his faults. "You didn't win, I just don't see any point in arguing about this dumb subject. So, I'm going to leave it alone."

"Okay we will call it a tie then." Jasmine replied, smiling.

"Sounds good to me," John said fist bumping Jasmine. "Alright let's go eat, I mean practice," John finished his sentence grabbing Jasmine's hand and pulling her in the direction of their house.

Chapter Four

"Well one son knows, "Lucifer said, appearing on the throne. "The other will soon enough."

"Okay," Hades said. "Why don't you just go right now and tell him?"

"Because I have business to attend to on Asgard", Lucifer replied.

Asgard Hermes said, "what business do you have there?"

"Thor, and Loki are reforming. I sent a spy there years ago and they have been reforming very slowly, but they are almost completely rebirthed now."

"Um, are you sure you want to be there when they reform?"Aphrodites asked, with concern clearly showing on her face.

"I have to be there to inform them on the situation. I mean, like it or not, they fought against the creator alongside us. Besides, I don't need a war between you and them going on right now while we are trying to win our freedom from the lake of fire."

"Okay, so when will you go and talk to your son?" Zeus asked Lucifer, feeling that Lucifer was putting it off.

"Well here is the thing," Lucifer said. "One of you will have to go to inform him, because Asgard takes precedence for me."

"I figured you were going to say that." Zeus said, shaking his head.

"Well, it is what it is." Lucifer coolly replied before disappearing.

"Hermes, I have a job for you!" Zeus yelled into the crowd of Greek Gods.

"I'm on it!" Hermes yelled from the back of the throne room. He was gone before Zeus got a chance to see him.

"Asgard resurrecting cannot be good, and I don't care what Lucifer says. Asgard is not going to just let go of what we did to them, especially Thor." Hades proclaimed from his seat on the throne. "Thor has a temper like none other and likes to win even more than our brother Victory."

"I know." Zeus replied, placing his elbow on his chair's rest with his fingers to his chin as he thought to himself. "I'm thinking we need to send someone to check on our Giant counterparts, especially Typhon. Actually," Zeus said in a more serious tone," I need somebody to check on our ancestors, the Titans. They are the ones who actually fought against the creator, we weren't even around yet. I imagine that the ones who have died in the past, will be reforming and will join the others."

"I'll do it." Poseidon volunteered. happy to leave the throne room. He pretended to be fine with everyone, but his last memory of Zeus was when Zeus had tricked him and trapped him in the enchanted cave. Any chance to get away from Zeus was a chance for him to breathe, because he planned on killing Zeus once the tournaments were over. And pretending to love his youngest brother and obey him for the time being was strenuous, yet necessary.

"And as Lucifer said we do not need another war going on during these tournaments." Poseidon shook his head expressing his concern for them possibly being overwhelmed. Then disappeared to check on each of the Titans.

Zeus wondered what Lucifer's plan was, especially since Thor hated him. Zeus wouldn't be surprised if he never saw Lucifer again after Thor finished forming.

Zeus fidgeted his fingers, he was anxious but there was nothing to do, until Hermes, Lucifer and Poseidon came back. How could they stop the titans if they were reforming? That would be a battle against Asgard and the Titans all at once. That would be way too much for the Greek Gods.

***

"David! David!" Hermes yelled as David attempted to turn a corner, headed towards a grocery store. It was 2:00AM and David had the sudden urge to eat. David paused in his step and slowly turned to see who was calling him. He was a great magician but he stayed as low key as possible. Unlike his brother. David didn't want people figuring out his secret.

"Can I help you?" David yelled back to Hermes, as Hermes jogged across the street towards him.

"You are David Angel, are you not?" Hermes asked, with a look in his eyes that forbade David to even think about lying. Hermes' eyes were like a fireball that hit David right in the heart as he penetrated him with his stare.

"Yes, I am. May I ask if I did anything to make you upset with me?" David didn't feel right about the man in front of him. Something about him made David very uncomfortable. I need to get him out of the public eye so I can use my powers without exposing myself. David thought within himself.

David took off in a fast run. Somehow, he knew the man would follow. David ran between two building's, into an alleyway. David had no idea how he knew it but the man chasing him had powers too. They radiated off of him in very powerful waves.

David disappeared into an abandoned building but Hermes could feel his power too and punched the door in.

Hermes was a scary sight. He was around six foot six inches, with a Conan build and a fiery red beard that covered his face. He was wearing a tight athletic bodybuilders shirt that exposed his muscles and black sweat pants with white stripes down the side.

David, who was only five foot seven inches and nowhere near as athletic. Prepared to use his powers. David, lifted the man off of the ground and slammed him into the wall with a lift of his hands. To David's surprise the man got up quickly and looked completely unphased. David began to use his powers again but Hermes beat him to it this time. A fireball blasted David through the wall of the building, where he lay unconscious in the back-alley way.

Hermes picked David up and disappeared with David into the night, taking him to Olympus to speak with Zeus. As the two appeared, with Hermes holding David over his shoulders, Zeus and the rest of the Greek Gods just stared at Hermes with confusion etched into their facial expression. Nobody could figure out why Lucifer's son was unconscious. All Hermes was supposed to do was go talk to him.

"He tried to use his powers on me", Hermes defended himself quickly seeing everyone staring at him.

"So, you thought it best to kill him?" Zeus asked half chuckling very low to himself.

"No. I just blasted him with one fireball. This kid is not tough at all. He might make it through the first ten minutes of the Labyrinth, if he even makes it past training." Hermes very seriously stated. Shaking his head in disappointment.

"I hate to burst your bubble", Aphrodites interjected herself into the conversation, "but you are a God and he is a demigod. You really can't compare his abilities against yours. Especially since you don't know how to hold back."

"One should Never hold back. Winning is all that matters." Nike said holding up her hand, as if she had just won something.

"Yeah anyways", Aphrodites continued, "we will see what he has in training."

"Yes, we shall." Zeus said looking down at the demigod from his throne. "Someone take him to a room until he wakes up and I can talk to him."

"By someone he means you Hermes," Aphrodites stated. while pointing to the unconscious demigod. "You are the one that did this to him, so get to it."

Hermes wanted to argue but seeing Zeus nod his head at him in a warning, indicating that it probably wasn't the best idea to get into it with Aphrodites. Aphrodites may not have been the most powerful God, but when she was mad, she had been known to do some damage.

Zeus patiently waited on his throne for Poseidon who had not yet returned. Zeus was beginning to get worried. However, he could still feel his brother's presence so he at least knew Poseidon was still alive.

"Hades, Aires, Orion; you three gather twenty minor gods of your choice, and your soldiers. Go see what has happened to Poseidon." Zeus finally said after two more days had passed and Poseidon had not yet returned.

"And exactly what are we supposed to do when we get there?" Hades asked, with his hands held in a way that spoke for themselves, indicating that he felt Zeus' plan was stupid.

"What do you mean?" Zeus asked Confused about what Hades was asking.

"Well in the Titan war, it took all of the Gods and demigods to defeat the Titans and the Giants. So, if they have reformed or escaped for the ones we couldn't kill, there is no way in hell that just one of us major three, your son Aires, and a bunch of minor Gods will stand a chance."

"I see your point." Zeus replied. "Well everyone gear up then and we shall all go together."

"Um, shouldn't someone stay behind for Lucifer's son?" Athena asked, pointing out the obvious.

"Good point." Zeus said not sure of what to do because they would need all of the Gods if the Titans or Giants were free.

"Okay someone volunteer to stay and watch the Demigod." Zeus bellowed to the other Greek Gods.

Every hand in the room went up in the air.

Hades hit his knees laughing. "Well I guess nobody is going to check on Poseidon." Hades shouted while still laughing so hard his stomach ached making him hold it.

The entire room began to laugh but Zeus silenced them. "Since Aphrodites was the first one to show concern for the demigod, she can stay and babysit him."

"I have no problem with that arrangement at all." Aphrodites said with a smooth cocky attitude. She really didn't care, babysitting an unconscious demigod was sure to be easier than fighting with the Titans.

Chapter Five

Zeus and the gods headed to find Poseidon, as Aphrodites settled herself in a vacant seat on Olympus. "This should be rather easy." Aphrodites said to herself, as she sat back in her seat yawning.

"Aaaaaaaahhhhhhh!!" David Angel screamed at the top of his lungs. As his eyes opened, he jumped up out of the gigantic bed he had been lying in.

David's last memory was of a giant size being, shooting something out of his hands at him. Now he was somewhere else but didn't know where. This must be the home of the giant's. David thought to himself. His bed was three to four times the size of the tallest human. There were no decorations in the room, just pure cold grey brick walls, and a big stone bed with a regular sized blanket and a pillow for David.

Immediately David's mind went to Jack and the beanstalk. The fear surged through his body. What if they try to eat me? David thought to himself. I need to get out of here.

David climbed down from the stone bed and slowly began to inch his way along the walls of the strange, huge place he was in. David pictured a large invisible castle floating above earth in the sky. The thought of the fiction book was really getting to him. The further David got without running into anyone the more comfortable he became. That is until he stepped outside and saw a giant statue at least a hundred feet high holding a lightning bolt, in a position that looked like he was about to throw it.

With a turn of his head David saw another giant statue and then another. One was of a giant holding a Triton. The other of a giant holding what appeared to be the spear of death.

"Oh my God!" David shouted in what sounded like a Selena Gomez singing whisper." Oh my God!" He shouted louder. I must be a Demigod! That would definitely explain my powers.

"Mom!! DAD!! I'm awake. Mom, Dad!!" David shouted again and waited for an answer but none came.

A thought crossed David's mind. "Maybe I am the last demigod left and this now is my kingdom", he said out loud.

Aphrodites who was watching him, did her best not to fall over laughing. She had summoned a video Camera and was recording David for the other gods to see.

David raised his hands in the air, and shouted in his mightiest voice, "I declare unto the Universe that humans must make supplements to me every Saturday. Provide me with unlimited snacks and the rulers on land, must bow before me and bring me tribute of their greatest treasure. This I, David Angel DECREE!!" David shouted the word decree with all his might.

Aphrodites' laugh echoed through the halls of Olympus.

"Hello is someone there?" David whimpered. All of David's mighty confidence had vanished faster than he could count to one, realizing that he was not alone.

David backed up until he was leaning against one of the Giant pillars.

Aphrodites appeared to him in her best human form. She didn't want to scare him just yet.

"Hello, David. It's alright, you can come forth."

"Who are you?" David asked, feeling a bit easier seeing the person before him was a beautiful woman and not some fierce God about to attack him again.

"I'm sure Hermes failed to explain to you as to why you have been brought here to Mount Olympus?"

"Mount Olympus? Am I a Demigod, or a full God?"

Aphrodites smiled at David. "You are a Demigod. You are the son of our leader Lucifer. You have been brought here because we Gods have a mission for you."

"A mission?" David asked. He was a bit confused, but he couldn't stop looking at how beautiful Aphrodite's was.

"Yes, a mission." Aphrodites repeated.

By the time the other gods returned to Olympus, Aphrodites had already explained everything to David in a way that wouldn't scare him. It took David a moment to take in what was happening as Zeus and Hermes, who he immediately remembered being the one who attacked him, stood near him. They were towering over him as they both stayed sixty feet, rather than shrinking down to human size. For any regular mortal seeing them in their natural state would kill them, but not a demigod. They were half angel and half human.

"Well since it has already been explained to you, if you don't have any further questions, you have seven months to prepare yourself for the tournament. It's your dad's responsibility to get you ready."

"So pretty much I don't have a choice?" David replied feeling a little woozy in the pit of his stomach.

"Exactly", Zeus replied.

"And according to you, Chris Blaine is my brother?"

"That is correct". Hermes said impatiently. "Enough with the dumb questions. I'm going to take you back now."

"Does this make Lucifer a Greek God?" David asked, continuing to be confused.

"Oh my goodness", Hermes replied." We have been over this. We told you, Aphrodites told you. What are you not understanding?"

"You don't like me very much do you?" David replied to Hermes.

"He doesn't like any Demigods. Not even his own." Hades said, smiling. "However, he is right. We need to get you back now. We have explained everything to you. You and your brother Chris will be competing in a death race through the Labyrinth and into Tartarus. You must rescue Apollo from Tartarus in order for it to be a win."

"Everything else will be explained to you in your training sessions." Go ahead and get this Demigod out of here," Hades said to Hermes, who gladly grabbed David before he could move out of the way. The next thing David knew, he was in his house waking up in his bed.

David sat up in his bed trying to decide whether it was a dream or not. He looked around the room. Nothing seemed different. He looked at his clock, it was 8:00PM. "Wow," David said to himself. "I don't even remember falling asleep."

Even though he wanted to believe it was all just a dream, David knew deep down that it was not just a dream.

Chapter Six

"NOOO!!" Jasmine screamed in her sleep. "NOOO!" She screamed again as she began groaning and crying hard. "I don't want to go in there. Please let me go."

John shook Jasmine awake from her sleep.

Jasmine opened her eyes which were filled with tears. "Same dream?" John asked Jasmine.

Jasmine nodded her head. "This mission is impossible. There is no way to escape Tartarus, especially not with Apollo. Every night in my dreams we are there and get captured. They torture us. They make me bathe in hot lava and it burns so bad, but they won't let me out of it. I just melt and reform. Every time I reform Tartarus forces me back into the lake all over again."

"Every dream means something and maybe Tartarus is trying to scare you to keep us from going down there."

"Scare me for what?" I am already scared. I don't want to go down there Jonathan. Please, let's get Michael to find somebody else to do these tournaments."

Michael appeared in the room as he normally did when his name was called.

"Jasmine, Tartarus is messing with your mind." Michael spoke looking at Jasmine with a ton of concern. "Nobody wants to go into battle, but somebody has to in order to save their country. Nobody wants to go to work but they have to in order to feed their families. Right now, you and John are the ones who must win these contests to keep

Lucifer and Zeus from avoiding the lake of fire. Because believe me, they are going to send you to Tartarus regardless because they hate Demigods. If they win this tournament, they will torture you and your families for all eternity because The Creator will not break his word. He will not send them to the lake of fire if they win the tournament., They will be able to do whatever they want to you humans here on earth with zero worries about consequences because there will be none." With those words Michael disappeared.

Michael's words did not comfort Jasmine but she at least stopped crying and now sat staring blankly at the wall. "You know in one of these tournaments, either I or you are going to die, right?" Jasmine's voice was full of sadness and heartache as she spoke those words.

"No, I don't know that." John said tensely. He was upset. John did not want Jasmine thinking that way. He had enough trouble fighting those thoughts off on his own without Jasmine putting more of the thoughts into his head.

They both laid back down in the bed and as Jasmine laid her head down on the pillow, John leaned over and kissed her lips before placing a shield bubble of air around Jasmine to block Tartarus from being able to plant dreams or visions in her head.

The sun rose in the sky shining through the bedroom window passing over Jasmine's entire head and brightly shining into the eyes of John. John stretched as he opened his eyes, yawning. John looked over at the clock, it was 11:30AM.

"Wow", John said jumping up and getting out of the bed. "It's late." John removed the air shield from Jasmine's head then proceeded to wake her up. "Wake up," John said gently pushing against Jasmine's shoulder. He kind of didn't want to get out of bed yet. Their room was very cozy. Everything was Gold and Silver.

"What is it?" Jasmine asked, as she rolled over on the bed.

"It's almost noon. We have to get up."

Jasmine slowly got out of bed. John was nervous as Jasmine was giving him an evil stare the entire time. Jasmine was not happy about having to get up at all.

John shrugged his shoulders, "I'm sorry but it was your idea to go to the library at noon because there are not very many people there during that time."

"I know. I just still feel tired. I'm not mad at you."

"Well if you want to," John replied, "you can lay back down and get some more sleep." John raised his eyebrows and bit his lip while he held his hands out towards the bed.

"No, I can't." Jasmine replied. "We still have to do a lot of studying on the catacombs, and the Labyrinth."

"Yeah I know. It's just we have been studying for a while now and there is nothing on the Labyrinth." John replied hoping Jasmine would take him up on his offer of getting more sleep so that he could as well.

"I know there isn't but today I was kind of thinking that we could find some of the entrances to the Labyrinth and go and check them out."

"Jasmine you are crazy!" John said louder than he had intended to. His eyes were fierce as if he were angry but in reality, Jasmines suggestion scared him more than anything. "Jasmine, you want to go into the Labyrinth seven months early? Are you serious right now?"

"Yes John. Wouldn't you rather be over prepared than under prepared?"

"Yeah but I think that's pushing our limits just a little too much John replied. His eyes pleading with Jasmine like a child begging their dad not to spank them. "You do remember they are keeping Arachnid and her babies back from us for a reason. If we go now, they will be able to hunt us."

"I know but we can get out anytime that we want as long as you can focus on..."

"No Jasmine." John said cutting her off. "That's too dangerous. Marcus and Ho-Young are dead, and...."

"And I am trying to keep us from dying too John. This is the only way I can possibly see us escaping by mapping out the entrance to the Labyrinth."

John bit his lip as he always did whenever he was considering doing something that he didn't want to do. His mind was telling him no but his heart was beating the hell out of his mind and causing him to surrender against his better judgement.

"Fine." John said. A fierceness resting upon his eyes. Though he was agreeing to do the task "If we die doing this, I want you to know that both of our death's and the extinction of the human race will be all your fault."

"We are not going to die, John." Jasmine said giving John an evil glare. Her eyes were piecing as if they were the freshly sharpened blade of a Samurai warrior on its way to battle. She hated that John was making it seem like she was sending them on a suicide mission. She was the offspring of the

Goddess of wisdom. She was sure that if anyone could come up with a plan to win this tournament, it would be her. She trusted her judgement and inwardly began to hate John a little for his doubt in her abilities.

"Well there won't be any books on where the entrances are. Except fiction books, which are made up. So, there is no guarantee any of them have the correct location."

"Well can you just try to focus on the Labyrinth and maybe teleport us there using your powers?" Jasmine asked, giving John her best puppy eyes., They normally got John to give in and give Jasmine whatever she wanted.

John, without so much as a word, reached out and held Jasmine's hand. He focused his mind on Greece and on a symbol that he had seen in one of the books he and Jasmine had read at the library during their studies. It was supposedly an indicator letting everyone know that it was an entrance into the Labyrinth."

John and Jasmine did not appear at any cave as John had expected. Instead they landed in front of what looked like a haunted house. It was dark outside. Slowly John and Jasmine approached the house, careful to keep their eyes on their surroundings. This large house definitely had the feeling of Evil all over it.

"Get away from that house!" An elderly woman came screaming out of her house with tears in her eyes. "You cannot go in there!"

"It's okay," John said to the woman. "We are not scared." John was lying through his teeth. He was petrified.

"Well you should be very afraid. Nobody that has gone in there since Hercules has ever come out alive."

John was about to ask her how she knew about Hercules but then remembered reading it in a book and just assumed she was referring to the legend.

"Let's just say we are special." John replied, smiling.

"No kidding Sherlock" The elderly woman replied very roughly. Jasmine looked at John with a worried look on her face.

"John." Jasmine whispered and beckoned him to lean in closer. "I can't get a reading off this woman."

"A reading? What do you mean?" John whispered back louder than he had intended to.

"I can't read her thoughts. Something is wrong."

"Yes. Something is wrong", the woman warned. "If you go in there, you will not make it out alive."

"Okay, I understand." John replied, as he grabbed Jasmine around her shoulder and walked them away from the haunted looking house.

"Where are we going?" Jasmine asked John, looking up into his eyes. Her eyes seemed to be concentrated in a mixture of worry, fear, and questions. Questions in which she may never find an answer to. She was confused as to why John was taking them away from the Labyrinth but she was also glad that he was. Because there was something about that woman that scared her and chilled her bones.

"To go and buy weapons and to get some rest so we can come back later in the morning and sneak in while she is asleep. I mean, if we went in now it might still be blocked off depending on what time the cave opens in the morning.

Look, the sun is already setting." John pulled his cell phone out of his pocket to see what time it was there in Greece.

"Holy crap, it's 7:00PM here." John said, shocked at the time difference, between there and Chicago from where they had just left from.

"Oh wow. Well, I guess I can go back to bed now." Jasmine said laughing.

"Yeah we can." John said, getting a serious face.

"What's wrong?" Jasmine asked.

"You mean besides us being here?" John replied, giving Jasmine a dissatisfied look.

"Yes, besides that." Jasmine smiles, choosing to ignore John's sarcasm. She didn't like the way John was talking to her but she also knew John's fear of spiders and knew he was just scared because they would be walking right into Arachnid's den. The queen of all spiders. Jasmine was also still sure that going into the Labyrinth was the right idea.

They found a hotel and used the unlimited credit card given to them by Michael the Archangel.

"Let's get some sleep." John said to Jasmine as he shut the light off. John was scared Jasmine would have more bad dreams so he caused the air around the room to form a shield to keep anything from entering while they were asleep and to keep any magic from entering their minds.

John and Jasmine slept as if they hadn't just woken up in the United States at noon. They slept until 3:00AM. Jasmine woke up first. She looked over at John who was still fast asleep. Jasmine smiled at John. She knew that no matter what happened down in the Labyrinth, no matter how scared John was, that he would protect her.

John woke up shortly after Jasmine and sat up in the bed before looking to where Jasmine should have been sleeping. At first, he panicked when he didn't see Jasmine lying next to him. All kinds of thoughts began racing through John's mind. Maybe his powers somehow broke during the night and something got in and took Jasmine. Another possibility was that maybe Jasmine got up and walked out of the room sleep walking.

John's heart was beating too fast. He was scared and on the point of having a panic attack until he heard the shower water running in the bathroom. His panic quickly subsided then he stretched and got out of the bed.

"Jasmine," John said as he walked in the bathroom.

"Yes?" Jasmine excitedly shouted over the sound of the water.

"Why are you so happy?" John shouted back as he laughed to himself because of the way that Jasmine was acting.

"Oh no reason." Jasmine replied as she looked around the curtain. "Can you hand me my towel?" Jasmine flirtatiously asked John, blushing and smiling from cheek to cheek as if they were not about to go on a suicide mission in the Labyrinth.

"Well I'm glad to see you are having fun." John joked with Jasmine as he pretended to pop her with the towel before handing it to her.

Once Jasmine was out of the shower and dry, they started prepping to go into the Labyrinth. They debated about whether they would need lights or not because they both remembered Michael saying that the Labyrinth would mimic the sunlight on Earth and darkness of the night. They were confused about whether it was like that all the time or specifically just for the tournament. They decided to buy flashlights just in case. Finally, they stopped at a gun store, which was also closed, and borrowed a few shotguns, shotgun shells and dynamite.

John teleported them back to the haunted looking house. He scoped out the perimeter of the house to make sure that the coast was clear. The woman who had hassled them the night before was nowhere to be seen.

"Come on", John said as he began a light jog towards the house. He wanted to get in the house before the strange woman caught them again. Most likely she was someone working for the Fallen Angels, trying to keep them from getting an early start on mapping the Labyrinth out.

As John and Jasmine reached the house, they cautiously entered. Every floorboard creaked as they stepped on them, surely alerting the monsters below to their presence.

"Are you sure you want to do this?" John said to Jasmine as they neared a pitch-black opening in the wall. John's eyebrows were raised and his teeth were gently biting his bottom lip as he silently argued with himself in his head. One part of him said to go in, the other part was yelling for him to grab Jasmine and run.

"No, I'm not. But I know we have to." Jasmine didn't look at John as she spoke, because she didn't want him to see her watery eyes that had become a flood being held up by a dam that was full to the brim and ready to pour over.

"I guess." John replied.

John shined his flashlight into the darkness ahead of them. They were not going to have much visibility at all. It was pitch black everywhere except for the small skinny line of light preluding from his flashlight. Jasmine shined her flashlight into the tunnel as well but it wasn't much better.

"Let's put on the helmets too," John said to Jasmine. "We are going to need more light than these two flash lights."

"Yeah, I agree." Jasmine replied without argument and immediately grabbed a construction hard hat from their travel bag that had the flashlight on it. She handed one to John and then placed the other one on her head.

"Okay, let's do this," Jasmine took a step towards the opening in the wall. A small spider scurried into the tunnel before them. John looked up at Jasmine wide eyed.

"It's fine John. It was a regular spider." Jasmine said, urging John to continue walking forward.

"Yes, a regular spider that can communicate with Arachnid according to the book we read in mythology class about our ancestors. A book that was supposed to be fiction but happened to be true."

They entered the darkness slowly. Their hard hat lights were actually producing a good amount of light and they could see quite well once they had fully entered into what appeared to be a mine. As they walked John and Jasmine began to see symbols on the walls that looked nothing like the symbols signifying the entrances to the Labyrinth. Instead of a round maze, it was a symbol for a square maze.

Words were written on the wall next to the symbols. As Jasmine and John passed them, they tried to read what the words said but they were in another language.

"Well, we have seen the Labyrinth we can go now." John stated, tensing up, getting a really bad feeling in the pit of his stomach. They were walking down a long and wide passage or tunnel. It was dark except for their small lights and John just did not like it. He felt like spiders were already crawling all over him though he knew it was just his imagination because he checked twice with his flashlight.

"Hold on." John said to Jasmine as they neared the end of the passageway. "I'm going to teleport ahead to see if there is anything up there." John tried to teleport, but nothing happened. John tried again but still nothing.

"Okay", Jasmine said. "What are you doing? I thought you were going to do your teleport thing." Jasmine asked thinking John was playing some kind of game pretending that his powers didn't work. A loud screech pierced the air from around the passageway corner. It was a deafening and shrilling sound that sent a chill down to the bone.

"John, stop playing. If you are going to teleport now would be the time to do it."

"I am not playing. Something is blocking my powers down here." John said looking at Jasmine. John looked like he was about to throw up. His eyes dropped towards the ground as he stumbled a bit trying to keep from fainting. He was either having a heart attack or a panic attack. Whichever one he didn't know. But it didn't matter, thanks to Jasmine pressuring him into going down there they were about to die anyways.

"Here." John said, finally pulling himself together and grabbing a bottle of water dumping it on the ground. "See if your powers work, because mine aren't."

Jasmine tried to raise the water, but nothing happened.

John looked at Jasmine with more fear than he intended to. "Run." John mouthed, as the screech sounded again but much closer this time., John didn't even need a guess he just knew it was the spiders.

John and Jasmine left everything they had except for the dynamite and shotguns and took off running back the way that they had come in. As they made some distance, John looked back, and about forty giant spiders of all poisonous breeds, were very quickly running after them.

"Faster!" John shouted as he grabbed Jasmine's hand and picked up his speed to a full sprint pulling her along with him.

Jasmine looked back "NOOO! Michael please!" Jasmine screamed as she saw the spiders. Jasmine began crying as she ran. There was no way that they were going to be able to outrun the spiders as fast as they were catching up to them.

"Keep going," John said to Jasmine as he let go of her hand and stopped running. John took a few deep breaths to catch his breath. He wanted to fall over but there would have to be time to breathe later. Right now, he needed to kill the spiders. Within no time they were upon John. He had pre lit a few dynamite sticks and was launching them as they tried to get to him. John was able to fire only one shot with his shotgun before he was tackled from behind by a giant brown recluse spider.

John screamed as he closed his eyes and prepared for the spider to bite him. It never came. Instead, the spider was lifted in the air and thrown by a giant being in a white robe. As John got to his feet to see if Jasmine was okay, he noticed an army of beings dressed in white. Michael the archangel was with them slashing at spiders, with their swords.

The angel who had just saved John scooped him up in one arm and sprinted for the exit. John saw the angel by Jasmine do the same. The other angels did the best they could to protect the angels running with the two Demigods in their hands. John helplessly watched as a few angels went down and were dragged off by the spiders. As they exited the Labyrinth and then exited the haunted looking house. The angel put them down.

"Stay here." He very sharply said. "Do not move from this spot."

John and Jasmine stayed in place. Both too scared to move. After a few moments John randomly fell to his knees, tears pouring down his face. John was traumatized. He had just nearly been killed by the creature he was most scared of.

The angels after another twenty minutes finally came out. They were battered, tired and many of their pearly white robes were no longer white. Michael looked furious.

"What do you think you are doing?" He questioned the two demigods.

"What were we doing?" Jasmine roughly replied back. "We were planning on mapping the Labyrinth out so that we would be able to have an advantage over our competition. I'm sure Lucifer will be mapping it out for his son's."

"You know nothing about Lucifer. He is my brother!" Michael shouted as he furrowed his eyebrows. "I grew up with him. The Christians think that we were created full grown, but that is not true. We were created as infants like humans are and we grew up. Don't ever talk to me about my brother Lucifer as if you know him better than me." Michael spoke quietly, but you could feel the anger and sharpness in his voice. "Today is the first time since the war in Heaven took place, that an angel has been killed. Thirteen angels died rescuing you."

"Wait, I thought angels couldn't die? They only reform." John said to Michael, remembering that he had once said that.

"Oh no, angels can be killed but it is just harder. You have to have a certain kind of dagger or sword to kill them. However, the exception is in the Labyrinth because in there, we angels have no powers including healing powers. The Labyrinth is designed to block all power, which Lucifer obviously has forgotten, unless he knows his sons will be killed in there as well." Michael bit his lip like John did when he was in deep thought or angry. "This tournament I believe isn't about winning at all, but about killing you two. Lucifer is willing to sacrifice his own sons to kill one of you or hopefully both of you."

"We are not going back down there." John said to Michael. "That was a life experience that I never want to ever have again. I could do it if things were fair, like if we were allowed to use our powers. But without our powers we are nothing.

Why did you and your fellow angels not just grab us and teleport out, like you guys teleported in obviously?"

"Because you can use magic to get in. How else do you think that we got all of those monsters down there? But on the counter side, once inside you cannot use magic at all. Not even us as I just had previously explained to you while you obviously weren't listening. There is a spell that would allow you to use your powers in there but the Father has forbidden anyone to use it.

And as far as you not going back in there, that is not optional. On the day the tournaments start no matter where you are, you will be teleported into the tunnels. And when you leave at night if you do not go back you will be teleported back and then not allowed to leave at night. Then you will be stuck in there with Arachnid and her not so little babies."

"In which case," John replied sharply, "you guys lose, and Zeus and Lucifer don't go to the lake of fire. I'm cool with that." John stated as he grabbed Jasmine's hand and prepared to teleport away.

"You don't know how Lucifer is. Or Zeus," Michael began. "Lucifer especially hates humans as does Odin. If they win a single tournament, they will be free to do as they please to humans. They hate humans and my Father, which is in Heaven, will have to turn Earth over to them and Just focus on his other creations. Which means, that while you may be dead. Your mom," Michael said pointing at John, "and your dad," he said pointing at Jasmine, "will still be alive. And you better believe they are the first ones my cousins and brothers go for. They will gain control of

Tartarus and they will torment you every day down there for all of eternity."

John didn't speak for a moment as he thought. They didn't have any choice, but he could at least hustle Michael into helping them have a better chance of surviving.

"Well, here is the deal," John finally said without consulting Jasmine. Which he normally would do out of respect for her, but he had an idea that couldn't wait. "If we go in there un-prepared, we are going to die anyways. All of that will happen regardless. Not to mention, a deal could be struck between us and lucifer while we are alive to where he will reward us and our families for throwing the tournament and letting him win, rather than torture us. So, if you want us to go in there and fight this battle with the intent to win. We will need an accurate map of the Labyrinth and indicators to tell us which tunnel is which so when they change, we will still know where we are. Second, we will need to know every beast that is down there and we will need weapons that can kill them and training in those weapons on how to beat them."

Michael looked at John for a second at first with no sign of considering John's suggestion. But then out of nowhere Michael smiled. "Deal. We will have the list of monsters in the Labyrinth to you on Wednesday, two days from now."

"Awesome!" John said looking down at the ground, concentrating on his last question. "Okay, my final question is this, if we cannot use our powers in the Labyrinth, is it the same in Tartarus? Because I don't see any way of making it out of Tartarus alive without our powers."

"No, you will have your powers there. The reason nobody escapes from Tartarus is because once you die you lose your powers. So, nobody can escape. Like you pointed out, without powers there is no chance in hell of you or anything escaping Tartarus alive. However, when you go in there you will still be alive, so you will have full control over your powers. I dare say that your powers may even be stronger down there. Now here is a bonus. Apollo is not the only one down there that you can save. Ho Young and Marcus are down there as well. You both can save them along with Apollo. If they escape from there, they will live again."

"Really?" Jasmine asked, smiling. She missed Marcus and Ho Young and thought about them every day. The chance to get them back was almost too much for Jasmine to bare.

"Yes," Michael said, "Now go and get some rest, you have a lot of studying to do tomorrow."

"Okay," John replied, touching Jasmine's shoulder. He teleported them back to her dad's house and into Jasmine's room. They both brushed their teeth and said their prayers before they laid down to sleep.

That night John dreamt a dream. He and Jasmine were in the Labyrinth fighting against the Minotaur and just as they were about to beat the Minotaur three hundred large spiders came speeding around the corner. They ate them and the Minotaur.

For once John was the one who woke up screaming and Jasmine had to calm him.

"I'm sorry." Jasmine said to John. "You were right. We should have never gone down there."

"No, actually I was wrong. Yes, we almost were killed, but if we hadn't of went down there, we would not know that our powers don't work in the Labyrinth but do work in Tartarus. We wouldn't be getting a map of the Labyrinth or a list of the monsters down there. Now go ahead and get some sleep." John said closing his eyes.

Jasmine stayed awake for a while. Lying on her back and contemplating the new information they now had concerning the tournament and drowning herself in thoughts of seeing Marcus and Ho Young again. Her hands were gently folded across her stomach as she just laid there deep in thought. She had managed to play it cool all day, but now her mind was wondering and wound up back on the Labyrinth and how they almost died. Tears finally began to soak her cheeks. She didn't care that she was almost eaten by a spider. She was hurt deep down in her soul for making John go. Especially since John was already scared of regular sized spiders.

John, who had only been half asleep, heard Jasmine silently crying, just loud enough to barely make a sound. He slowly turned his head in Jasmine's direction. For a moment John hesitated to make an attempt to comfort her. He assumed that she was crying because she did not want to do the tournament. Somehow John knew and felt that it was because of something else.

"Jasmine", said John softly as he placed his hand on her shoulder. She quickly tried to sneakily wipe her tears without letting John know she was crying but John reached over further and wiped a streak away from her cheeks as it was racing down.

"Why are you crying Jasmine?"

"I'm sorry John. I am so sorry. Please forgive me? I think I know everything and I almost got you killed today. You expressed multiple times that you did not want to go in there and you only did to protect me." Jasmine started crying harder, "you almost died because of me John. How can you not hate me?"

"Because I'm in love with you which leaves no room for hate." said John sincerely. John leaned closer into Jasmine and kissed her cheek. "You are not always going to be right, just like I am not always going to be right. We will make bad decisions but as long as we make them together that's all that matters."

"John, I know you are trying to make me feel better, but I have a pain deep down in—"

John interrupted Jasmine with a soft kiss on her lips. "Listen, I think I have proven that I will die so that you can live. Let it go. What you did today, as I have already told you a million times, was give us an actual fighting chance in the tournament."

"You are right John but you dying for me is not what I want. I don't want to die and I don't want you to die either. John we cannot go back in there unless we are allowed to use our powers."

"I know." John said." That is why you aren't going in there."

"What do you mean by that is why YOU aren't going in there?" Jasmine asked with an expression of worry in her facial features.

"I mean that we did not ask for this and you definitely did not ask for this. So," John hesitated for a moment before finishing, "I am going in alone. There is no rule saying that we both have to go in."

"I do not think so." Jasmine stated very angrily, hurt showing in her eyes. "You are not going in there alone."

"Jasmine, it is the only way."

"No, it is not!" Jasmine desperately replied in a shouting voice.

"Is everything ok up there?" Jasmine's dad yelled up the stairs making sure his daughter was okay.

"Yes, sorry dad. Everything is fine."

"Okay, well if you need me, you know where to find me."

"Yeah dad, I know, but everything is fine." Jasmine yelled back down to her dad before she turned her attention back to the conversation she was having with John. "As I was saying." Jasmine looked at John seriously, "either we die together or we live together. But no matter what we do, it has to be together."

John looked down at the bed, he knew Jasmine was going to end up in the Labyrinth whether she went with him, or after him.

"Besides." Jasmine continued, "we are both required to be in it. Remember? Michael said when it is time, we will both be transported into the labyrinth."

"Dang it." John said. "You sure are right. Jasmine, I don't know what to do then." John said flailing his arms as helplessly as he felt.

"For now, just lay here with me." Jasmine replied. "I love you. And should we die this time, I want to enjoy you as much as I can before this tournament ruins our lives again." John cuddled up next to Jasmine. He stared into her wonderful face. All of his life he had wanted to date her and now he was and if this tournament didn't go in their favor, he could die saying he was with her till death did them part.

Chapter Seven

Lucifer entered the throne room of Olympus bleeding angelic golden blood from his head. He looked around surveying all that was present in the room but specifically looking for Zeus.

"Something you want to tell me, cousin?" Lucifer said with his hands on his hips. Lucifer was hot, he had been jumped by Odin and Thor.

"We kind of were involved in the whole Ragnarök prophecy coming true. We may have played a small hand in it being destroyed." Zeus said grinning. "Just a tiny bit," Zeus used the space between his pointer tip and his thumb tip to show how little of a role they played in it.

"Oh, I don't know why you are grinning." Lucifer said laughing. "They were right behind me, headed here, as I came. When they found out I was locked away in the bottomless pit during that incident, they reluctantly let me go."

As Lucifer finished speaking Odin, Thor, and the Asgardian army stood outside of the Olympus' gates dressed in full battle attire. Loki winked at Zeus from outside of the gate, giving Zeus a hint that he was still on their side.

"Now that you are here, we must talk", Zeus yelled out to Odin from inside the palace.

"Oh, dear cousin, there will be plenty of time to talk centuries from now," Odin yelled back. "When you and your brethren reform."

"There will be no more reformations." Zeus yelled back. "I'm going to assume that Lucifer failed to disclose to you what is happening right now between the Creator and all who fought against him, which includes you."

"Well, no. He never got the chance. We fought him on site and then as we were about to kill him, Loki informed us that he was not a part of it. He reminded us that Lucifer had been in the bottomless pit during the time of Ragnarök, making it impossible for him to have been involved in the attacks."

"As much as I would have liked to kill him," Thor interceded, "my father Odin forced me to release him. Without a word he fled from Asgard. We decided to attack you and my, what a coincidence, this is exactly where he ended up as well."

"Well if we fight now and you kill Lucifer or myself," Zeus yelled back, "the deal will be off and it will be off to the lake of fire for us all. Lucifer and I have a deal with THE FATHER, THE CREATOR, and if we are not here to continue it, well, you can guess what happens. It will be considered a broken deal. Our side will automatically be forfeited and sent to the lake of fire."

Thor looked at his dad Odin. "Father let me send Zeus to the parts of Tartarus in which not even a God can reform."

"Speak on this deal that you have with Father." Odin began," tell us how you begged for mercy and to be forgiven. I'll bet you even tried to make it seem like we all were responsible and you an innocent victim, but Father knowing all things did not fall for it. Then you included everyone else in this 'so called' tournament, realizing you could not win without them. In my years as ruler of Asgard, I have learned but one thing, cowards make deals and plead to save themselves while warriors fight to the death."

"Oh, I did not beg. And from what I have seen in your many years as a ruler, all you have managed to learn to do is die. Which is why you are just now reforming." Lucifer shouted down from the top of the palace's steps. Lucifer thought it best to begin taking control of the conversation before Zeus could utter another word. "You see, next to Father I am the brightest and most intelligent angel. What I learned over many years is how to stay alive."

"Put it how you wish." Odin said. "But if this deal doesn't strike my interest, we Asgardians will attack. And I promise that your destruction will be much worse than the one that my people suffered during the time of Ragnarök where you Greeks cowards, smiled in our faces, but stabbed us in the back."

"We know it was you." Odin said pointing at Athena, "who freed Fenrir the werewolf. It was you Greeks who coerced Leviathan against us. Bribed the dark elves into warring the elves of the light to separate me from my son Thor. Loki's acts in this are only forgivable because he is my son. I know he has much to be angry about. I killed his real father during war. I couldn't bring myself to kill him, so I brought him back. Then I imprisoned his son, Fenrir. Had it not been for all of these events, he would still be the responsible and good son that I once raised before he learned of these mistakes of mine. If it would not have been for my mistakes," Odin said very sadly looking at the ground, "perhaps my son would not have been so easily persuaded and eager to see my death."

Odin realized that he had made mistakes as had the Greek Gods in mid speech. "There will be no war," Odin finally said after a moment of silence.

"But Father," Thor pleaded.

"We all since before we fell from heaven, have been making mistake after mistake. How can I refuse to forgive you for your treachery against Asgard, yet expect my son Loki to forgive me for my treachery against him as a baby until the present?"

Loki silently sat in his chariot listening, but not speaking. Odin's words were appealing to the better side of Loki. The feeling was uncomfortable for him. He much preferred to be angry with Thor and Odin and having reason to plot against them.

"Fine you want peace Father? Have peace! But allow Zeus and I to battle like men. One on one combat!" Thor thundered angrily.

"Oh, I am perfectly fine with that," Zeus replied, before Odin could answer Thor.

"If it is a one on one battle, then you shall have it. But after it, I will hear no more about any private wars. Pride will have its way today, but tomorrow strategy and intellect must take the lead. Pride is for fools and wisdom for those who wish to succeed." Odin addressed Thor and Zeus.

"Perfect Father. Tomorrow we will drink as Gods. But today Zeus will be shamed a second time by me."

With those last words, Thor flew at Zeus at a great speed with his hammer in the lead. Zeus held his hand out as his lightning staff flew to him. Thor barely missed hitting Zeus in the center of his face with his hammer as Zeus ducked just in time upon grabbing his staff.

Thor turned and swung his hammer down with full force in an attempt to crush Zeus' skull but Zeus blocked it with his staff. The blow from Thor, however, was very strong and it brought Zeus to his knees.

Zeus rolled over to avoid the third strike and hit Thor with lightning from his staff. Thor flew back and yelled in rage. Zeus fired another lightning strike from his staff that Thor dodged with the speed unmatched. Thor threw his hammer at Zeus full force hitting Zeus right in the center of his core. Zeus flew through the palace walls of Mount Olympus.

Realizing that Zeus would have been hurt badly by that blow from his hammer. Thor without hesitation charged in after him. Zeus was too quick and was back up to battle Thor in combat. Zeus' staff verses Thor's hammer. They wound up back outside of the palace and fighting on the steps. Giving their all, each trying to outdo the other. Zeus slipped a mighty swing by Thor with his hammer and did a spinning ground kick tripping Thor and causing him to tumble down five rows of steps. As Zeus flew towards Thor, Thor blasted Zeus back with lightning of his own. Zeus was blasted back to the top of the palace steps, hitting the palace doors hard, causing them to break. As Zeus attempted to get back to his feet, Thor took to the skies. He began to twirl his hammer in the air, creating a Tornado of wind, filled with thunder and lightning. Zeus had been waiting for this. Their last fight Thor had completely caught Zeus off guard with it, But not this time. This time he was expecting it.

Zeus fired six lightning bolts at Thor, Thor was hit and fell from the sky landing hard on the stone staircase of Olympus. Thor sat up slowly dazed. Zeus not wasting any time, charged at Thor. Zeus was determined not to lose this time. He raced towards Thor and oh how he could see, smell, and taste Victory. As he drew near to him Thor looked up and saw Zeus just in time and moved to the side very swiftly, leaving a bit of his leg behind to trip Zeus.

Zeus tried to avoid Thor's leg but he was just moving too fast to adjust in mid run. As his foot tripped on Thor’s leg Zeus banged his head hard on one of the cement stairs. Golden blood oozed out of Zeus’ head. Zeus stood up just in time to see a flash of silver. Thor had flown at Zeus with lightning speed with his hammer leading the charge. This was a favorite move of Thor’s.

The hammer connected with Zeus’ chest and Thor just kept flying forward with the hammer pushing hard against Zeus. Thor flew Zeus right through his own statue causing the statue to explode with gold bursting in every direction from the exploding statue. Zeus attempted to get up but fell back to the ground. Thor charged again mustering up all of his might, with his hammer aimed directly at Zeus. He was lying on the ground with more golden blood preluding from different parts of his body.

As Thor charged, Zeus held his hand out and his staff flew to him. Zeus without even aiming, shot Lightning bolt after lightning bolt into the sky. The third strike hit Thor directly in his mouth. Thor blacked out in midflight and fell to the ground and bounced high off of the first few steps he landed on.

As Thor opened his eyes, he too was having trouble getting up. Both Zeus and Thor began crawling their way towards one another.

"That is enough!" Odin yelled. "You both have had your fight. Neither of you proved your point. Neither of you in that fight did anything productive towards winning this tournament that I am still waiting to hear about. The tournament that determines our freedom from the Lake of Fire that FATHER promised to send us to."

Thor attempted to crawl again towards Zeus but Odin blasted the steps between them, causing both Zeus and Thor to fly backwards away from each other. "I said enough! The next time I have to speak, you will be fighting me instead."

Though Thor wanted to finish Zeus off, Odin's threat of battle was enough for him to submit. The only angel who could compete with Odin, was Odin's brother, Michael the Archangel.

"Okay then," Odin said, addressing everyone present, "let us go inside, have drinks and discuss this tournament."

"That sounds like a plan to me," Athena, the Angel of Wisdom said appearing next to Zeus and helping him up.

Chapter Eight

"Duck!" John yelled at Jasmine as a giant spider lunged at her from the darkness. John tried to get to Jasmine but he couldn't without his powers he was not able to teleport. John watched as Jasmine was eaten alive by spiders. What was he thinking bringing them back into the labyrinth to try and map everything out a second time?

"NOOO!" John yelled into the darkness as the spiders lunged at him. Where was Michael? John assumed that if they got into trouble that Michael would save them. But he wasn't coming? Jasmine was dead and now the spiders that had leapt at him were inches away.

John leapt up, swinging wildly in the air, to hit as many spiders as he could before they could kill him, but there were no spiders, just air. John looked down. He was inches from Jasmine's face who was sound asleep in their bed.

John plopped down and wiped the sweat from his face. It was just a dream, a very real dream it seemed like. John wondered if the dream he just had was anything close to the ones Jasmine kept having, before he put the protective air shield around her when she slept.

John watched Jasmine sleep for a second. He knew what he had to do, but was scared out of his mind. John teleported himself back to the house in London. He slowly crept up to the house. John knew that he would have to sprint in and sprint out. He needed pictures of the spell at the entrance to the Labyrinth to see if he could find a counter spell.

As John took another step towards the house a familiar voice yelled from behind him.

"STOP!! DO NOT TAKE ANOTHER STEP!"

John froze in mid step. He slowly turned around to face the elderly woman dressed in white.

"Listen I'm not going all the way in. Just to the beginning part right before the maze begins to take a picture of the words written on the wall. I believe those words are the source to why no powers work in the Labyrinth."

"Wrong. That spell is what imprisons the monsters in the Labyrinth. If you undo that spell you will only release all of the beast back into the world and still not be able to use your powers in the Labyrinth. Not to mention the spiders are waiting at the entrance into the Labyrinth hidden by the darkness."

"Well since you know so much, what spell will allow us to use our powers in the Labyrinth so I don't have to get killed by the spider ambush? Because we die if we go in there without the use of our powers."

"Come and follow me." The woman in white said. Without another word she turned and walked towards the blue house across the street. John followed. As they entered the house the entire scenery inside changed into what looked like a castle.

"What is going on?" John asked, scared and confused. He began to wonder if it was some kind of trap. But if it was a trap, why did the woman stop him from walking into the Labyrinth where a ton of spiders were waiting to kill him at the entrance? Was she lying about the spiders at the entrance to keep him from going into the Labyrinth and to keep him from finding out the spell that would allow them to use their powers?

"Feel free to sit." The woman said calmly. John quietly sat down studying the woman as she took her hood off. She was an elderly woman with long white hair and ears that narrowed to a point and were long enough to touch the top of her head. Her face was wrinkled and her jawline narrow.

"You are an elf." John finally said as he finished examining his host.

"That is correct. I'm an elf of light. When Leviathan fell after Asgard The Creator entrusted us Elves of the Light to guard the entrances to the Labyrinth and also guard the portals between realms."

"You mean the nine realms?" John asked the woman, remembering studying Asgard and the nine realms.

"No. I mean the various realms that preside in each and every Galaxy."

"What do you mean?" John asked.

"Well, in each Galaxy there are multiple realms. Here in the Milky Way there are thirteen, but only nine connected to earth. There is an angel that THE FATHER has appointed to rule over each Galaxy. Those angels meet with THEFATHER and give reports for the Galaxies and creations that THEFATHER has created.

"Oh, I see." John said. "You are here to guard this particular entrance to the Labyrinth." John said piecing everything together.

"Yes, that is correct." The woman replied. "My name is Qkertayluor."

"Do you have a nickname?" John immediately asked knowing he was not going to be able to pronounce whatever name the woman had just said to him.

"No." Qkertayluor replied.

"Okay then I will call you Q."

"That is perfectly fine." Q replied.

"Okay, so back to my reason for being here," John began, "I need to find a spell to allow Jasmine and myself to use our powers in the Labyrinth."

"Actually, you need to find a spell and someone to cast it. You have powers but you have never performed ritual magic, which requires perfection in pronunciation and perfection in the motions."

"I'm guessing you know the spell and are more than capable of performing the spell?"

"You are correct, but I will not do it. The rules have been set by The Creator and I will not go against The Creator of all things."

"That is dumb. If we lose, Lucifer and all of your enemies win."

"How are you sure that they are my enemies?", Q said, baring her sharp teeth as she leaned forward scowling with a fierce look in her eyes.

John wasn't scared though. John knew elves were powerful but they were not as powerful as Leviathan, who John had recently beaten.

"Well," John said ignoring Q's change in attitude towards him. "Because Zeus and the other Gods are the ones who orchestrated the attack on your world by the dark elves and the giants. They did it so they could separate Odin and Thor."

"Your knowledge is very admirable, but as I stated before, I cannot help you." Q said to John leaning back in her chair. "Believe me I cannot wait for those self-proclaimed Gods to be thrown into the lake of fire."

"Which they won't be," John interrupted, "without us being able to use our powers."

"Either way, I cannot disobey The Creator. Not even in such a case as this."

John made an agitated noise of exasperation. "Fine." I'll just figure it out myself."

Without another word John teleported out of Q's basement and back to Jasmine's house. Jasmine was wide awake and sitting in a corner. When John appeared, Jasmine ran at him.

"Where have you been?" I wake up from a dream that you went back to the Labyrinth alone and were ambushed by spiders and killed. And sure enough, you were gone. I called Michael and he said that you had gone back to the Labyrinth but that one of the guardians prevented you from going in."

"Yeah, that old woman who stopped us last time stopped me again. Apparently, she is one of the Elves of Light."

"Really?!" Jasmine responded with pure excitement.

"I don't know why that excites you. But she admitted to being able to perform the spell that could lift the spell blocking us from using our powers in the Labyrinth."

"Well I expect that she wouldn't." Jasmine replied, not sure why John would think she would. "I mean she is there on orders from God. So, if she is working for God why would she go against him?"

"I don't know. Maybe for honor, to get revenge for the Greek gods initiating the attack on their world by the Giants and Dark Elves."

"Well I'm sure that she wants revenge but knows that the Greek Gods and other Fallen Angels with them are going to pay in the end regardless."

"Jasmine why are you so calm?" John finally asked. She was just hysterical before falling asleep, and now she was calm. It didn't make sense to him.

"Look." Jasmine replied pointing to the desk in the corner of her room. There was a pile of books on the desk and stacked up on the floor next to the desk.

"Every creature in the Labyrinth is in those books, including their strengths and weaknesses. Also, we have several maps of the labyrinth."

"I see Michael kept his word."

"Yes, he did." Jasmine replied joyfully with a beautiful smile on her face. John chuckled to himself as he watched Jasmine with her new found confidence in their mission.

John looked at the books again, and using his power summoned the top book to him. The book was about the demon Leo. A twenty-foot lion who was solid muscle. Leo was very fast and very strong. His roar had scared more than hundreds to death. Leo's weaknesses were not very many things. But the horn of an African buffalo could kill him on contact Also Leo tired very easily. So, if you could survive for more than twenty minutes, he would tire giving you a chance to kill him. The book then went on in chapters.

John closed the front page. He was drowned in despair. There was no way that they were going to win. One look at Jasmine and John did not want to discourage her. John sat on the bed and laid back on it with his eyes looking up at the ceiling. Jasmine, climbed on top of John.

John wrapped his arms around Jasmine. "You know I love you right?" John told her.

"I know." Jasmine smiled as she replied. "But I also know that I love you more."

"That is not possible." John said, kissing Jasmine on her lips soft and slow.

"Oh, I think it is." Jasmine replied. Jasmine kissed John back on his lips. "All I want John, is your love forever."

"You already have that." John replied, as he began to lift up Jasmine's shirt.

"Awesome!" Jasmine replied jumping up. "Well I guess it is time to start studying."

John sat up with his mouth open. "Really Jasmine? You know that was messed up. You tease me and then get off as soon as I make a move."

"We need to study right now. That can wait."

John sighed as he got up. "Fine, we can study but you owe me."

"I don't owe you anything. If we should by chance mess around afterwards, it will be because we wanted to, not because of any debt."

John picked up the book about Leo's History and began to read it as he sat in a chair that was in the corner of the room. After reading for a few hours John asked Jasmine if she was ready to go to their house.

"John, you just don't like studying," Jasmine replied, frowning.

"That is true, but I did study. Look, Leo the Lion is none other than the Nemean Lion killed by Hercules. Although in many pictures it depicts the Nemean Lion as walking on all four legs, he really walked on two like a human. He has the strength of five strong men. He can run up to twenty-five miles per hour in short distances. Leo is also the son of Typhoon and was sent to Nemea to terrorize the town. His skin is made from gold, and no human weapons can kill it, except the Scythe Sword."

"Okay so maybe you did read." Jasmine replied, smiling. "But I still have reading to do on Cerberus who is in the Labyrinth. Apparently, he was placed there after the great flood."

"You have got to be kidding me. There is no way even Lucifer's sons will survive five minutes in the labyrinth."

"That's what has me nervous." Jasmine replied. "Lucifer knows all of the beasts in the Labyrinth and is the one who picked the Labyrinth to be the place of the tournament. From what Michael says, he is very crafty. I'll bet he is going to find a loophole to cheat for his son's so that they can use their powers if he already hasn't."

"I'll bet the same." John replied furrowing his brow. He was certain of it.

"Did Michael tell you the story of him and Lucifer growing up, that he promised to tell us."

"No, not yet. He said he would do it when he came back."

"Good, because I did not want to miss it. Now how do we beat Cerberus?" John finished his question.

"It says by playing music."

"That's it?" John replied. "Well that shouldn't be too hard then."

"I wouldn't be so certain. One of the books I read while you were gone was about Medusa and she is attracted to music. If we play music to put the three headed dog Cerberus to sleep, Medusa will show up."

"That sucks," John replied. "How do we beat her?"

"We have to cut her head off and burn it. We can look at her through mirrors and through sunglasses, but if you see her with your bare eye, you are turned to stone. So, if we use sunglasses, we cannot look out of the sides of them as we are turning, otherwise we are turned to stone."

"Okay, well then, there must be another way to beat Cerberus because no way in hell am I calling Medusa."

"I didn't see any, other than stabbing Cerberus in the heart. If you cut off a head it grows back."

"Doesn't it grow back two heads, every time you cut one off?" John asked, thinking he was correcting Jasmine.

"Good guess. But no." Jasmine replied. "That is the Hydro Dragon."

"Yeah, you are right." John replied thinking about it. "It was the Hydro. He isn't down there, is he?"

"I don't know, let me see the list." Jasmine scanned the list for at least two minutes. "No, he is not on here."

"Thank God." John replied.

"Oh. I wouldn't thank him just yet. Some of the beasts and monsters down there are pretty scary and dangerous. Here." Jasmine said reaching out to hand John the list.

"I'm actually okay for right now. I don't want to see that list."

"Are you sure?" Jasmine asked, surprised at John's unwillingness to look at the list. Normally John would have been the first one to look.

"No, I'm okay, really I am."

“Okay,” Jasmine replied. It will be where you can find it if you need to.”

“Do you like to get these books to our house or leave them here?”

“We can take them. I mean we will have to take them little by little, but we can take them home. We have a lot of studying to do.”

“I know.” John replied as he walked over to the first pile of books. John teleported back and forth until all of the books were at the house he and Jasmine lived in.

Chapter Nine

"So, your plan is to go to the Dark Elves and ask them to give you a spell that will allow your sons to use their powers in the Labyrinth?" Thor asked Lucifer as all of the Gods sat around a large dining table on Mount Olympus.

"Yes, that is the plan."

"And why would they help you?"

"I'm not saying that they will. I'm saying that we need to attempt to get them on our side. Remind them that they did assist us in the first and the second war and I'm sure that they will be counted among those cast into the lake of fire that fought against God."

"As much as I hate to admit this," Zeus said slamming his fist on the large meeting table, "Lucifer has a point."

"He always has a point," Poseidon interjected, "but as clever as his plans are, whenever they are against the FATHER they tend to backfire."

"Another good point." said Odin.

"Exactly." Zeus stated. "We need a full proof plan. Not just one that sounds good, but also one that has the least chances of failing."

"You Gods can come up with a plan then. But as for me, I'm going to go speak with the council of the Dark Elves." Lucifer said.

"What about training your sons? When exactly where you going to start doing that?"

"What is the point in training them if they cannot use their powers? Without our powers each beast down there could kill us Gods easily."

Thor sat back in his chair and looked towards his father Odin. "I have to agree with my cousin Lucifer on this one Father. Without being able to use their powers they will easily be killed in the Labyrinth."

"Okay." Odin finally said after sitting silently in thought for a minute as the other Gods argued back and forth. "So, we must either convince the Dark Elves to help us, or force them, but either way we need a Dark Elf to lift the curse on the Labyrinth that blocks the use of power in there."

"Wait a minute," Hades finally spoke up for the first time in the meeting." If we lift the curse, then the demigods will be able to use their powers as well. It would give them the advantage. No offence Lucifer, but their power far exceeds that of your sons."

"Ok, this is the plan," Lucifer finally said. "I was going to go and not talk to the Dark Elves about lifting the curse, but about participating in the next tournament. Without the use of their powers as you all have pointed out over and over again, both sides will be killed. Which means we will rid ourselves of these demigods.

It sucks that I have to sacrifice my sons, wait, no it doesn't." Lucifer said laughing.

"You are a piece of work," Thor finally said, shaking his head in disgust. "You would sacrifice your own sons for you to live. It is not that way on Asgard. We give our lives to protect those who cannot fend for themselves and definitely for our family and friends."

"Okay, what would you have me do?" Lucifer asked, as his face blushed red.

"The Labyrinth is too dangerous without any of them being able to use their powers. I say we catch us a Dark Elf and force him to chant the spell that would free all of the monsters in the Labyrinth onto Earth The tournament will be on both sides. Recapturing all of the beast and they can attack each other while the tournament is in play. In the end, whoever captures the most monsters wins the tournaments."

"That is actually a good idea." Lucifer said as his face was frozen in amazement at the idea. "Let's do it. I will go and tell The FATHER the change in plans." Lucifer told all of the others in the room.

"That really is a good idea." Hades said. "I like it."

"Thank you." Thor replied. "I tried to imply my father Odin's wisdom to this situation as he taught me to do. If Lucifer's sons, who are less experienced than the Demigods, would have died before the Demigods did, the tournament would have ended within the first day. I was just thinking about how easily that tournament could have played against us. I don't like depending on luck and that tournament was depending 100% on luck."

"I agree." Zeus said. "It definitely could have gone either way."

Chapter Ten

Michael appeared between John and Jasmine as they were walking.

"Whoa!!" John yelled, jumping back and grabbing his heart after realizing it was Michael.

"Michael you cannot be doing that. You need to appear at least fifteen feet in front of us so that we can see you coming. "

"That is not important." Michael said, brushing John's comment aside. "Listen, the tournament has changed."

"What do you mean?" Jasmine asked, concerned that it had somehow become worse or somehow more impossible.

"Well it will be similar to the last one, accept a lot more beasts."

"Oh," Jasmine replied looking down at the ground. The last tournament nearly killed them with only three beasts.

"That sucks," John replied. "But it's better than fighting them in the Labyrinth without our powers."

"Yeah, I would say so." Michael replied. "That version of the tournament was a suicide mission. Lucifer was going to risk losing his sons just so the two of you would be killed."

"Wait. What?" John asked. a look of bewilderment etched across his face.

"Let us be honest, you have read the books. You know at least some of the monsters that are down there. Neither side would have lasted more than thirty minutes in the Labyrinth and that is stretching it. Lucifer was depending on the two of you to die first. I'll bet his plan was for his sons to remain by the entrance of the Labyrinth while you two would naturally immediately start jogging through the Labyrinth to win the tournament getting you killed first while his sons lived."

"Wow," John replied. "That's pretty messed up. So, God changed it to stop his plan?" asked John.

"Well, no." Michael replied. "Thor and Odin reformed and Thor was disgusted with the idea of Lucifer risking the lives of his two sons just to kill the two of you. Truth be told, even at the entrance the beasts can smell when someone is in the Labyrinth. They would have most likely been killed to."

"Okay, so to this tournament," John said, changing the subject. "How many beasts are we talking about and are they allowed to attack the humans?"

"No, they are not allowed to attack any humans, only Demigods. You two and Lucifer's sons are the only ones they are allowed to attack."

"That definitely will make it a little easier."

"Oh, and just a heads up, from this day forward, bath in mint oil before you go to sleep and when you wake up. Because until the tournament starts Arachnid's babies are allowed to bite you if they come across you. So, I'm sure you know what I am indicating."

"Yes," Jasmine interjected. "You are saying that she will most likely send a few of her babies after us while they still are allowed to bite us, meaning they are not allowed to attack us during the tournament."

"That is correct." Michael replied, smiling.

"Arachnid will not be one of the beasts?" John asked, hoping she wasn't.

"Oh, trust me she will be one of the beasts." Michael replied. "Her babies however, are not part of the tournament, only her. They are forbidden to interfere."

"Thank God," John replied, after making a sigh of relief.

"I have to be going but study the books I gave you.

"Okay," John said, waving at the air sarcastically, as Michael had already left.

"That is much better news." John said to Jasmine knew it would still be tough and very dangerous for them, especially since Ho-Young and Marcus had died in the previous tournament.

The only issue with not going through the Labyrinth into Tartarus was that they would not have the chance to save Marcus and Ho-Young.

"You know," John began as he turned towards Jasmine," I believe that all things happen for a reason, don't you?"

"Yeah, I guess. Why?"

"First off, since the angels were going to save us in the Labyrinth anyways, Q didn't have to reveal herself to us. I don't know exactly why, yet but I think that we met Q for a reason. Q actually may be able to help us in the instance if we should decide to maybe go into Tartarus to save Ho-Young and Marcus."

"Do you think we can?" Jasmine took in a deep breath, "the thought of saving Ho Young and Marcus seemed too good to be true. I mean, we don't know how to get in or out of Tartarus without going through the Labyrinth. You heard Michael. We would be killed in there within the first five minutes without the use of our powers."

"I know." John replied, with a smile on his face. "But since the Light Elves are the guardians of all of the entrances to the Labyrinth and into Tartarus, I'm betting that Q knows a way in and a way out."

"I can see where you are going with this, but why would Q help us?"

John replied to Jasmine's question, "Q hates the Greek Gods and definitely hates Lucifer. If Q could help us get Ho Young and Marcus, it would give us full strength and increase our chances of winning this tournament."

“That makes sense, but I’m still a little doubtful about Q helping us.”

“There is only one way to find out.” John said, holding his hands at chest level in a pleading kind of way with a facial expression to match.

“I really don’t want to. My gut is telling me that even though Q may be an Elf of Light, that she may still be deceptive. From my research on the Dark Elves and the Elves of the Light, I have learned that they are not named with light or darkness because they are good or bad but because of how they are born. The Elves of Light are born from the sun while the Dark Elves are born from the darkness. One book even suggested possibly from black holes.

“I didn’t know that.” John replied, with a look of bewilderment. He looked down towards the ground realizing the danger he had put himself in by allowing Q to take him down into the cellar of her home. John remembered the look of evil that came over Q’s face. A shutter ran down his body.

“That option is out then.” said John.

“I want to get them out too,” Jasmine stated. Her eyes were filled with sadness and began to water. The thought of not being able to save Ho Young and Marcus was too much for her. Jasmine’s insides quenched together as she spoke.

“We just have to accept that we cannot save them”, Jasmine finally managed to say.

John wanted to argue back, because Marcus and Ho Young being tortured in Tartarus was not acceptable to him, and not going to save them was even more unacceptable But Jasmine was right. They knew nothing about Tartarus and saving Ho Young and Marcus would prove to be near impossible.

John and Jasmine continued their walk. The wind began to pick up a bit and after a bit of nagging from Jasmine, John used his powers to push the wind away from them. The tricky part was doing it without being seen, because there were others walking along the sidewalk not far from them. John was forced to use only his mind A trick that he had been working on over the prior few months. John didn't like always having to use his hands telegraphing his every move, so he began focusing on using his mind which he knew was the source of his power. John figured that since the mind could control every little bone and muscle in his body, that it also could control his power as well without him having to motion everything that he wanted to do.

Chapter Eleven

David Angel found himself on the edge of a cliff standing next to his newly discovered brother Chris Blaine. The surrounding scene was beautiful but their positioning was scary. There barely was enough room on the cliff for either of them to move.

"What is going on?" David asked Chris, his eyes twitching as they always did whenever he was nervous.

"I honestly don't know dude. I just appeared here seconds before you did."

"I see." David replied. He had always seen Chris do his televised magic shows but this was his first time ever speaking to him in person or at all. David wondered if the Gods had told Chris that he was his brother as they had done with him.

"Uh-um," David cleared his throat, "so I guess we are brothers?" He insecurely asked Chris as he reached out to shake Chris' hand. David's voice was a bit hoarse from nervousness.

"Yeah, I was told by Lucifer himself who is supposedly our dad." Chris replied.

"Wait, you got to meet our dad?"

"Yeah, he was going to go to you next but he said something about the Asgardians rising, so he had to rush there or something before they fully formed."

"Oh, I see." David replied. "And when you say Asgardians, are you referring to Asgard like with the myths Odin & Thor?"

"Dude." Chris replied, "our dad is supposed to be a myth."

"That is true." David replied. "I still can't believe that our dad is Satan."

Chris flinched at the name. "I prefer to call him Lucifer. He explained to me that he started both religions, Luciferian and Satanism and did so to keep people confused because another God who calls himself the Father or Creator, started Christianity naming him as the bad guy."

"Yeah, but Zeus and Aphrodites told me that, that God is the Creator and their father." David replied.

"Wait! You got to meet Zeus? The God of the sky and of lightning?!"

"Yeah I did. He is pretty cool actually, scary as well. I actually got into a fight with Hermes before I knew he was Hermes. He was following me, so I walked into an alley and blasted him back into a wall before he knew what hit him."

"You beat Hermes?" Chris asked with a doubtful look on his face.

"Well no." David replied. "After I blasted him, he got up and that is all I remember. Next thing I know I woke up on Olympus with a big headache."

"Hey, at least you can say you blasted a God." Chris chuckled.

"Yeah, that's true." David replied while laughing.

"What are your powers?" Chris asked David, curious to know who was the more powerful brother. In his mind he was but he knew deep down there was a chance that David had been down playing his power during his performances as he had, just a lot more.

"I can shoot fireballs, turn into fire, breathe underwater I can make anyone hallucinate and see things that aren't there. I can even make them think they are somewhere that they are not."

"We pretty much have the same powers. Can you walk on water or command ghosts and other dead things?"

"Yup. So yeah, we have the same powers it sounds like."

"All of my kids have the same powers." Lucifer's voice boomed as he appeared floating in front of them.

Both Chris and David stepped back in fear as Lucifer's sudden appearance frightened them both. As they stepped back on the cliff, they quickly remembered that they were standing on a very narrow part and they both fell backwards.

Lucifer with a quick whisper summoned two demons who shot out of the water with lightning speed, catching Chris and David in mid fall. They flew them back up to the top of the cliff.

"Why are we meeting right here?" Chris asked his dad, very upset at literally almost falling to his death.

"Because I said so." Lucifer replied, eyeing Chris with a look that even made David tremble. David looked from Lucifer to Chris as sweat poured down his head.

"Please." David said to Lucifer. "Chris didn't mean it. He was just shaken up, as I am from the fall."

"I can accept that, but don't ever talk back to me or get an attitude with me." Being my son's does not give you any favoritism with me. If I didn't need you for this tournament, I would kill you right now. Don't think I have to use you, because I have sixteen other kids that I could use. You all have the same powers. You two just have more experience using even the little bits of your power that you know how to use."

"Can I ask a question?" Chris very shakily raised his hand.

"Ask."

"I have served you in the Luciferian religion most of my life and I was taught that they are waiting on a son to be born from you. But if you have so many kids already born, is that real or was it made up?"

"No, it is real. I have one son who will be born and will rise up turning the Nations against The Creator. All will be drawn unto him and he will kill all who oppose him. Christianity in his time will meet its doom."

"Is it either one of us?" Chris asked, hesitantly still not wanting to get the death stare or something worse from Lucifer.

"No. If it was you, do you think I would waste you on a tournament such as this? He has yet to be born. I assume that it will be before the last tournament, if the Oracle is right in her prophecy."

"Oh," Chris said looking down.

"So, pretty much, it doesn't matter whether we live or die." David said in a voice that sounded as weak as he and Chris felt. There dad Lucifer didn't care even an ounce about them. If they died, he would just prepare for the next tournament without a second thought. If they won, he probably would just go back to ignoring them or use them for something else even more dangerous.

"You both are sulking like two little babies. At least wait until I tell you why I brought you here." Lucifer began to explain to Chris and David why they were there on the cliff. "This tournament is a very dangerous tournament. Seventy-three monsters and beasts are being released from the Labyrinth and they will be hunting you. The tournament only requires that you kill them before they kill you, in which case they will automatically reform in the Labyrinth. Here on this Cliff, you can create the illusion that there are more cliffs behind you. You can enchant the water into a tunnel leading into the Labyrinth."

Both Chris and David looked at each other and silently motioned with their bodies, mouths, and hands asking each other if the other knew how to make the tunnel to the Labyrinth.

Lucifer clapped his hands very loudly together to regain both Chris and David's attention. "If you two idiots can focus long enough, I will show you how." Lucifer forced a sarcastic smile. Both David and Chris had to hold their hands over their ears to stop the loud ringing noise that now sounded in both of their ears. It was quite loud and painful.

Lucifer began to chant in a language they had never before heard.

"Now you try," Lucifer said, looking to both of his sons.

Chris and David both looked at each other with wide eyes. "I'm sorry dad. I have never heard such words. Could you please say them slower?"

"I don't have time. Learn them or die. I will write them down for you. The thing to remember is every letter is not what it seems. For instance, the K makes a cru sound, the n makes a pre sound, the w makes a shir sound, and the S makes a blospre sound. You have a week to learn it. If you don't know it, you will be punished severely." With that Lucifer disappeared without another word.

"What in the actual hell just happened?" David asked Chris looking at the words that were carving themselves into the cliff that they were standing on.

"Dude, we are not going to be able to pronounce those words. We might as well just join the other Demigods and fight against dad. Whatever protection they have from dad and the other Gods I'm sure that they will offer us that same protection as well."

"I agree," Chris and David both left the mountain through teleportation. Which went unnoticed by Lucifer who was on a mission headed to a Galaxy on the other side of the Universe to persuade an old friend of his to join in the fight against The Creator, for the next tournament in case they lost this one.

The entire journey Odin's words to Lucifer after asking about his plans are away at Lucifer. Cowards always have a backup plan because they never plan to win. Lucifer had to keep convincing himself on the journey that it wasn't so much that he didn't expect to win, but more him being prepared in the case that they didn't win. His plan with his sons waiting for the beasts and the monsters on the cliff was a near perfect plan. There was almost no way of losing. But the demigods showed in the last tournament that they were capable of pulling off the impossible.

David and Chris appeared in Chicago. They had no idea where to look for the demigods. They didn't even know their names.

"Can you feel when you are in an area where magic has been used?", David asked Chris. Chris shook his head yes in response. So, they journeyed through the city of Chicago finding traces of magic and following the scent back to its owner. There seemed to be a lot of Demigods in Chicago. Most didn't even know they were Demigods or did magic. Chris and David didn't have to ask them because they could somehow both tell that the power in the magic that they had been tracing weas from Demigods who were not anywhere near as powerful as the Demigods they were looking for.

After six days of searching Chris and David were near the point of giving up, but as they found themselves walking across the street on Martin Luther King BLVD, they both caught the scent of strong magic. The scent was very Powerful. Both Chris and David looked at each other and followed the scent far to the other side of the city. They didn't care who saw them walking sniffing the air. They knew they were on the right scent and were only concerned with finding the Demigods.

After an hour of walking the scent disappeared but they continued in the same direction and found the scent again on the south side of Chicago. They followed the scent for another hour and a half until they appeared in front of a bluish, greyish house. The house was a two story, and looked to be one of the finer houses. David was worried that the Demigods lived in a section of the Southside that would have had Chris and his self-dodging bullets but they didn't. The Demigods lived in one of the nicer neighborhoods on the south side of Chicago.

Chris rang the doorbell. Both Chris and David stood back away from the door, not sure what kind of reaction they would get from the Demigods.

"Can I help you?" John asked after quietly appearing behind the sons of Lucifer.

"Oh- um, do- you... uh, live here?" David asked after nearly jumping out of his shoes at the sound of John's voice.

"Depends on who is asking?" John said looking sternly back and forth between Chris and David. John had half of a mind to attack them. The only thing stopping him was he knew nothing would happen to him or Jasmine before the tournament because of the rules. Instead he decided to give them a chance to lie and make up some lame excuse for visiting before demanding them to leave.

"You know exactly who they are Joh." Jasmine said, opening the door. "Come on in guys."

"Jasmine, what are you doing? They are our competition. They probably came here to study us, and to find out our strengths and our weaknesses."

"Oh no," Chris started, but Jasmine interrupted him.

"They actually came because they are being forced to be in the tournament by their dad Lucifer and they want to know if they can join us to gain protection from him."

"Really?" John asked, not wanting to believe that they weren't there for any sinister plan. However, since Jasmine could read minds and partial futures it made it very hard to argue.

John walked in behind Chris and David. As they both walked in, they kept their eyes on John. Both of the brothers could feel the radiance of John's power. Chris momentarily locked eyes with his brother David. His right eyebrow raised higher than his left eye. David quickly nodded his head in a short up and down motion to indicate back to Chris that he too felt how powerful the two Demigods were.

"Have a seat. And don't worry about our powers. As long as neither of you tries anything against us, we won't have any need to use our powers against you."

A single stream of sweat rolled down Chris' eyes as he realized that Jasmine could read their thoughts. David also realizing that Jasmine could read their thoughts, immediately began trying to close his mind but the more he tried not to think the more he seemed to.

"Have a seat." John irritably repeated what Jasmine had just said to the guys. "I will be frank. I don't like the fact that you are here at our house. More than half of a year prior to the start of the tournament. I don't trust either you and I want you to be honest and tell us why you are here." David and Chris focused on John as he spoke. John quickly blinked three times which was a power that he got from his ancestor the Demigod Vanessa. Three blinks and a person would be under John's control and would do anything that he wanted, including telling the truth.

"Why are you here?" John directed his question at David since he was not as known as Chris and assumed that he was likely the less powerful of the two.

"We came to you hoping that you guys could help us get out of this tournament. Our father is Lucifer and he has devised a plan for us to win the tournament. The catch is however, that we have to memorize a spell impossible to pronounce. If we do not memorize the spell which is made of words that do not exist in our world, before midnight tonight he has sworn to punish us. He did not say specifically what punishment but we know that even the lightest punishment from Lucifer would be impossible for any human or Demigod to endure."

John blinked three times again to release David and Chris from the spell.

"Um, what just happened?" Chris asked as he looked back and forth from John to David.

"I can control people." John very arrogantly replied. "But that is beside the point. You guys came here looking for us to get you out of this tournament and I honestly don't think that we can help. We have been trying to get out of it ourselves. From what we were told by Michael, if we don't compete, we will be cast in Tartarus with our two friends who died in the last tournament."

Chris stared straight in front of him as if he were in a trance as he heard the news. They had just wasted all of their time to learn the spell looking for the Demigods who were now informing them that they were being threatened to compete in the tournament as well. They couldn't help them get out of the tournament.

Just as Chris was beginning to come out of his trance a frightful voice filled the room.

"So, you want out of the tournament and came to your enemies to help you? HAHAHAHAHA!" Lucifer laughed as he appeared in the room. His appearance was a thousand times scarier than his voice.

Lucifer was not just the red beast with horns and a tail that you saw in movies. He had a face like a dragon. His head split into ten heads. His waist up to his neck was that of a human body builder. While his waist down he seemed to be a goat. On the top of Lucifer's head, he had two horns. Lucifer did not wear any fancy robe but just a cloth wrapped around his waist that covered him down to his knees around his entire body.

"So, you Demigods are being forced to as well? How about we make a deal. You submit this tournament and I will assure you are not cast in the lake of fire. I will also bring back your friends Marcus and Ho Young."

John looked at Jasmine for an answer. The deal Lucifer had just offered was a much better deal. Jasmine lowered her head as she considered what Lucifer had just said.

"The deal will not be on the table long. You must decide right now."

John without thinking blurted out an answer to Lucifer's question. "NO! You are the biggest Liar that exists. If you're not lying there is some loophole in your deals that always plays in your favor."

Lucifer stepped forward menacingly but was blasted through the wall of John and Jasmine's house. John turned around to see Michael standing in their living room in full battle armor.

"Lucifer, I believe that you know the penalties for breaking the rules."

"I have broken no rules brother." Lucifer said, walking back into the house menacingly. His mouth was showing a sadistic smile while his eyes were as cold as Alaska. "My sons came here to escape the tournament and your Demigod used his powers on them. Which is where the rule was broken since the tournament has not yet started."

"Wrong. The rules were broken when your sons encroached on my Demigods, making pre contact with them before the start of the tournament. However, since the male Demigod did use his powers on your sons when no threat was present, your sons will not be penalized for making contact." Lucifer's smile disappeared, and an angry face replaced it. Without a word the ground disappeared beneath the feet of his son's and they disappeared from site.

"This tournament I will ensure that you lose, brother. You will find that you cannot always win."

"Yeah that is nice. Either leave these Demigod's house or take a penalty in this tournament."

Lucifer disappeared while giving Michael the middle finger.

Chapter Twelve

"You guys just met my brother Lucifer." Michael addressed the Demigods.

"Is he really going to torture them?" Jasmine asked. She was reading Lucifer's mind before he left.

"Yes, he will. Be glad he is not your parent. He will torture them in some really cruel way for disobeying him and for coming here. Anytime they mess up he will torture them. That is just how he is."

Jasmine paced a few steps in the direction opposite of where Michael was standing. "I wish we could help them." Jasmine spoke out loud as she came to a full stop.

"Not happening," Michael replied. "After whatever Lucifer does to torture them, I promise you they will never disobey him again. If he tells them to kill you, you better believe that they will."

"I understand." Jasmine replied. "I have one more question though if you don't mind?"

"If it was John asking, I would have minded but go ahead."

"What the heck?" John, who had just turned to walk into the kitchen said, turning his head sideways to look back at Michael, with his hands held out.

"My question is, If God is so merciful as the bible says, forgiving and kind, why are we all being forced to fight a battle between you guys? I hope my question is not disrespectful."

John was in the middle of making a sandwich in the kitchen, but stopped to hear the answer. The question Jasmine had just asked was a question that had been burning inside of him. John was sure he had asked it before but couldn't remember if Michael had answered him or not.

"The answer is simple really," Michael said. "Picture you invented something. Let us say you made something to generate electricity and that was its sole purpose. If it was good for nothing else, what would you do if it did not work?"

Jasmine had a blank expression on her face. She was almost past the point of not caring. She just wanted to know the answer. "I guess I would trash it," Jasmine replied after a moment.

"Good and truthful answer," said Michael. "Now let's see if we can keep the honesty going. What happens to the trash after the garbage man picks it up?"

"It is taken to the dump and then crushed or thrown in the furnace and burned."

"Exactly." Michael replied. "So, your question about the creator is therefore an unjust question. Humans do the same and nobody judges one another for putting their inventions in the furnace to suffer"

"But trash isn't alive," Jasmine replied, finally showing just a tad bit of emotion as she spoke with a tint of sadness in her eyes. Her tears definitely wanted to fall but she fought them back.

"But isn't it?" Michael again replied, for the first time looking sad himself. Michael didn't want to keep replying to Jasmine but he knew he had to. "There is nothing made that isn't alive. Molecules and atoms are all alive. Now tell me, anything made by humans that is not made of molecules and atoms." Michael sadly finished.

"I see." Jasmine said, finally letting her tears pour down. John, who was now in the living room standing next to Jasmine, wrapped her up in a hug.

"I have to finish explaining." Michael spoke softly. "Demigods should not exist. Angels and humans were never made to reproduce together. So, to The Creator Demigods are defects in his perfection. Had these tournaments not taken place all Demigods would have only wound up in the lake of fire but yet you, John, Ho Young and Marcus are here fighting for The Creator. I can tell you this, I believe while this tournament is going Father will leave things as they are with all Demigods being cast into Tartarus, awaiting final judgement and the lake of fire. But you four will be spared from the lake of fire as will your immediate families."

"Really?" Jasmine said, through her tears but there was no answer. John looked over his shoulder to where Michael had been standing, but he was gone.

"He is gone." John told Jasmine, as he kissed her on her forehead.

"This isn't fair." Jasmine said to John, but he was 100% right. "We do the same thing that God does with things that don't do what we want them to."

"I know." John replied, still holding on to Jasmine hugging her.

Thoughts were racing through John's mind. Wow, we were on our way to the lake of fire and didn't even know it, just because we were born outside of the norm. As unfair as John thought that was, he thanked God in his mind for giving him, Jasmine, Marcus, and Ho Young a chance to escape the lake of fire.

Chapter Thirteen

David woke up. He looked around. He had just had the strangest dream that he had been attacked by a giant spider and eaten alive. It was the most painful thing that he had ever felt and it felt so real. As David sat up, he looked behind him and fear shot through his entire body.

"No", David whimpered to himself. The cave that he had just dreamed of was no more than fifteen feet behind him. David jumped to his feet to run and just like in his dream, before he could even run a few feet a giant Brown Recluse shot out of the cave and ran him down within seconds.

The Recluse dug its pincers into his flesh. Immediate pain shot through his entire body. The flesh on David's body began to eat away at itself as the acid in the venom from the spider began to quickly go to work on David's body. The pain as the acid ate away at his flesh was a thousand times worse than being burned alive. Though the entire process of David dying was less than a minute, the pain made it feel like hours to him.

"Aaaaaahh!!" David woke up screaming in pain as he could still feel the burning sensation of his body being destroyed by the acid in the venom of a giant brown recluse.

"Stop please! Dad I am sorry. Please make it-- Aaaaaahh! No more. Please no more!" David stood up to a horrific scene a few feet from him. His brother Chris was being beaten with a whip that had huge claws on the end of it. The claws were the size of a huntsman spider. David watched as his brother screamed in pain again as the whip hit his back. Chunks of flesh flew from his body with streams of blood following it. David was just about to throw up as the giant recluse pounced on him again from behind while he was watching his brother. Pain again shot through his body and it was no less painful than the times prior. The acid didn't numb him to the pain of the spider's fangs piercing his skin with each bite. The pain was too much, David blacked out.

"Please! Stop!" Chris was able to scream in between swings of the demonic whip. The beating stopped for a second. Chris was less than an inch away from dying. He looked over as he heard a loud scream that sounded like his brother David's voice. He saw his brother David being eaten alive by a large spider. Chris threw up in his mouth. Chris screamed louder than he ever had before as a monster poured alcohol on his bloodied back. It burned, causing Chris to fall to his knees. He looked up just in time to see the axe head swinging towards his neck before everything went black.

Chris opened his eyes thinking he had dreamed everything but quickly felt the chains holding his arms to two wooden post, twice the size of him. His legs were chained together connected to another chain that was bolted into the ground. Chris was suspended in the air held three feet above the ground by the chains. Sweat poured down Chris' face as he realized that he had not dreamed his death several times in one night, but was literally being killed over and over in the same way, and it was about to happen again.

Chapter Fourteen

"John." Jasmine woke John up from his sleep.

"Yeah?" John asked, warily as he turned his body over in the bed to face Jasmine. His eyes were only part way open, as Jasmine began to talk.

"Earlier, while you had Lucifer's sons in a trance, I used my powers to go into their past. Lucifer has an airtight plan for them if it works. There is a spell not from this world, that creates a portal into the Labyrinth. Lucifer showed them a certain cliff to stand on and told them to just wait for the monsters to come to them. Part of their powers are they can make people see things that aren't really there, including making their environment change.

John sat up in the bed. Jasmine's news worked like coffee waking him up completely. "I see." John said. "Well, that is something that we will definitely need to prepare for because in the case they do not stick to the plan, or the plan changes because we are killing more beasts, I'm sure that they will come after us."

"Yes, I completely agree." Jasmine said as she began to think of what else she had wanted to tell John. "Oh yeah. Also, when they were sensing our powers, they both noted in their minds that we were much more powerful but their powers, if used right, could be very challenging to overcome. Which I'm sure Lucifer will be teaching them how to do."

"Yeah, he will," John replied. "But in this tournament, we will have the upper hand. One, because we have more experience. Two, because we do have superior powers. Three, because we know what their plan is. All of that means we could use Lucifer's plan against him and trap them in the Labyrinth."

"John, they came here for help. We are not going to send them into the Labyrinth. I cannot believe you just said that".

"Jasmine, you know as well as I do, that Michael said when Lucifer finishes torturing them, they will never disobey him again and will kill us if he tells them to."

"Yes, that is true but we are not going to kill them. We will find a way to subdue them because they are being forced to do this tournament just as we are. If we killed them just to get them out of our way, we are no better than Lucifer."

"Okay whatever you say. But mark my words, you are going to regret not listening to me."

"And what does that mean?" Jasmine asked, placing her hands on her hips and rolling her eyes as she spoke with an attitude.

"It means that you are putting my life in danger by having a soft spot for those two. If I die you will be forced to realize that it was your fault because you didn't listen to me." John replied back, angrily raising his voice. "Maybe you need to join their team and the three of you can team up on me. since I'm obviously the bad guy here."

"You know what? Screw you!" Jasmine yelled at John, placing both of her hands up and sticking her middle fingers out at John.

John stuck both of his middle fingers up at Jasmine in return.

"Oh, that is it. I'm out of here," said Jasmine as she stormed out of the door.

"Bye!" John said turning and walking back over by the bed. John was not about to risk his life because Jasmine had a soft spot for the sons of Lucifer.

"Michael!" John yelled as he stood next to the bed.

"I heard the argument between you and Jasmine," Michael said as he appeared without so much as a hello. "Lucifer is teaching them spells to manipulate the Labyrinth. Which in turn means that they could trap you in the Labyrinth. It looks like you will get your wish," said Michael, smiling at John.

"What do you mean?" John replied back, curiously.

"If they can use a spell to trap you in the Labyrinth, I can technically teach you a spell that will allow you to use your powers in there. One that Lucifer does not know. We kept it hidden from him.

"What can you tell me about Q?" John suddenly asked. When Michael mentioned a spell that would allow John to use his powers in the Labyrinth it made John think of Q.

"If you are referring to the Elf of Light that you met, I can tell you this, if you didn't have the power that you have, where you can teleport in and out of places, you would be dead right now. Q, as you call her, is neither good nor bad. Q's job was to ensure that nobody cheated in the tournament, when the tournament was set to be in the Labyrinth. And to keep all from entering the Labyrinth. You attempted to enter the Labyrinth twice. Q was going to kill you for attempting to trespass."

"Oh, I see." John replied.

"Yes. So, from now on, make sure you listen."

"I will", John honestly gave his word.

Michael surprisingly never brought up the subject of Jasmine leaving. Instead he just disappeared as he always did.

John sat on the bed thinking about the argument with Jasmine, eventually falling asleep. The next morning John woke up and rolled in the bed. He considered getting out of bed, but seeing Jasmine's side of the bed empty, he decided to stay in bed.

A week later Jasmine had not yet come back and still had not spoken a word to John. She would see John walking in the street and would walk on the other side and John was no better. John would be playing basketball with his friends and see Jasmine but would act like he didn't see her.

Michael was getting frustrated. He kept trying to convince both John and Jasmine to talk to each other, but neither would budge.

"John you have to talk to her. This tournament is far more dangerous than the last one and this time there are two less of you." Michael said to John.

"Nope. I'm done with her being selfish. She is not about to risk my life because she has a soft spot for them."

"Have you ever consid—" Michael stopped in mid- sentence because John had teleported out of the room tired of hearing Michael defend Jasmine.

Next Michael went to Jasmine. "Listen Jasmine—"

"No. I will not." Jasmine interrupted Michael. "John isn't who I thought he was."

"Yes, he is." Michael interjected. He was speaking truthfully. "They are going to come after you guys and you guys don't have time to waste figuring out how to capture them, which I guarantee you will be near impossible."

"That is nice. Are you done defending John?" Jasmine angrily asked. "If you want to talk to me about this tournament, I'm up for it but if you are only here to talk about John, then you can do your disappearing act."

Michael raised his hands in the air frustrated, very upset and disappeared.

Chapter Fifteen

"Look I don't care how we learn this. I am not getting tortured again." David said as he failed a fourth time in a row to perform the spell to open a gateway into the Labyrinth.

"Me neither." Chris seconded David's statement. "Let's get this dang spell right."

"You know what would be nice? If we could trap those Demigods in the Labyrinth as well. Without the use of their powers they will be dead within no time, leaving us the victors." Said David

"Yeah. I would love to get those Demigods." Chris replied. "They didn't even try to help us."

"They sure didn't." Lucifer said as he suddenly appeared. "Keep working on this spell and you will get it. Those Demigods will find that this tournament may just be too much for them."

Chapter Sixteen

John looked up as he and his friends were walking in the neighborhood of south Deering. Jasmine was hanging with some guy John had never seen before, most likely from a different neighborhood.

"Aye homie." John's friend C-4 said, pointing at Jasmine and her friend. "You want us to show him what's up?"

"No. It's good. If that is who Jasmine likes, then she can."

"Nah lil homie. That Yuppie needs to dip or get his wig split. Them Riverdale fools ain't got no business in these parts."

John turned to walk the other way, but addressed C-4 first. "C-4 I may be fighting with Jasmine but she is still close to me."

"If you say so, mane. Come on," C-4 said to his crew as they walked the other way with John. The boy walking with Jasmine looked in the direction of John and his friends C-4 couldn't resist the urge to lift up his basketball jersey, flashing the butt of his gun for Jasmine and her friend to see. "Wrong side Homie," C-4 yelled as they walked away.

Jasmine watched John walk away with pure hatred for him at that moment mixed with a single drop of love that was fighting against her hate for him. She shook her head disgusted. She couldn't believe that John was back to hanging out with his gangster friends.

As John entered his house that night, Jasmine was there with Michael.

"Where is your boyfriend?" John said as he walked past Jasmine.

"At a hotel room waiting for me. We will be spending the evening together. I hope he has protection though." Jasmine added to get into John's head. She knew that John knew she was lying. She also knew that her last words would still cut John deep and hurt him.

John didn't reply, instead he just walked past Michael and sat down on the bed.

"Okay." Michael sternly said to both John and Jasmine. "I'm going to need you both to put your differences aside for this tournament. Especially right now since I'm about to explain the rules to you so that you don't get disqualified."

"More rules than we already have been told?" John asked with his 'are you serious' look he had a high tendency to make. John's right eye always squinted down and his left eye would fully open. His hands shooting out and his palms facing the ceiling.

"Here are the rules." Michael began. "I just explained them to the other team no less than an hour ago. Anytime the two of you are in this house, you are safe and the monsters and opposing Demigods cannot attack you. You cannot attack the other Demigods in their safe house either, which is located in Boston. Your families and their families are off limits in this tournament. If either team breaks that rule their team will automatically be disqualified and the other team will win."

"Lastly, there is no time limit on this tournament. However long it takes, it takes. Oh, actually there is one more thing." Michael said, handing Jasmine a blank piece of paper. "Every time a monster or a Demigod is killed, it will keep the tally on this paper."

"Oh okay," Jasmine replied as she placed the paper in her backpack.

"You guys have the credit card. I suggest you use it to get whatever you need. If you sleep in a hotel, I suggest you make sure you have some kind of protection around you. A lot of the monsters probably are not just going to go straight into towns and attack people. They know that you Demigods must kill them to complete the tournament and many of them don't want to go back into the Labyrinth. So, they will hide the best they can and make you have to find them. Here is a completed list of the monsters so that you will not have to take those stacks of books with you to know what beasts to look for." Michael, for once, handed the paper to John rather than Jasmine hoping that by doing so he would be able to get them to interact with each other again.

"And this really is the last thing. The most dangerous power that your opponents have is the power to make you see things that are not there. They can make you think you are on a cliff separated from each other even if you both are standing next to each other. They can make you think you are being attacked by things that aren't there and can even make you attack each other by making you look like the enemy. So please keep your minds focused and in check. Do as we practiced use the signal to indicate to one another whether you are friendly or not. Jasmine, protect yourself the minute you suspect you are in an illusion because John can teleport far enough away for the spell to break with him and be back in seconds to get you to safety."

"Assuming he chooses to come back for me." Jasmine very down heartedly said giving John not so much a look of hate but a look of disappointment. Her eyes were not looking directly at John but through her peripheral vision she could see him as she focused the main part of her eyes on the ground. A very sad look rested upon her eyes. This was the first interaction her and John had since they stopped talking to each other and without words un-officially broke up with each other.

Surprisingly to Jasmine, John didn't answer. For the first time he didn't make any rude or snide comment towards Jasmine since the ones he made at her when the meeting had started.

"Look." Michael said. "You guys fought because you are both stressed but you cannot let your emotions get you killed in this tournament. This is the most dangerous tournament that you have done. You are two Demigods down from the last tournament. John, I promise you your pride is going to get Jasmine killed and Jasmine I promise you that your pride is going to get Jonathan killed. Is that what you both want?" Michael sincerely asked looking back and forth between Jasmine and John

Neither Jasmine nor John spoke.

"Say something, please." Michael begged. It was quite strange to see Michael the Arc Angel beg. Michael standing next to Zeus made Zeus look like a nerd. That is how radiant Michael's powers were. So, to hear him reduced to begging to save their lives, John and Jasmine both knew he was being sincere

"Before I speak, who was that guy that you were with today?" John asked Jasmine.

"He is my cousin John. He lives not far from us. I have not been able to see him since these tournaments started."

"Oh," John said.

"He doesn't live far from here."

"I know." John replied. "He stays in Riverdale. C-4 recognized him. He wanted to shoot him but I talked him out of it."

"John, why were you hanging out with those guys again? Even if we did break up with each other, though we never said we did, why would you go back to hanging out with them after you have made so much progress?"

"I actually wasn't." John replied. "I was walking because I got bored and I guess they saw me and noticed that you were not with me and kind of tagged along. You remember I used to be good friends with Chris when we were kids before he became the leader of the gang and became C-4. I guess maybe he missed that friendship we had or something. Something like that is hard to let go. I have gotten arrested in the past protecting him and he has done the same for me. I know he can change if I help him but I also know you saved me from that life whether you know it or not. Long before these tournaments started. I knew that I wanted to marry you and I made the conscious decision to stop hanging out with all gang members because I knew you didn't like gangs. I'd say what's up to my old friends but just wouldn't hang out with them anymore."

"Oh my God! That's so sweet. Do you mean it John?" Jasmine gushed.

"Yes of course I do."

"I mean the part about wanting to marry me."

John froze and slowly turned towards Michael looking for an escape. "We can talk about that in a minute." John said. "Michael finish what you were saying." John said.

"Oh, I was done. It's all you right now." Michael said smiling.

"Don't worry about it." Jasmine said before John could say another word. "It is okay. I understand."

"Do you?" John replied as he stepped towards Jasmine. "I didn't walk to talk about it here in front of Michael because I get uncomfortable talking about my feelings but I won't have you thinking that I don't want to marry you. Jasmine I want to marry you with every bone in my body."

"I see." Jasmine said as she allowed herself to blush.

"Listen Jasmine, I'm sorry for what I said. I know I was out of line. I was angry and I said some things that I shouldn't have."

"I did too." Jasmine said as tears rolled down the right side of her face. "John, I love you. I was miserable without you. I wanted to talk to you each time that I saw you but I guess I let my pride take over each time."

"I did too." John replied. "And you already know that I love you. Jasmine." John softly said her name as he beckoned for her to come to him. Jasmine walked over to John still wiping her eyes.

"I thought I had lost you." Jasmine said as she started crying a bit harder against John's shoulder as they hugged.

"I'm an idiot." John said to Jasmine. "I should have been more considerate with how you felt and you will never lose me. I will always love you no matter what we go through."

"Okay," Jasmine said as she continued to cry. Michael disappeared after saying, "Oh goodness get a room." As John and Jasmine laid on their living room couch together cuddling.

***

"Okay John we need to study this list all over from scratch, just to make sure we didn't miss anything. If you don't mind helping me study." Jasmine blushed and added as she realized that part of John's attitude had come from her being so demanding.

"I completely agree with you on that." John replied as he grabbed a book from the stack. The first book John studied was about Harpies which John had once thought were beings the size of fairies but this book described them as human size women with bodies like birds. Apparently, the Harpies enjoyed torturing people.

"I get the feeling that we are going to have to go after the Harpies first because they like to torture people," John said to Jasmine.

"We are going to have our hands full because Chimaera from what I am reading, will definitely go after people. She is similar to Leviathan just not as smart. So, we know how to beat her. The Sphinx and the Nemean Lion will go after people as well. We won't be able to save everyone but we know which monsters we will most likely have to fight first."

"Yeah those are some tough creatures. But all I should have to do is do like I did with Leviathan, teleporting in and out dismantling each monster's body piece by piece." As John spoke a letter appeared on the bed. The letter was from the Angel Gabriel.

To John,

Lucifer has complained that your power to teleport parts of creatures' bodies is an unfair advantage in the tournament. To keep things fair The Creator has agreed to ban the use of that power in the tournament. You will still be able to teleport yourself, as well as others, just not single body parts from your opponents.

John stood up. His brows furrowed in anger as his hands balled up the letter from Gabriel. "This is stupid!" John said out loud.

Jasmine, who was reading the letter at the same time that John was, was a bit flustered as well about Lucifer adding rules to cripple their chances.

"Well the bright side of this is that if certain powers can be considered a disadvantage, I'm sure that the power of illusion is as well because that certainly isn't a fair fight."

"Michael." Jasmine said in her normal voice not raising it at all. Michael appeared in the room before even a second had gone by.

"I just finished arguing your case to Father and he has agreed that Lucifer's sons cannot use their power of illusion against either of you and that they cannot use their power of illusion against any monster except in defense. They cannot attack any monsters while they are using their powers over illusions on them."

"That sounds pretty fair to me," John replied. "How did Lucifer take it?"

"Oh," Michael replied, smiling from one cheek to the other. "He did not take it well at all. He walked off yelling at Father and talking to himself about the unfairness of Father."

"Good." John said laughing. "That is what he gets." John turned to thank Michael but he was gone.

"At least the tournament is back to even but now we will have to really come up with strategies to beat these beasts without you being able to just separate them piece by piece."

"Yeah, not to mention we need to find ways to avoid certain monsters all together, such as Medusa," said John

"Yeah. I'm not looking forward to facing her. I'm not looking forward to facing the Nemean Lion either. He is almost indestructible, not many things can hurt him."

"So, we need to make a list of monsters to avoid, monsters to attack right away, and the ones that we will have real trouble with. Ones that we cannot avoid. like the Sphinx, who can appear to you anywhere and the only way to beat it is to answer its question correctly."

"Michael." John shouted. "You don't have to come just send a letter like Gabriel did. I know I cannot teleport body parts in this tournament but say I wanted to teleport a monster or either of Lucifer's sons whole to a place, could I do that?"

A note formed on the bed. It was a square note in the shape of a Christmas or Birthday card, dark emerald green with the words engraved in solid gold.

YES. The note read.

"Awesome." John said.

"What's up?" Jasmine asked, seeing John's excitement. She tried to read John's mind but John, out of habit to keep Jasmine from reading his mind to win arguments, kept a protective molecule shield around his head. It was invisible but worked very well.

"I figure if they plan to cheat most of the time by staying on that rock, I can teleport to them and teleport them to the monsters far away from their cliff. If we both ever agreed to do so." John finished seeing the look on Jasmine's face. Jasmine's face scrunched up a little and her eyes looked pleading as if she wanted to interject and say no but didn't because they had just reunited. Jasmine didn't want to ruin it with an argument. "I won't do it unless we both agree to." John repeated, making sure that Jasmine heard that part loud and clear.

"Okay," Jasmine replied. "And if it does come down to it that would be a really good plan."

Chapter Seventeen

Time passed by very quickly with so much to do for both sides. John, Jasmine, as well as for the sons of Lucifer. Within no time they were days away from the tournament. The sons of Lucifer learned the spell to open the portal into the Labyrinth and learned how to multiply their powers. They learned to use powers that they never even knew that they had.

John and Jasmine mastered the spell to use their powers in the Labyrinth as well as how to open the portal that led into the Labyrinth. Jasmine made sure she studied every monster and beasts' strengths and weaknesses. While John focused on Arachne who was John's biggest fear from the Labyrinth. He studied other beasts as well but he really focused on beating Arachne.

The nerves were compassing both sides. David was so nervous he had to be calmed down by Aphrodite because he wanted to quit the tournament and didn't care about being tortured. Zeus and Odin had a time keeping Lucifer away from David. Lucifer wanted to give David a twenty-four-hour torture session as motivation to wish for the start of the tournament.

Storm clouds began to form as the final twenty-four hours hit before the start of the tournament. Zeus was excited and ready for what seemed like a very good chance for the Gods of the Earth to get a win. Lightning and thunder storms happened worldwide as Zeus could not restrain his excitement. Even Odin was anxious for the tournament to begin.

Chaos, who had been quiet in the tournaments up to this point, found himself standing on the edge of Mount Olympus yelling, "Victory for Olympus! Victory for Olympus!"

Victory joined Chaos in chanting. The Gods of the Earth were excited to the point of losing control.

***

John took a long walk by himself, far away from Chicago, along the beach in Hawaii where he had once beaten Leviathan. He was excited and nervous. He wanted the tournament to begin so it would be started and the wait would be over. At the same time, he didn't want the tournament to begin because that meant that the battles would begin. The best thing that Michael had given the Demigods was a map that kept track of all of the beasts that would be released from Tartarus. Now John and Jasmine would know when any beasts were near. Lucifer's sons had the same map as well.

"Man, I can't do this again," John said to himself as he plopped down onto his butt on the beach. "We are going to be killed this time. This tournament is too much. Whatever." John thought within himself. We won the last tournament against impossible odds. Even Thor couldn't beat Leviathan but they did. "We can win this!" John shouted out loud to himself. A few homeless beach bums looked at John like he was crazy. He kept jumping up and then plopping back down shouting at times and at other times talking quietly to himself, trying to motivate himself one minute, and then tearing himself down the next moment.

Jasmine stayed with her dad and John's mom while John was out collecting himself. Once John returned to the house, Jasmine went into the bathroom to be alone for a second. She grabbed her hair and pulled it part way back and screamed a noiseless scream. Jasmine fell to her knees before falling against the wall next to the shower. Jasmine began to sob, as she remembered Marcus and Ho young who had died in the last tournament. "Please God," Jasmine prayed. "Please don't let us die in this tournament, please."

John could hear Jasmine but he knew as she needed a moment to be alone and stopped her dad and his mom from going up to interfere with Jasmine getting all of her pre-tournament fears out.

"We have to let her be. I just did the same thing far from here. Tomorrow is tough and Michael said angels will be guarding you guys until the tournament is over."

"I wish that they would just find other Demigods to do this tournament thing." Jasmine's dad said with a hint of anger in his voice.

"You know." John replied to him. "I did too, until I found out that all Demigods go to the lake of fire automatically. But this tournament allows us to bypass that and get us, as well as our immediate families, into Heaven."

Jasmine after some time finally came out of the bathroom.

"Oh honey," John's mom ran up to Jasmine and hugged her. Jasmine's dad ran over and joined in. "John, come over here too." They beckoned him. John didn't like emotional moments but he knew that it was possibly their last time seeing them in the case that they died, so he walked over and joined his mom and Jasmine's dad in hugging and all of the emotional stuff they were doing.

***

Chris paced back and forth for a while only a mile from the cliff where he and his brother would start the tournament. Both he and David were camping out near the cliff. Chris kicked a few rocks before finally lying down and trying to go to sleep. It seemed no matter how many sheep he counted or no matter how much he tried to empty his mind, he just couldn't sleep.

John and Jasmine stayed up through the night as well. They wound up going for a walk and then laid back down in the bed staring into each other's eyes. The only Demigod who got sleep that night was David.

***

John and Jasmine awoke to the sound of a loud booming voice. The voice repeated the phrase several times and each time it was more heart pounding and soul dredging than the time before.

"THE TOURNAMENT HAS BEGUN. THE TOURNAMENT HAS BEGUN.

John looked at Jasmine with a tinge of fright in his eyes. John didn't know why but his eyes watered a bit and he could not stop them. His stomach churned as did Jasmine's.

"John," Jasmine said very hoarsely. "It is only midnight." Jasmine's voice was very shaky.

Chris looked over at his watch, "are you kidding me?" Chris shouted. He had just fallen asleep and it was only 1:00AM in Rhode Island. He had assumed that the tournament wouldn't start until a decent hour where everyone was awake.

***

Monsters began to race out of the Labyrinth at every opening in every country that there was an entrance in. The cool breeze and the fresh air were something some had never felt before and others not in a long time. The beasts immediately began attacking people. The police and militaries were getting so many calls that they couldn't keep up.

In the Netherlands an entire family was taken by Harpies and tortured in midair while police shot at the Harpies. The bullets had zero effect on them. One Harpies ripped an eleven-year-old boy in half while the others laughed before picking up on their original job and transporting the boys two sisters and the parents to hell.

The Nemean Lion took on ten thousand British soldiers and eight thousand U.S soldiers in the UK. They unloaded thousands of bullets into the Nemean Lion and dropped countless bombs but none of their weapons even scratched the lion.

John and Jasmine watched the events from their house which was their safe zone.

"John, we have to do something." Jasmine said as her eyes were still glued to the T.V.

"I agree. But what?" John replied as the T.V switched to a seven headed dragon, which clearly was the Hydra.

"I have an Idea. I know the chant to open the portal to the Labyrinth and you can teleport monsters as long as you do them whole. I figure that you can teleport to monsters and teleport them above the portal and drop them in the portal that leads into the Labyrinth. What do you think about that plan?"

"It sounds like a good plan. I believe it will work for some monsters but not so much for others. It's better than staying here and waiting for the sons of Lucifer to take the lead though."

"Okay so here we go." Said John as he teleported to the Nemean Lion. John appeared right behind the Nemean Lion and touched him and attempted to teleport the Nemean Lion to where Jasmine hopefully had the portal opened and waiting for John to drop it in. But nothing happened except for a very angry lion turning towards John with a quickness John was not prepared for.

The Nemean Lion barely missed John's entire head with its teeth as it lunged at him. With a quick pushing motion of his hands John lifted the Nemean Lion into the air and threw him, a good ten feet away from him. The Nemean Lion hit its head pretty hard on the curb but the only damage that was done was to the curb which broke into pieces as if a bomb had hit it. The Nemean Lion was completely unharmed.

The Nemean Lion again charged with super speeds. This time John was ready for it. John teleported out of there with a quickness back to his home where Jasmine was waiting.

Jasmine was shocked as John popped up behind her empty handed. "It didn't work." John said to Jasmine as he shrugged his shoulders.

"I know I was watching it on T.V. That was too close." Jasmine said breathing hard as she tried to catch her breath. John popped up right behind her while she was watching him battle the Nemean Lion on national T.V. The camera had focused on the Nemean Lion as John had used his power to throw it far away from him. Jasmine thought John was still there and her eyes were glued to the T.V as John teleported only feet behind her causing Jasmine to nearly jump out of her clothes.

"What happened? Are you okay?" John asked as he noticed Jasmine was out of breath.

"No. You just scared me. I was watching you fight on T.V and while I was watching it you appeared behind me. I wasn't expecting it."

"Yeah, after seeing that the Nemean Lion wasn't even hurt off of what I did to him, I decided to bounce and see what other plan we can come up with."

As John and Jasmine talked the next news segment caught their attention causing them both to stop in mid-sentence. On the screen the U.S Military was fighting alongside Chris Blain and David Angel against the Hydra seven headed dragon.

Every time the beast would get near them the helicopters would draw its attention by hitting it with missiles.

"Turn that up." John suggested to Jasmine since she was closer to the remote.

As Jasmine turned the volume up, they both began to hear the news anchor speaking in the background.

"This is amazing," the newscaster said into his microphone." As the world is being attacked by monsters, that we thought were only fictional creatures, two magicians who until today were just mere entertainers, have stepped up in the wake of these recent events where countless people all over the world have been killed. Right here on this cliff in Arizona they are helping our military fight off this creature. From what we have heard fifty feet below the cliff is a portal and anything that falls into it will disappear into the Labyrinth. Another place supposed to be nothing more than a myth."

"Christians, I imagine, cannot be taking this quite well right now. For a long time now, they have fought to be the only legitimate religion but with these Greek mythology monsters appearing I can only imagine that Zeus and the other Greek Gods must be the real Gods who created the world. The proof of Greek Gods is right here before us. My question is where is the proof of the Christian God?"

Jasmine was about to turn and say if only they knew, to John but before she could move John was flying in the air on Television. John with a swipe of his hands through the air caused the wind to push the Hydra monster into the Labyrinth. Next John teleported behind Lucifer's sons, reached out and touched both of their shoulders with his fingertips careful not to make a sound and teleported them both to a beach in Maui Hawaii then teleported himself away before they knew what was happening.

John re-appeared next to the camera man. "You wanted proof of the Christian God, you just got it. David Angel and Chris Blaine are not just magicians as you said earlier, but they are the sons of Lucifer. I cannot go into details but I will say this, God is real and he is the one who created all things. Zeus, Poseidon, Hades, Thor, Odin, and all other religions with living being's as their Gods are real as well but are the fallen angels from Heaven."

"So why doesn't God just stop this?" The camera man asked. "How is this fair to us?"

"This is happening because of dumb questions like that." John replied. "You don't want to acknowledge God, yet want to ask dumb questions like what kind of God allows stuff like this to happen. Maybe an ignored God who doesn't lie. He said if you won't seek him and serve him then he will not hear your cries and will not help you in your time of need. I don't know what verse that is and I probably quoted it wrong. But you can't ignore God and do what you want to do and still expect God to acknowledge you. He is God not you. So, it needs to be the other way around. If someone creates something you better believe that nobody is going to do what their creator wants them to do, but my creation does what they want it to do." With that John disappeared and teleported again behind Jasmine.

"That was a really good speech." Jasmine said and look, she held out the parchment that was keeping score and it read

Team 1... Jasmine and John... 1 point

Team 2... Chris and David... 0 points.

"Awesome." John said. "So, we are up one to zero and it will be a while before they are able to get back to that cliff. Now we have a little time to work on that Nemean Lion.

John and Jasmine watched the news for more major events but nothing was popping up as far as out in the open attacks. A week went by and there were many reports of disappearances but no sightings of monsters. Chris and David had returned to the cliff but no more monsters seemed interested in going up there. It seems that in trying to use the tournament to get more famous by putting it on the news the sons of Lucifer had actually alerted all of the monsters to their plan. The Harpies were the ones who saw it on the news first as they were abducting another family to torture and take to Tartarus. When they saw what the sons of Lucifer were planning with the secret portal back into the Labyrinth the Harpies spread the word to all of the monsters and beasts. After that the Nemean Lion had disappeared.

"This makes it really hard." Jasmine said out loud to John one day. "We know where some of the beasts are because of the number of missing persons' reports in those areas but the problem is that we don't know which monster is there. There is no way to properly prepare."

"Yeah, I know." John replied. "We are going to have to figure something out."

"If we go to those areas do you think you can focus on the events and the people taken? Then travel back through events that previously happened there, like you do with books and stuff so we can see what beasts are there?"

"I don't know I have never tried before and I'm not even sure if I can. What about you? Can you focus on the beasts and maybe just Teleport us to them?"

"Yeah, I can but the problem is, we don't know where the beasts are. If they are in a small cave not big enough for us and I teleport us there I don't even want to think about what could happen. Don't think for a second that we are ever going after Arachne. She is off limits to us. That is a death trap waiting to happen. We need to try and convince Michael to convince God to reverse Athena's spell and turn Arachne back human."

"I'm definitely for that plan." Jasmine replied to John. "I was not planning on going after her either. I would rather take my chances against escaping Tartarus."

"Me too," John replied.

"Our best bet is to go to the places where the most disappearances are being reported and just sit and wait. The monsters will be able to feel our presence there and I'm sure will attack at some point. Let's make them come to us when we get to these places rather than us going to them."

"That might work." John said as his thumb and his pointer scratched his chin indicating that he was pondering the idea. "That just might work."

"How long until we should start?" John asked Jasmine hoping that she would say a few weeks.

"Today." Jasmine said as she turned away from John to get her clothes ready to pack.

"I figured you were going to say that." John dully said.

"Well I mean how many people do you want to let die before we begin saving them?"

"Twenty." John jokingly replied.

"Ha-Ha." Jasmine faked laughed. "Now go get packed Mr." Jasmine finished her sentence with a smirk on her face.

John went upstairs into their room and began to pack a few of his clothes. John wondered what beasts they were going to run into first. Just as John finished packing, Jasmine came up the stairs and into the room.

"Okay I googled a list of the most recent missing persons reports, and twelve people have gone missing in the Amazon just this morning. Another twenty-three in the last seventy-two hours. Sixteen people have gone missing in Big Trees California. Forty-two have gone missing in the last forty-eight hours in Toronto, Canada and seven have gone missing in Boston Massachusetts. I have a whole list but I thought it best to start in those places. Which one do you want to go to first?"

"Let's do Canada and get it out of the way before winter hits." John replied.

"Okay." said Jasmine, holding her suitcase in hand. John grabbed his bag of clothes off of his bed and softly took Jasmine's hand into his own. Seconds later they were both in Toronto Canada. John had Teleported them two miles out of Toronto city limits. Nobody was around in the area that John and Jasmine teleported to so they began to walk the two miles into town doing the best that they could to appear normal.

As they walked two cars drove by them both of the car's occupants stared at John with their mouths open.

"I wonder what that is about?" John casually asked Jasmine.

"I don't even have to read their minds to answer that one. But since I did it is about you being an international hero and proof that there is a God. Also proof that aliens walk among humans."

"Wait what?" John asked, confused about the alien part.

"NASA is apparently saying that you are an alien and that you have escaped from Area 51. They are also telling people to stay clear of you because you are dangerous and came to our planet with one purpose and that is to conquer Earth."

"Are you kidding me?" John replied. He laughed to himself as he spoke. "I told them who I was and who I was fighting with. If they would rather believe that the idiot Zeus is a God, or that I'm an alien that is up to them."

"John you know how people are. They believe anything negative about anyone."

John shook his head. "Please remind me of why we are trying to save these people again, because we really can just sit back and relax for a while, because those Demigods Chris and David haven't killed a single beast yet."

"Well that is not the only reason that we are doing this John." Jasmine reminded him." Just because people have evil hearts doesn't mean that we have to as well."

"I know." John replied. "It's just frustrating for people to make stuff up and then have people believe it. They were praising Chris and David as hero's but because I proved them wrong about the Gods and God, they want to lie about me and try to make me sound like I'm an alien out to destroy the world."

"They are going to do it to me as well," Jasmine replied sincerely. "You just have to ignore it and know that you are better than them. That is why they are doing it. Insecure people talk about people and place themselves in drama and that includes the government. They couldn't even beat the Hydra Dragon with the help of Chris and David but you showed up and beat it with one move. That had to have upset them when you did it and then said you were proof of the God that they were trying to discredit."

John smiled because he knew Jasmine was right. "Yeah I guess so," John said as he continued to smile as they walked. "Since everyone knows there is no point in us continuing to walk." Before Jasmine could contradict him, John touched Jasmine's shoulder and teleported them both right into the middle of the Toronto police station. The minute the officers noticed John and Jasmine appear out of nowhere they all drew their guns and began firing bullets at Jasmine and John with the intent to kill.

John caused all of the bullets to freeze in the air before making them fall near the guns they were fired from. The police officers all looked at each other debating on whether to try shooting again or to try something else.

"Listen." John yelled. "I know you guys can't be dumb enough to believe I'm an alien. My great, great, great, great, grandpa is Aeolus the God of the winds, and my great grandmother is Aphrodite's. Believe me when I tell you that I'm not an alien like they want you to believe. I have never been to Area 51. You can look it up. I was born in a hospital on the Southside of Chicago, and I grew up on the Southside of Chicago. I went to Elementary School there, middle school and high school. So, at what point did I come from another planet and escape from Area 51 if I was in school the whole time? With me being the great grandson of Aeolus on my great grandpa's side and Aphrodites on my great grandma's side and Jasmine here being the great granddaughter of Hades on her great grandma's side and Poseidon on her great grandad's side, you might want to stop listening to NASA who has no idea what they are talking about. You may want to start listening to us on what is really going down."

The police did not dare say a word but remained motionless and speechless with their guns still pointing at John and Jasmine.

"Okay," Jasmine said, taking over the conversation. "Zeus, Thor and all other religions were started by fallen Angels who wanted humans to worship them as Gods. They wanted to be Gods so bad that they attempted to de-throne The Creator who they call Father. They lost obviously, and were cast down to earth. The reason humans stopped hearing from them was because the great flood was actually another war which they lost and were imprisoned in. Now they are trying to avoid the lake of fire and it's them who have released all of these monsters and John and I are trying to save you guys from them."

"What about David Angel and that Chris Blaine fellow? Are they working with you as well?"

"No." John quickly answered. "They have not been honest with you. They are actually the sons of Lucifer, who is the fallen Angel responsible for all of the beasts attacking humans right now."

"Now you guys have a bunch of missing people and if you would be so kind as to show us where the majority of them went missing, we would greatly appreciate it." Jasmine took back over the conversation.

The cops remained in silence for a moment before one of the officers finally stood to his feet. He walked over to an office, grabbed a piece of paper and walked back.

"Hey what the hell do you think you are doing?" One of the officers a little on the chubby side asked the first officer.

"My daughter is missing and I saw how powerful this Demigod is in that video, against that seven headed dragon."

"You mean how powerful this alien is?" another cop said looking at his fellow officers for support.

"Yeah, definitely an alien." A few cops shouted in the background. At that point John lost his temper. Without using any of his body motions John focused his mind on all of the surrounding police officers and with a single thought the air obeyed John and retreated away from the police officers and surrounded itself around John and Jasmine.

"John, they can't breathe!" Jasmine yelled with panic in her shaky voice.

"So what?" John said. "If these officers are too stupid to see that I'm not an alien then their lives are not important and they are not intelligent enough to figure out the locations of the missing people."

"John, please. I know you are upset but please let them live this is not you. Remember just because others are evil that does not mean you have to be evil too. Your actions define you."

"Give them air." John angrily ordered the air. The tone in his voice was very sharp and you could clearly hear his frustrations in his voice.

"Thank you." Jasmine said to John with a shy look in John's direction. She wanted John to be the boy that she had fallen in love with but the tournament was making John act angry quite a bit.

"You can breathe now." John said to the police officer his expression still one of being upset. "In the future use your brains and not your ignorance. The army and the sons of Lucifer could not beat the Hydra Dragon. I did it with ease, what on earth made you idiots think that you could insult me without consequence? Now I'm upset and the only reason you are still breathing is because of my girlfriend, Jasmine." The police officer remained silent. Some looked upset and like they wanted to do something while others now had fear in their eyes. The officer that seemed to be on the Demigods side whose daughter had been taken, quietly smiled to himself. He knew that John doing what he did to the department was going to play in favor of finding the missing people including his daughter.

"So, this is what is going to happen," John continued. "You all are going to assist my girlfriend and myself in finding these missing people. We have seventy-three monsters to catch that have been released from the Labyrinth. We need to be in and out of here as fast as possible. Some of these monsters will be harder to kill than others, like the Nemean Lion, Medusa, Arachne, the Sphynx, and a lot more. In such cases it will take much longer to defeat them."

As John spoke Michael appeared standing less than two feet away from him in the midst of the Toronto city police station.

"What's up?" John asked, surprised to see Michael. Unlike the last tournament Michael had to promise not to assist the Demigods at all during the tournament. Since they were seasoned in their powers now. Lucifer felt that any assistance from Michael in this tournament was unnecessary.

"I have good news and I have bad news," Michael said to both John and Jasmine.

"Is that Zeus?" One of the officers asked loud enough for everyone to hear. Michael slowly turned towards the officer.

"Don't ever insult me like that again. Zeus wishes he was me. I can beat Zeus in battle on my worst day only using thirty-seven percent of my strength and powers. I have done it already so that is a pretty accurate calculation."

"Then who are you?" Another officer asked.

Michael got a mischievous look in his eyes. "I'm Batman." Michael placed his hands on his hips as he spoke. Michael had been waiting for generations, since the first batman movie had come out to say that and now, he had his chance and he did not miss it.

A few of the officers laughed while others remained frightened.

"He is Michael the Arc Angel." John finally said, realizing that Michael was enjoying that moment a little too much to remember he was there to tell them something.

Michael turned and looked at John. His expression spoke for him. It was the look you give someone in chess when they interfere in the game and give your next move away before you can do it.

"Remember, you have bad news for us." John said, as his hands made a circular motion in front of him motioning for Michael to tell them the news.

"Yeah, well, I have some possible good news actually and some possible bad news. It all depends on you and they are both tied together."

"Okay." Jasmine said. "Tell us. What is the bad news first?

Michael hesitated, "before you answer, allow me to finish, and tell you both sides of the news." Michael was more looking at John than Jasmine when he said it.

"Okay, okay, I will wait." John agreed.

"The bad news," Michael began. "Is that Lucifer wants to speed up Leviathan's re-birth since you cannot beat him piece by piece like you did the last time." John started to speak to protest but held his tongue in order to keep his promise.

"The good news," Michael began again, "is that I bargained with him. If he gets Leviathan for this tournament, you guys get Marcus and Ho Young back."

"There is no question." Jasmine quickly said. "Bring them back."

Michael looked at John to see what his answer would be.

That wasn't that great of a deal to John from the aspect of winning the tournament because John was sure that Leviathan would not play any games with them this time. They would most likely beat all four of them together easily since John couldn't teleport body parts of monsters away from their bodies anymore. However, John also missed Marcus and Ho Young and so he nodded his head in agreement to make the deal.

"Why did you hesitate?" Jasmine asked John angrily. Her hands were on her hips and her very light brown skin was bright red.

"I was going to do the deal but I paused for a second to think. The Leviathan is going to kill all four of us this time. I was just weighing that. I mean, what is the point in saving them from Tartarus if it gets all four of us killed and right back in Tartarus together this time?"

"I can't with you John," Jasmine said after a moment of silence as a stream of tears joined together flowing down her eyes. "I think we need to call it quits for now."

"Are you serious?" John asked Jasmine. "You are breaking up with me because I paused?"

Hurt was building up in John and his eyes watered but he fought back his tears. He was not going to show weakness. "I'm sorry for wanting to live. We could have found a way to get Marcus and Ho Young after the tournament is over." John replied. "As we had already planned to do."

"No John. Not because you paused but because you have changed and not for the better. You have become an angry person. These tournaments have turned you cold hearted. I'm sorry. I just can't date someone like that. You were quick to want to kill the other Demigods, almost killed those police officers and now you didn't even want to save your own friends because you are scared that we will be killed."

"Excuse me." John replied. "I have the spell that allows me to use my powers in the Labyrinth so I was already going to go and get Marcus and Ho Young out of Tartarus. Once I entered the Labyrinth. All I would have had to do was focus on the entrance to Tartarus and teleport there."

"Not the point." Jasmine stated with authority giving John the impression that her mind was set. "The r—" before Jasmine could finish her sentence John was gone and back in Chicago. John teleported himself out of Canada, leaving Jasmine in Toronto with no money because he had the card on him. When they had packed John saw the card on the table and had put it in his pocket but in his feelings, John forgot that he had the credit card.

Jasmine was standing alone when Ho Young and Marcus appeared. Both having looks of horror on their faces. Marcus looked at Ho Young and then at Jasmine.

"Is this real?" He asked, scared to hear the answer. In Tartarus Marcus was tortured day and night. Giants would chase him and catch him every day and without his strength or speed Marcus was completely defenseless.

The giants would catch him and would first yank his legs off of his body one leg at a time. Next, they would grab large sharp knives and would cut three quarters of his arms off each. On earth Marcus would have bled out and died, but in Tartarus he lived through it. After cutting his arms the giants would roast Marcus over an open flame while pouring salt on him. Marcus would scream in pain and agony every time this happened which happened every day. Every time the giants would eat Marcus, they would start with his legs up to his head so that he felt the pain of every bite. Then the day would start again with Marcus running from the giants. No matter how fast he ran or how good he hid they always found him.

Seeing Jasmine and Ho Young on what seemed to be earth was a sigh of relief for Marcus. He was hoping it wasn't a hallucination and that he really had been freed from Tartarus.

Ho Young fell to his knees. He didn't know what was going on. He knew he had been killed by Leviathan and then taken to Tartarus. Nonstop Ho Young was tortured in hot lava. inch by inch he was lowered very slowly. From the moment his toes touched the lava his entire body felt like he was on fire and it just got hotter and more painful as he was lowered into the hot lava. Ho Young never died until his head completely went under with him screaming. Each time Ho Young was lowered into the lava it was from twenty feet above the Lava to add the suspense of waiting for the pain. He could see others being tormented. One person was being attacked by a spider and every time the spider ate him, he would reform, run from the spider who would magically wind up back in the cave and the spider would rush out and eat him again. Another person was trapped in a flat giant-sized portrait.

The entire portrait was painted a dirty dainty brown color including the man. He could not move to the back or to the front but could only move flatly to the side as the portrait allowed him to do. Every hour and eleven minutes the portrait would begin filling up with water and the man, though he tried. could not cover his nose or swim above the frame of the portrait. He drowned over and over again.

"You guys are really free." Jasmine said as her eyes welled up with tears for Ho Young and Marcus. You guys were in Tartarus but Lucifer wanted Leviathan back in this tournament. John and myself agreed to do it on the condition that you both were released from Tartarus." Marcus and Ho Young both ran to Jasmine and hugged her. Ho Young and Marcus were crying.

"Where is John?" Ho young finally asked, taking notice that his friend John wasn't in the room.

"We kind of had a falling out and broke up. He left," Jasmine vaguely stated not wanting to go into details.

"You broke up?" Marcus asked, with a look of concern on his face. He didn't know what but he knew that there was something that Jasmine was not telling them.

"Yeah. We broke up," Jasmine stated again.

"But why?" Ho Young asked, allowing his curiosity to get the best of him.

"Because these stupid tournaments have changed John. He just is not the same person that he was before the tournament."

"How so?" Marcus asked, though he knew he would need John's side of the story to get the full picture.

"He just has, he acts worse than the enemy does and he is ready to kill innocent people just to win a tournament."

"What innocent people and how is he acting worse than the enemy is?"

Jasmine sighed and then went into a detailed explanation about Chris Blaine, David Angel, and about how John hesitated to accept the deal releasing Ho Young and Marcus.

"I see. Marcus said, as Jasmine finished.

"That is messed up." Ho Young said. "If John knew how it was down there, I don't think he would have hesitated."

"No. I believe John knows about how it is down there and maybe that is the only reason he did agree. Because Leviathan sounds like the ultimate monster. With John not being able to use his signature move that he used to defeat Leviathan the last time, he maybe feels the tournament would be a guaranteed loss with Leviathan in it."

"Of course, you go right to defending John." Jasmine said with an attitude.

"No. I 'm just speaking the truth. You being able to read my mind know that."

"John is more in love with you than anything or anyone and if he wants to kill those two Demigods, I don't know them personally, it's because he is trying to protect you. It's not about winning the tournament with John. It's-"

"Stop right there." Jasmine said. "You have been in Tartarus you don't know what is going on with John, but-"

"But he is right." John interrupted Jasmine. John summoned the winds to bring Jasmine, Marcus, and Ho Young together with his hand touching Jasmine's shoulder. John teleported them back to

John and Jasmine's house in Chicago. John shook hands with Marcus and Ho Young teleporting them with him to another room away from Jasmine. He chatted with them for a while.

John explained his side of everything and why he hesitated to accept the deal. When Jasmine came into the room, John teleported away but he left them the credit card because they would need it more than he would.

As Marcus turned the T.V on the same story popped up all over the news. An entire town had become stone and it was the town John had just taken them from.

"Whoa!" Ho young yelled. "It's a good thing John rescued us otherwise we would be right back in Tartarus." Ho Young nearly fainted at the thought of going back to Tartarus as memories fluttered across his mind.

"No, it is not. We could have saved those people," Jasmine defiantly replied.

"Not according to John." Marcus stated very strongly. Michael told John it was Medusa there and that in the state that you and John were in that we would have lost that battle to her."

"I'm glad you got us out of Tartarus Jasmine," Ho Young said with a blank expression on his face. "But I am in no hurry to go back."

"I'm not either," Marcus seconded Ho young's statement.

"Well either way, we cannot just sit back and let people get killed. We have to stop as many monsters as we possibly can." Jasmine said.

Marcus was not excited about this news. He leaned against the wall and allowed himself to fall to the ground until he was in a sitting position. "You know," Marcus began. "When I first got these powers, I was excited, but now I really wish I never had them. If we fight again, we are risking dying and that is too much too face knowing where we will wind up." Marcus finished.

"Not just risking but we will be killed without the help of John for sure." Ho Young added his two cents in.

"Michael!" Marcus shouted loud enough for the entire block to hear.

"What?" Michael said with a bit of an attitude as he showed up with a quickness. "I'm in the middle of getting ready for the next tournament so this better be important."

"It is. We need you to find John and bring him here."

Michael disappeared for less than a second and was back in the living room with John not looking too happy about it.

"What do you want?" John looked back and forth from Jasmine to Michael His hands were out with his palms facing upward his body language clearly showing he was frustrated and did not want to be there.

"All four of you are in this tournament together, whether you want to be or not. As punishment for leaving the group from this point on the member that leaves will be handed over to Lucifer to be tortured by him for no less than seven days."

John sighed a sigh of frustration. "That is bull and you know it. Why can't we just fight these monsters on our own?"

"Because this is a team tournament. You must work as a team."

"Fine, I'll stay here with them. Marcus is my friend as is Ho Young so I have no problem with that."

Jasmine noticed that John left her name out of the list. "Oh, so because we are not dating, we aren't friends?"

"Do you guys hear something?" John said to Marcus and Ho Young who both looked very uncomfortable about being brought into the middle of the argument. Michael vanished the moment John said he would stay.

"You are stupid." Jasmine said to John very aggressively with her middle finger sticking out as she walked away.

John didn't even bother to respond to Jasmine. "Okay you guys." John said, addressing Ho Young and Marcus. "We need to figure out a game plan. Medusa will have moved on from that place and Leviathan needs to be the last monster we attempt to engage. We can cheat with the Sphinx." John said as his mind began to formulate his plan of attack. "Jasmine can read the Sphinx's mind so she can know the answer to any riddle the Sphinx asks. Once we kill the Sphinx, I'm sure that Chimaera and Leo the Nemean Lion will come out from hiding to get Vengeance because Chimaera is the mother to the Sphinx and the Nemean Lion is the Sphinx's brother."

"Wait a minute." Marcus said. "Are you saying Leo the constellation is the Nemean lion?"

"I am. You and Ho Young were fortunate enough to miss all of the studying that Jasmine and I had to do to prepare for this tournament. We discovered that Leo is the Nemean Lion. Apparently after Hercules killed him, he was given a lace among the stars."

"How is he in this tournament then?" Marcus asked, even more confused. "I thought you guys said that only monsters from the Labyrinth were being used in this tournament?"

"Only monsters from the labyrinth are being used." John replied. "Stars for the angels and God's are like statues for humans. They are not the real beings or monsters whose shape they are made in the image of but only ways of honoring certain creatures or beings."

"So, Leo was in the Labyrinth but now is out and has already easily kicked my butt. It will take teamwork for him or since your ancestor Hercules beat him maybe only you can. We need to start studying how Hercules beat him so that you can do the same thing but with our help."

As John finished talking Jasmine walked in the room and the whole atmosphere changed. A sharp tenseness filled the room that could cut through a forest of trees in one swing.

John looked away from Jasmine in the direction of Marcus. John was facing Marcus but his eyes were looking towards the ground. John's lip leaned to the left side of his face showing that he was disappointed about her choice of timing to enter the room.

"It's a good plan." Jasmine said, addressing John. "And it will work I believe."

John acknowledged Jasmine's approval with a simple nod of his head but made no attempt to look in her direction.

"Look John, I know that we are not going out anymore and that you apparently hate me now, but just because we are not boyfriend and girlfriend anymore does not mean that we have to stop being friends. It definitely doesn't mean that we stop speaking to each other in the middle of a tournament that we can be killed in."

John remained silent. Jasmine was his life and losing her was his fall. She took away his aspiration to dominate the tournament. The fact that she broke up with him because he was trying to find ways to end the tournament as soon as possible to protect not himself but Jasmine, destroyed John's heart. His emotions were now nothing but a past history lesson that taught John to never love again.

"John," Jasmine said his name again. "We have to talk, please. Marcus and Ho Young do not want to go back into Tartarus and all of our lives depend on us talking."

"Fine." John said. "For that cause, we can talk but about nothing else."

"If that is how you want it to be between us, that is fine. But at least treat me like a human, please." Jasmine's eyes had a blank yet pleading look.

"I'll try my best but I can't guarantee anything. You did me wrong and I don't want to talk about it. You have broken up with me twice within the last seven months and I'm not going through that again."

"I won't argue or defend myself. Let's just start planning for the battle."

"Okay. The way I figure it." John began," Jasmine doesn't need to have her eyes open. She can read Medusa's mind and can tell us when she is about to do something. We can use code words to know when Medusa is near us."

"I don't like that plan all the way." Marcus cut in. "Ho Young for one is bound to mess up whatever code we come up with and he will be right back in Tartarus."

"Hey!" Ho Young quickly rebuked the notion that he would mess up any plan that involved intelligence.

"No offence Ho Young." Marcus said. "But this is not about pride. I don't want you to die again. I know what it is like in Tartarus. I was there myself and I am going to do everything I can to never go back."

Jasmine watched John with a little bit of sadness in her eyes. She in no way wanted to break up with John and regretted what she said to him out of anger. It didn't seem to matter though because John was determined to hate her and shut her out. How could she apologize a second time to John for breaking his heart, not once but twice in such a short time.

"Yeah. I'm going to have to agree with Marcus," John said to Ho Young. "I want you to stay here in the land of the living and Medusa is way too dangerous for us to take any chances."

"I guess so." Ho Young said. He looked disappointed but John, Marcus and Jasmine could tell that he understood.

Jasmine wanted to add her input but for the first time she felt uncomfortable speaking. She knew deep down that the plan was not air tight but she felt it best for her just to keep silent.

John, even though he agreed to communicate with her during the tournament, kept his eyes in every direction but hers while he talked. John was trying to get past Jasmine breaking up with him but he just couldn't.

"Are you guys ready?" John said to the group, everyone nodded their heads yes but nobody dared speak. They were going on a mission that was near suicide. Medusa was crafty and if she got you to look at her, you were dead. You would instantly be turned to stone.

"Wait, how are we going to know where she is?" Marcus asked, just realizing that Medusa turned an entire town into stone so most likely she had moved on.

"If I focus on anything, I can teleport to it, including Medusa."

"Oh wow." Marcus replied. "I see your powers have gotten stronger."

"Yeah after Ho Young died, I had to master my powers and take them to a whole other level to defeat Leviathan."

"Man, that must have been tough fighting him. I remember how we were dreading his coming and were trying to get rid of the other beasts before he was released from his prison."

"Yeah. He was really scary." Said Ho Young more to himself than anyone else as he remembered Leviathan killing him just a year prior.

"Okay, well if we are going to do this," Jasmine said. "Medusa is in an open field right now but she is very fast. We need to hurry if we are going to catch her in the open."

"Okay." Marcus said. John just stood where he was with a disgruntled look on his face. He wasn't ignoring Jasmine as she thought that he was because he didn't answer but he was trying to focus on Medusa. He had to picture the actual Medusa and focus on her in order to teleport to her otherwise they would all wind up in some art gallery with a painting of her or at someone's house who had a book about Medusa. As John searched through his mind to remember her picture in the books, Marcus interrupted John's meditation.

"So, are we going?"

"Yes." John replied more in a sort of aggressive tone. His voice was higher than normal and his body gestures suggested he was frustrated in which he was but he had not meant to show it.

Of course, Jasmine, who could not read John's mind because of his protective bubble, only saw that John answered Marcus and not her and seemed very agitated most likely because she had suggested they go at that moment instead of him.

Why didn't I just keep quiet Jasmine thought to herself.

"Let me see that book." John said to Ho Young, as he pointed at the top book on a stack of books.

"Okay." Ho Young said running towards the books. It should have been a simple process just run over, grab the top book and run it back, but Ho Young tripped on a flat piece of paper on the way, fell into the books and knocked all of the books on the floor.

John put his hand to his face and just began to laugh into his hands. "Yup it is great to have you back Ho young." John managed to say after a moment.

"Uh, hey! Thank you," Ho young replied as he did a salute. Ho young rummaged through the fallen books and surprisingly found the book on Medusa pretty quickly.

"Okay." John said, focusing on her picture. "Everyone come in close and link up." As every touched one another's shoulders John teleported everyone to Medusa. They appeared behind her since she was moving so fast.

"Close your eyes!" John yelled as he could feel through the wind that her head had begun to turn towards them.

"John!" Jasmine yelled. She is coming and she has claws, very long claws. She is going to swing at you first. Count to forty-five then duck. Then count to ten and turn around and kill her from behind. Marcus and I need to turn and run away as fast as possible the minute I say go."

"Why are we running?" Marcus yelled.

"To distract her so that she will chase us and so that John and Ho Young can kill her."

"Ho Young." Jasmine tried to hurry and say his instructions before Medusa reached them. "Turn into a dragon now. Turn into a giant fire breathing bat because bats are blind and.... Marcus, run!" Jasmine yelled.

John hit forty-five second in his head and ducked. He really didn't even need to count because he felt Medusa swing in the wind as if he could see it in slow motion and could have easily ducked her swing. It was as if John and the air had become one.

After missing, John felt Medusa swoop past him chasing two individuals which John of course knew were Jasmine and Marcus.

John turned just in time to see Medusa less than an inch from reaching Jasmine. John commanded the wind to hold Medusa in place. As John did this, he felt a giant creature fly past him in the air towards Medusa.

"Good." John said looking up and seeing a giant bat flying quickly through the air at Medusa.

Medusa shrieked as the bat grabbed her head with its talon feet and tossed her high into the air. The talons pierced Medusa's thick neck on all sides but not enough to kill her or decapitate her.

As Medusa fell from the sky to the earth Ho Young began cooking her as he circled her breathing fire on her. Medusa burned to death long before she ever hit the ground.

"You can look now." Jasmine yelled at the top of her lungs.

"I thought that even if she was dead that if you looked at her face you would still turn to stone?" Ho Young questioned.

"No, Ho Young." John answered. "That was just in a few movies. In real life when a monster or Demigod dies their powers die with them."

"Oh, I see." Ho Young said as he and Marcus both opened their eyes at the same time.

As the four Demigods stood around Medusa's body, her body disintegrated before their eyes. A loud voice sounded throughout the sky.

"**Two points for team one, and zero points for team two. Medusa has been sent back to the Labyrinth**."

John, Jasmine, Marcus, and Ho Young decided to go to the movies once they were back in Chicago. The battle seemed to work some kind of magic over John because he was talking to Jasmine now as if they had never stopped talking. Marcus dared to smile because things were finally getting back to the way that he remembered things being before he died, with Jasmine and John on talking terms again.

"Oh man this is going to be amazing. I haven't been to a movie in years." Ho Young said in a volume just short of yelling.

The four of them stood in line to buy tickets to a movie called Black Out. The movie was a futuristic type of movie. "That movie looks pretty dope." Marcus stated with his eyes wide open to show his appreciation for how good the movie sounded.

"I'm down to watch it. You Jasmine?" Asked John.

"Yup." Jasmine replied with a smile.

"What about you, Ho Young?"

"Yeah I would like to see that." Ho Young replied.

"It's settled then." Jasmine said, pulling out their Gold credit card as they reached the booth to buy tickets.

"Hello welcome to Chicago's affordable motion pictures, how can I help you today?" The ticket agent asked the four Demigods.

"We would like to see Black Out." Ho Young said as he saluted the ticket agent, a tall boy with reddish hair and freckles.

"Okay." He said as he took the card from Jasmine and charged the tickets to it. "Here you go," the agent said as he handed Jasmine the card back and four tickets along with receipts.

"You guys want snacks?" John asked as they entered the main lobby of the theatre.

"Yeah." Marcus answered.

"You know I do," Jasmine said grinning and blushing at the snack stand. Well John thought she was blushing at the snack stand until he saw a tall Hispanic boy standing in the line smiling back at Jasmine.

"Do you guys know each other?" John asked as he forced a grin hoping the boy was an old friend of hers, But Jasmine shook her head no without breaking eye contact with the boy.

As they moved forward in the line the boy waited on the side for Jasmine to get close enough for him to talk to her. John was hoping that Jasmine would tell him that she was with him. But even though they were on speaking terms again, John now realized that they never officially began dating again.

"Hi my name Hector." The boy said as Jasmine on purpose crossed to the side that he was on. John looked out of the corner of his eye and tried to eavesdrop but once the concession worker began questioning John, Ho Young and Marcus, he couldn't focus on Jasmine and the boy and pay attention to what his friends were telling him they wanted.

Hector just so happened to be going to the same movie so instead of sitting with the group Jasmine decided to sit with Hector a few rows behind them. John did his best to watch the movie but every giggle Jasmine did, pierced John's heart. Every time John felt Jasmine turn her head towards the boy John's stomach groaned but not from being empty. John fought his watery eyes. They were like a sprinkling rain attempting to penetrate past John's clouded eyes fighting to roll down his puffed-up cheeks.

Finally, Hector did it. He leaned over and kissed Jasmine. She didn't fight it but kissed him back. John began to breathe harder and harder as they kissed. When they finished Jasmine had no thoughts of John in her mind she was focused on Hector and nothing else.

Chapter Eighteen

"We need to be smart about this. There is a reason that I'm a warrant officer and you are not."

"Just because we have a hundred and thirty-two people freed doesn't mean we have an army and are ready to take on the Klu Klux Klan army. We are heavily outnumbered."

"What do we do? Leave them here until we have enough people to form a military? They will be found and killed."

Warrant Officer Jerry Johnikins thought to himself for a minute. "I don't know what to do, but I know if we attack now, everyone that we just rescued will be killed. We will figure something out. We have to."

The words **To Be Continued** flashed across the screen. The entire theatre booed because they were really into the movie. Everyone wanted the movie to finish.

"Dang that sucks," Marcus said to John but after not getting a response he looked over to find John's seat empty.

"Crap." Marcus said out loud causing Ho Young to look over.

"Hey," Ho Young half shouted. "When did John leave? I didn't even see him get up, that is crazy I must have really been focused on the movie not to have seen him go by."

"No," Marcus replied. "He left because Jasmine decided to be an ass and make out with that yuppie up there." Marcus made sure to say it loud enough for Jasmine to hear.

"Oh, so I'm wrong now?" Jasmine replied angrily. Jasmine was so flustered that she nearly tripped on the very narrow aisle steps leading down to the exit.

"Yeah you were. You guys finally got on talking terms and you pull this. John told me he is still in love with you, he just didn't know how to handle the break up. Then you gave him hope after we killed Medusa today and now you do this to him."

"Oh well poor sad John. I'm not going to wait on him to get out of his feelings." Jasmine continued.

"You big dummy." Marcus said walking up to Jasmine with anger in his eyes. His eyes were blazing so hard it looked to Hector like there were flames inside both of Marcus' eyes.

"Hey you better calm down homie before you get hurt." Hector said to Marcus.

Marcus without a word grabbed Hector and threw him into the movie screen." Hector died instantly.

"Marcus!!" Jasmine yelled as she wasted her time trying to push past Marcus." Fine you won't let me pass? How about I yell rape?"

"What is wrong with you?" Marcus angrily asked.

"What the hell is going on?" Michael angrily asked as he appeared his face was fierce. His eyes were like lightning.

"What are you mad at me too?" Jasmine asked laughing wickedly.

Marcus had to breathe before he spoke so he did not say anything that he would regret. "Jasmine do you know where John is at?"

Jasmine had been too mad at Marcus to read his mind. "I don't care." Jasmine replied.

"Good." Michael said laughing before Marcus could speak. "Good luck getting home without John's help."

"What do you mean?" Ho young said as he tripped trying to step over the seat to get to the top aisle where everyone was at.

"John is in Tartarus. Arachnid is in town and is on her way here right now." Jasmine's eyes went wide

"John is in Tartarus?" Jasmine began to breathe very heavily. She felt as though the weight of the world had just dropped on her shoulders. Jasmine could feel her heart missing beats. John had been the love of her life. She only did what she did at the movies to get John to react. She didn't expect John to go out and get himself killed.

"He will be in there for a week?" Marcus asked Michael.

"No. he has three weeks. He used his powers on a mortal, cussed myself and God the father out and he left the group. He received a week for each offence."

"What will his torment be?" asked Ho Young.

"Tartarus likes to make his torments a person or beings worse fear. John's is spiders. So I assume it will be him getting attacked by spiders."

"I'm confused. Is he dead? Why else would he be in Tartarus?" Asked Jasmine, trying to understand exactly what was going on.

"First." Michael said. "You could have figured this out at the beginning of the conversation, but you were so flustered that you didn't stop to think for even a second to use your powers to read everyone's minds to find out the entire situation. An enemy could use that flaw against you in the future if you do not learn to master it. Secondly, I just told you all the answer and you were so focused on John being in Tartarus that you stopped listening and didn't hear the reason why. You are so busy accusing John of changing that you haven't realized that it is you that has actually changed. You are not focused and John loves you with all of his heart but you are too hard headed to see that everything that he does, he does it for you. Whether to protect you or just to make you happy. The only reason Lucifer's sons have not attempted to kill you is because Lucifer told them to stay put on a cliff. But the moment he tells them that they can finally come after you they will. John knew this and that is why he was willing to send them to the Labyrinth to die. He was trying to protect you."

"I didn't know." Jasmine shyly said. "So, he is in Tartarus because of me?"

"Yes, he is," Michael said, not holding back or placing any sugar coating on his answer. "And he will probably go back again if you two do not find a way to make things work between you two."

***

John opened his eyes for the fifth time in Tartarus. "Dang it." John said realizing he was in hell and he was about to be attacked by spiders again. Aggressive wolf spiders began to crowd a hill in the distance. John knew that like the past times they would be on him within minutes.

The first time John thought he was in a dream as the spiders crowded on the same hill in the distance and he tried to run but they caught him very quickly. The spiders bit chunks of his flesh off and it hurt very much but now that it had happened a few times John knew he wasn't in a dream. And since he wasn't dead, he must be getting punished for leaving the group.

John watched as the spiders rushed at him for the fifth time but instead of running John sat down. Tears poured down John's eyes as the spiders neared closer to him. Not because of the spiders, John was crying because Jasmine broke his heart. Thoughts of Jasmine kissing the boy in the theatres was too much for him. He sat on the ground and wished the spiders would hurry up because he would rather face the pain of being eaten alive rather than suffer from his broken heart. The spiders eating him took his mind off of Jasmine.

The first spider reached John and very aggressively sunk its pincers in John ripping flesh from flesh. The pain was immense but John screamed more and more spiders joined in. The wolf spiders were the size of baby elephants. Their legs were very strong and carried them great distances at impossible speeds.

Within minutes John had been eaten. John woke up again as he had done so many times before for a brief second, he thought of Jasmine blushing in the line and purposely moving towards the boy. John couldn't take it and, in a hurry to get her out of his mind, John rushed towards the hill where he knew the spiders would be appearing at any moment. He reached the hill and the spiders appeared. They wasted no time and went right to eating John.

As John opened his eyes an eighth time in Tartarus, he was prepared to head towards the hill again, but everything was different. John was looking up into the sky and as if it was a virtual movie theatre. He saw Jasmine having sex with some random guy that he had never seen before. They were passionately going at it and John tried to turn away but no matter which way he turned the vision of them appeared in front of his eyes.

John closed his eyes hoping to rid himself of the visions, but in the darkness of his closed eyelids the vision appeared as if his eyes were open. Jasmine was still having sex with the boy, whoever he was. They had sex for hours and John was forced to watch the whole entire time. Constantly John yelled for the vision to stop. "PLEASE!! I'LL GO BACK TO THE GROUP! PLEASE STOP IT.!"

After many hours of watching Jasmine have sex with the guy the vision changed to a few years down the line. Jasmine was in the hospital a doctor and a nurse were present as was the boy that John had seen Jasmine with. John continued trying to escape the visions by looking in all different directions and by closing his eyes but nothing worked. John was forced to watch Jasmine have this stranger's baby and she was so happy.

John watched multiple visions of Jasmine. She married the guy. They had several children together and had a happy family. In one vision John himself was in it. He had just been freed from Tartarus.

"Hey Ho Young." John said as Ho Young, who looked much older, walked up to John with a big smile on his face.

"John. Wow, you are finally out man. Michael told us that you were being punished for cursing out God and hurting people."

"Yeah, I was hurt from losing Jasmine, speaking of Jasmine, where is she? And where is Marcus?"

Ho Young looked towards the ground.

"What is it?" John asked, seeing the hurt in Ho Young's eyes as they tried to focus on the ground.

"Man, I hate to tell you this, you just being freed yourself, but Marcus is dead."

"What?" John said in shock. "How? What happened?"

"A week after you were put in Tartarus Jasmine met another guy and she fell in love with him. She stopped focusing on the tournament. Leviathan showed up and Marcus and I fought against him. Jasmine had started helping us out but then another monster showed up Jasmine left us to save her boyfriend who was trapped in a car by a monster called Onocentaur."

"Hmm? What kind of monster is that? Is it one of the Centaur breeds?"

"No, it was half man and half donkey."

John looked at Ho young with the look he always gave him when he said something dumb. His mouth twitched to the left side of his face with his head tilted a bit towards the left and his left eyebrow was higher than his right.

Ho Young immediately recognized the look. "Oh man did I say something dumb?" Ho Young looked disappointed in himself.

"No, you didn't," John replied. "It's just that I'm sure that a half donkey/half man would be a breed of centaurs which is half man/half horse."

"Yeah that makes sense." Ho Young replied happily. "Wow they really could be Ho Young saluted John as he finished speaking. "You are really smart John. I mean it really smart," Ho Young saluted again as he ended his last word of his sentence.

"Where is Jasmine now?"

"To tell you the truth, she hasn't spoken to me in months. Her new boyfriend doesn't like me so she stopped talking to me."

"Stay here." John ordered Ho Young as he focused on Jasmine and teleported to her. A glass dropped behind John as he appeared in the living room. John quickly turned around to see Jasmine only to find the stranger she was having sex with in his visions while he was in Tartarus.

"What happened?" Jasmine said running into the room, with a baby in her hands.

Jasmine stopped as she froze seeing John standing in her living room. "What are you doing here?" She asked John, looking more disappointed to see him than he thought she would be.

"I was just released from Tartarus and I came to see you."

"You shouldn't have." Jasmine replied. "The tournament is over, and quite frankly so are we."

"So, it is like that?" John said not sure whether to be angry or hurt.

"John, I have a family now. I have no time for you or Ho Young anymore. I want nothing to do with that life."

"Why? Is it because you were the reason Marcus was killed?" John harshly replied, finally letting his anger win.

"Get out of my house!" Jasmine yelled at John. "GET OUT! GET OUT!" Jasmine yelled until John left.

"NOOO! SHE IS NOT LIKE THAT!" John yelled from lying on the ground in Tartarus.

"Oh. she isn't?" A voice said across the sky of Tartarus. "Watch this."

A scene unfolded high above John and some more familiar voices were talking.

"Shut up, Marcus it is not my fault that John is in Tartarus."

"Yes, it is. If you weren't acting like a hoe at the movies John would still be here."

"Excuse me? But did you just call me a hoe?"

"Uh, yeah, I believe I did."

"Guys!" Ho young yelled. "Stop fighting, please."

"Shut up!" both Marcus and Jasmine yelled together at Ho Young. Ho Young, offended and hurt by their response, went and sat in the bathroom so that he couldn't hear their argument.

"Go to hell Marcus!" Jasmine angrily yelled.

"Been there done that. But thanks to you, that is where John is now."

"What? Am I supposed to care? John made his choices in life. I'm not going to force myself to love someone that I am not in love with."

John turned his eyes from the scene but like before the scene followed. "Just bring the spiders back, please." John softly begged Tartarus in a whisper, completely heart broken.

John thought Tartarus had decided to honor his request because the scenes of Jasmine disappeared from before his eyes. Michael appeared behind John and placed a hand on his shoulder then teleported him back to the safe house where Jasmine, Ho Young and Marcus were waiting for him.

As they appeared in the house Michael sat John down in a chair close to a bed in the master bedroom that he and Jasmine shared. Jasmine, Ho Young and Marcus, who were already in the room, ran up and hugged John but got no response. John was in a vegetative state. The visions were too much for him, especially seeing them twenty-four seven non-stop for three weeks.

John stared blankly in front of him as they all hugged him, not even the slightest bit aware of their presence in the room.

Even though the visions had stopped, John still saw them in his eyes. He could not un-see what he saw. Jasmine did not love him.

"What is wrong with him?" Jasmine asked Michael.

"His torture was more than he could bear." Michael replied, without taking his eyes away from John.

"Oh no. Was it? Spiders?" Ho Young asked. "Because John is definitely scared of spiders. I remember one time, a long time ago, a giant spider tried to kill John but he was able to escape on a cloud."

Marcus turned around with a confused look on his face. "What?" He asked Ho Young. "When did that happen?"

"A long time ago." Ho Young said looking at Marcus as if he had asked something stupid. "Remember it was John and..." Ho Young stopped and focused his face and froze in mid speech. "Never mind that was in the book we read last year." He finally said after a few seconds of silence.

"Oh my goodness." Michael said as he shook his head and snickered doing his best to fight off a laugh. "It is good to have you back Ho Young." Michael said as he still was fighting the urge to laugh.

Jasmine and Marcus laughed. "Only you Ho Young," Marcus said.

Ho Young smiled and saluted.

"But," Michael finally began, after returning to his serious state. "The torture started with John being eaten alive by wolf spiders but he didn't mind that and Tartarus took notice of that. So, Tartarus dug deep into his innermost fears and found his number one fear and played it before his eyes twenty-four seven. No matter where he looked it showed and when he closed his eyes his worst fear showed there as well. It was obviously too much for him."

Marcus stared at Michael. "Well, let us know what it was? What was the vision that broke him?"

"It was of Jasmine dating other guys, having sex with other guys, marrying other guys, and having kids with other guys. The last one he had, the one I interrupted, was of Jasmine married with multiple kids and not wanting to see him when he was released from Tartarus."

"Wait a minute. John had no problem with the spiders eating him alive but he couldn't handle visions of Jasmine with someone else?" Marcus asked with shock, thinking in his mind that he would have been able to handle visions like that a lot easier than being eaten alive by spiders.

"It sounds like an easier torture than what you guys went through," Michael answered Marcus with a sad look upon his face. The wrinkles in his expression made him look much older than he normally looked. "It even sounds like a lesser torture than the spiders eating him alive. But to understand this, you would have to understand how much John really loves you Jasmine," Michael lifted his eyes towards Jasmine.

Jasmine's eyes were focused and attentive on every word Michael spoke. "Before this tournament began John attempted to bargain a deal with The Creator. He saw that the tournament was breaking you and hurting you. He spoke of the nightmares you were having and how scared you were at times."

Jasmine didn't speak a word but just listened. She knew what Michael was going to say but for some reason felt the need to hear it out loud.

"He tried to bargain a deal for him to spend years in Tartarus after the tournaments were complete if Father would release you from the tournament, and protect you."

Tears began to drop down her face as Jasmine looked at John. "Michael please. If you fix him. I won't hurt him again. Please I am sorry. I don't know what came over me." Jasmine began to cry hard as she rushed over to Michael grasping the bottom of his white robes. "PLEASE FIX HIM. PLEASE MICHAEL."

"It will take time but you guys need to not leave this house until I bring him back." Michael the Angel spoke.

Jasmine ran over and hugged John before Michael had the chance to take him. "John, I love you, I do. Please come back. I..." Jasmine had to pause as her lips quivered as the urge to begin crying again hit her stronger than ever before. "John I'm so sorry." As Jasmine expressed her love for John, John disappeared into thin air as Michael took him. Jasmine stayed in the chair where John was crying for a long while after he was gone. Marcus and Ho Young went downstairs to give Jasmine sometime to herself.

Chapter Nineteen

"Well this is completely insane. The demigods are in Chaos and are still winning with two beasts to your son's zero," Thor said out loud making sure that Lucifer could hear him.

"My sons will attack when the time is right. My plan is that when, and only when, the Demigods are fighting Leviathan my sons will join the fight. I have the perfect plan. While the demigods are fighting Leviathan my sons will cast a spell that forms an entrance into Tartarus, my sons will then trap the Demigods in the Labyrinth with all of the monsters that they have just killed and they will be dead in no time seeing as to how they will have no powers down there."

"Really?" Thor said mockingly. His hands stretched as he motioned with his body language to make his sarcasm even more dramatic. "That's it? You plan to let them kill all of the monsters stacking up all of the points on their side and then you think your sons will be able to just waltz in and steal the tournament from them? From what I have seen so far, these Demigods are good on their feet. I mean for goodness sake they beat a woman that turns anyone into stone if they so much as look at her. All this while fighting amongst themselves. I would hate to see what they could do working together as one."

"Oh, they can do quite a bit together with just two of them." Zeus said to Thor. "Lucifer here, keeps underestimating these Demigods. The only reason that there are only two beast dead is because they were fighting with each other and then the one demigod wound up in Tartarus. Lucifer having Leviathan put back in this tournament in exchange for the two Demigods who died in the last tournament was probably the most bone-headed move of all time."

"It was a wise decision and you will see why in the end." Lucifer said with his chest puffed out with pride and an ugly expression on his face.

"Lucifer and wise are not two words that I would ever dare put in the same sentence together." Thor said laughing. "A fool thinks himself wise, especially when all of his wise decisions in the end always turn out to be foolish."

A fire blazed in Lucifer's eyes. Anger was beginning to build up inside of him.

"Oh, poor Lucy is mad." Thor said as he laughed and mocked Lucifer.

"Be careful my son." Odin said entering the throne room. "Lucifer can beat you in battle. The only ones of us who can beat him in combat are Michael, Gabriel, and myself. I know you hear all kinds of rumors but he is actually smarter and craftier than most and can back it up with his skills in battle. The only reason he keeps losing is because he is going against the creator, who is all powerful and knows all things. I would even dare say that Lucifer is craftier in battle than even I am."

Thor stood dumb founded. He was not expecting to hear such things from his father. It was hard to believe that this same being that stood before him named Lucifer not long ago was cowering before the Asgardians begging for his life and throwing his Greek ruling cousins under the bus.

However, now that he thought about it, he was completely outmatched on Asgard, especially with Odin there one of the ones who could beat Lucifer by himself. Now Thor realized that Lucifer's craftiness in that situation saved him there to fight another day. Now Thor began to view Lucifer as a much stronger Loki, who because of his craftiness was far less powerful than Lucifer.

"I understand father." Thor responded to Odin's words. "At first I listened to rumors but now looking at Lucifer with the fire in his eyes, I realize that he is indeed a warrior."

"Forgive me." Thor said, turning towards Lucifer and bowing a short bow without going too low. It really was more just a nod of his head but indeed it was a bow to show respect.

The fire in Lucifer's eyes disappeared. "Thank you, Odin." Lucifer said. His eyes were sullen and dark yet focused showing his sincerity.

"No, need for apologies my dear brother. I was merely saving my son's life and sparing a battle between thine and myself, which would surely take place if such a thing were to happen."

Lucifer appreciated the compliment from his brother Odin, but also was very aware of the threat that Odin so slickly snuck into the compliment.

"Well, let us have our meeting real fast." Zeus said standing to his feet.

"Agreed." Poseidon said.

"Well this is your home." Odin said standing to his feet. "So, it is only fair if you take your seat at the head and conduct the meeting."

Zeus grinned and walked over to his throne room seat which Lucifer had forcefully banned him from. Lucifer did not like Odin asking Zeus back to his head position Olympus but he dared not say anything to keep peace between Odin and him.

"Okay," Zeus said as he looked over everyone, making sure to land his eyes on Lucifer multiple times. "We have much to discuss if we could all have a seat." Zeus asked as hundreds of chairs appeared out of nowhere.

"First before we begin to discuss this tournament, while we have a few of the sects of our brethren here, I would like to explain about the tournaments and their purpose and then extend the invitation to the rest of our brethren scattered around the world to join us."

Ares scowled under his breath. He had quite a few run-ins with a few of the Hawaiian Gods and the South American Gods. He disliked them almost as much as they disliked him.

"We will form a task force of our sisters and brethren to journey to their lands and extend an invitation to join us."

"What if they attack the messengers?" Asked Aeolous.

"If they attack. I am sure that most of you are far more than capable of defending yourselves. At least capable enough to be able to fight on the run as you get out of there."

"I see." Aeolous replied with a doubtful expression upon his face. He didn't like the sounds of this plan because he being the God of the winds knew all too well having had run-ins with some of the Gods in foreign sects, that some would prove to be very violent and hard to get away from.

"I have a better idea to spare any of us from getting hurt," Aeolous said out loud after a second of thinking. "I can just send messages to them through the winds letting them know exactly what is happening and letting them know if they wish to participate then we would love to have them."

Zeus started to protest the idea but Odin cut him off. "I sense that you being the God of the winds have had countless interactions with our former brethren as you have had with us. I also sense that you don't think sending any of the Gods will help much because you know how some of the other Gods have become. Am I close on my guesses?"

"Your guess is one hundred percent correct." Aeolous replied. "Some of the other Gods will attack on site and some are not as easy to get away from as others. I know for instance in Antarctica there is some sort of spell cast that prevents any kind of teleportation in or out. One of my sons has been held prisoner there now for over four centuries."

"Does our brother in Antarctica scare you that much that you would leave your offspring there to be held as a prisoner for so long?" Thor asked Aeolous with a look of disapproval upon his face.

"No that is not it at all." Aeolous lashed out in a very loud and booming voice. Thor's words had angered him. "I tried to rescue him. I sent an army but within seconds they were destroyed and my vision had been blocked from seeing what or who was there. I have been trying to figure out who of our brethren went to Antarctica but to this day I do not know."

"I like you Aeolous. You have always been an upfront person and are one of great powers. I therefore will accompany you to go and find your son when this meeting has passed.

Aeolous teleported to the throne of Olympus where Thor was sitting with Odin and the big three, Zeus, Poseidon and Hades. Aeolous extended his hand towards. "Thor, it will be a pleasure to have you accompany me on this mission to find my son and free him."

"It will be a pleasure to battle whoever this God is and to save your son my old friend." Thor replied as he extended his hand back and shook Aeolous's hand.

"Oh no. You two are not going to battle without me." Ares yelled as he flew to where Aeolous and Thor were standing.

"I have not been on a mission myself in a long time," Hades said out loud as he pondered going." I think I will join the mission as well."

"I think we all need to go." Odin with his powerful and very persuasive voice said as he stood to his feet. "Something tells me that this is not one of our brethren from heaven at all but maybe of another of his creations that I met once long ago."

"Who is it father?" Thor asked, impatiently wanting an answer.

"I need to go and I will return shortly. Continue the rest of the meeting so that by the time I return we can all prepare to go if need be."

"Okay." Zeus said as Odin left. "To continue this meeting, we need to discuss the next tournament, in the case that one is needed."

"One will be." Hades said. "Right now, all that this tournament has done is piss the Demigods off. John will come back to himself the moment Jasmine is in trouble and he will unleash hell."

"How do you know this?" Thor asked Hades.

"Because I have watched this scenario play out thousands of times with other Demigods. I have watched this John Demigod do it the last tournament and his powers just keep getting stronger and stronger. He is nearly as powerful as many of us are. He is easily the most powerful demigod ever."

"I believe you." Thor said. "And from what I have heard about him, he will definitely overcome this tournament."

"Am I the only one paying attention to the tournament?" Poseidon asked, not understanding what his brothers and cousins were thinking.

"We know he is in a vegetative state right now," Thor replied. "But he will come out of it and when he does, he will win this tournament if we are not careful."

"There is no way the Demigods win this tournament." Lucifer said, finally speaking after listening to everyone. "My sons will soon be attacking them as I have mentioned before. While the demigods are in a fight my sons will join the monsters against the Demigods. My sons will hide while using their powers to change the scenery for the Demigods. While the Demigods will think all of the monsters have disappeared because of my sons, the monster will kill the Demigods. They won't even be able to see the monsters."

"Hmm," Thor thought deep within his mind before speaking a sentence. "I like that plan." Thor finally said. "But only if we can get a fight going between the Demigods and a monster because right now, they are hiding in the safe house."

"Yes, that is a problem." said Hades. "We definitely need to draw them out and draw the monsters to them. But what can we do?"

"Why not create a scent to attract a monster? For instance, Chimaera cannot refuse the scent of fisherman on the sea."

"That actually is a perfect idea brother." Poseidon almost shouted." I can carry the scent of fisherman on the sea to Chimaera's nose and from there lead her to the city the Demigods are hiding out in. With their town under attack they will have to start fighting to save their friends."

"Are we all in agreement?" Poseidon asked the other gods."

"I am." Thor said. "That is a great plan."

"I am too," Lucifer said, sitting back in disappointment because he had not thought of the plan.

One by one all of the Gods agreed to the plan and Poseidon went to work. He caused a great smell of fisherman on the sea to enter into Chimaera's nose. As she followed the scent Poseidon led her to the southside of the city Chicago.

Chapter Twenty

Michael appeared before the Demigods as they all sat in the living room discussing how they could help John return to himself. "We have a big problem." Michael said, addressing the three Demigods who could respond to him. Chimaera the dragon has been led here by my brothers and cousins, the fallen few. She will destroy this city if you don't stop her."

Marcus looked a bit uneasy, "who is Chimaera?"

"She is the mother of the Sphinx, and the Nemean Lion known today as Leo."

"Oh." Marcus said as he sat down, a look of doubt sat upon his face as his lips curled inwards and his forehead became a den of wrinkles. If John being in a vegetative state wasn't bad enough, they were going to have to fight another dragon.

"You don't think we can beat her?" Ho Young asked.

"No, I believe you can. But you must understand if you beat her, the Nemean Lion and the Sphinx will come after you, both vicious and very dangerous."

"But isn't it against the rules for the Greek fallen angels, Gods whatever they call themselves, to interfere in the tournament?" Jasmine asked feeling that Michael would maybe penalize them for breaking the rules.

"No, they are forbidden from interfering from anything directly involving you in this tournament. They were smart on this one. They lured Chimaera to Chicago with her favorite scent and gave her no instructions, instead are leaving her free to do as she pleases. If they had ordered her or forced her to attack you then they would have broken the rules. However, all they did was put Chimaera and yourselves in a position where you would have to fight each other."

"I see." Jasmine responded to Michaels answer, in which she didn't like but she understood what he had just said. "And I see there is more news that you have kept from us."

"Good job." Michael said. "I could not tell you because of the rules, that would have been interfering but I am glad you listened because you need to really prepare for that part."

"What?" Marcus asked. "What did I miss?"

"She read my mind and will tell you what she saw once I leave," Michael said and then just like that he was gone.

"What is it?" Marcus asked Jasmine." What did you see?"

"Lucifer is setting a trap. His sons, David and Chris are going to sneak attack us while we are fighting Chimaera and use a portal to trap us in the Labyrinth."

"That is low." Ho Young said out loud.

"I know." Jasmine agreed. "You guys get some sleep. I'm going to spend some time with John before we go to face Chimaera."

"We actually don't have any time," Marcus said as his eyes passed over the T.V. On the television the news was playing. A twenty-five-foot dragon was consuming citizens with fire. People were running in all directions, many engulfed in flame.

Jasmine sighed in frustration. "Wow, Michael literally waited until she got here to warn us. So much for time to make a plan."

"No, we need to make a plan before going because I'm not trying to be killed and left in Tartarus again."

"Ho Young we need to find out what Chimaera's weaknesses are. Can you just grab me the book about her?"

"Yup, I am on it," Ho Young said as he saluted and ran upstairs to the stacks of books to look for the one about Chimaera.

"Marcus if the Nemean Lion should come, you will have to battle him. He is invincible against human weapons and

Demigod powers it seems. John fought him and nothing hurt him."

"If John couldn't do anything, what am I supposed to do?"

"Actually, the Nemean Lion has been defeated only once in history and it was by your ancestor, Hercules. We need to go through the books to see if we can find out any details on exactly how he did it. I doubt it was only muscles. He must have found some kind of weapon that could hurt and kill the Nemean Lion, but what?"

"Okay." Marcus said as he too ran up the stairs. While Marcus and Ho Young were searching through books, Jasmine began using her powers to read the minds of Chris and David. From what she could see, they were already in Chicago and were actually sitting by watching Chimaera the dragon, kill all of those innocent people.

Jasmine became very angered. Her fist balled up as she watched the horrific scenes through Chris' eyes as he laughed at people who were trying to get away.

"That is okay." Jasmine said to herself. "I know where you two are hiding and while Ho Young and Marcus attack Chimaera I will be attacking you."

Jasmine ran upstairs and sat next to John as she always did. "John, I love you so much. I have to go fight and if I don't make it back because I die, I want you to know that I am so sorry. You are the only man who will ever have my love. You were right about Lucifer's sons they are evil, but I will be putting a stop to them today."

"Jasmine, come on. We have to go." Marcus yelled up the stairs.

"Okay. I'm coming down." Jasmine shouted back as she embraced John in a long and final hug before she left. Jasmine wasn't scared of dying. Her biggest fear after everything that happened was dying without being able to get things right with John. The last time John had seen her with comprehension was the night at the theatre when she had left the group to spend time with the boy. She still didn't understand why she did. It was as if a sudden impulse came over her and as if she were present in her mind but was riding as a passenger.

She justified it to everyone as John had changed and they were broken up, so it didn't matter. But it did matter. She loved John with every ounce of her soul. John was her sunshine on a warm day. He was a cool breeze to her when one was needed. How could she have done what she had done that night at the movie theatres? She constantly thought to herself over and over.

She was the reason that John was in his vegetative state and it ate away at her conscience daily. The guilt trip she carried was a pain far worse than any anyone could ever feel and it was pitted deep down in her loins. Butterflies overwhelmed her stomach.

"Please God let me live at least long enough to get things right with John and please bring him back to his right mind. Amen." Jasmine prayed.

Jasmine slowly walked backwards away from John her eyes never leaving him. John, though he was in a vegetative state, could hear every word that Jasmine said. He tried to run, tried to teleport to her but he was immobile. He couldn't move a muscle no matter how he tried. He was floating in the present, past and in the empty darkness of his mind.

Jasmine, Marcus and Ho Young stepped outside and began walking towards Chimaera. They could see her in the distance. She was no more than eight blocks away from them.

"You guys walk ahead," Jasmine whispered to Marcus and Ho Young." I am going to linger back. Chris and David are hiding on opposite sides of that street up ahead. While you guys attack them, they will spend a few minutes looking for me before turning their attention back to you guys."

"Marcus, hold on. I need you to... "Jasmine stopped. Chimaera was a scary site. The book's description of her did not do her justice. Chimaera had the head of a lion with horns preluding out of it. She had a serpent's head where her butt should have been, that was breathing fire at people. The news didn't show Chimaera for some reason, only the people running while on fire. One of her legs was the leg of a goat while her other leg was a dragon's leg.

"We need to go somewhere else first." Jasmine demanded of Ho Young and Marcus as she began jogging down a side street. As they turned Chimaera turned as well in the opposite direction of them revealing a goat's head out of her side which had ten horns on it.

"Um, that is scary." Ho Young shouted as he sprinted to get ahead of Jasmine and Marcus. "I'm getting out of here, because I am not getting eaten by that goat."

Marcus stopped running, which caused everyone else to stop running. "Ho Young come here really quick."

"Oh, okay." Ho young said running up to Marcus. "Hello." Ho Young said as he saluted Marcus with the grin he always had on his face.

Marcus very quickly, before Ho Young could react, popped him in the back of the head with a very light hit just hard enough for Ho young to feel his hand but not enough to cause any damage.

"I had a strange feeling you were going to do that." Ho Young said as he rubbed the back of his head even though the hit didn't hurt his head. "You know John used to do that all of the time, but I am catching on to it."

"Ho Young." Marcus began.

Jasmine began to laugh her hardest in the background as she read Marcus's mind realizing why he had popped Ho Young in the back of the head.

"Ho Young," Marcus repeated himself. "There is a Lion's head on Chimaera and a giant Snake head. But the only one you are worried about eating you is the goat head? Which by the way, is the one that doesn't eat meat."

"Oh, they don't? What about that story with the troll under the bridge where the three goats ate the troll?"

"Ho Young." Marcus said as he laughed, "the troll ate the goats."

"Are you sure?" Ho Young asked, scratching his head.

"Oh my goodness Ho Young." Jasmine said as she continued to laugh.

"Listen," Jasmine said. "Chimaera was suffocated with lead a long time ago by a Demigod. I just entered her mind and traveled in it back to when she was killed long ago. Ho Young. can you turn into a big water hose that shoots lead out?"

"Yeah, I think so."

"Okay, we are going to rush Chimaera and the minute she opens her mouth to breathe fire, Ho Young you turn into a giant water hose and spray led into her mouth so we can suffocate her."

"I can do that.", Ho young said looking at the ground.

"Let's do it then." Marcus yelled.

Jasmine, Marcus and Ho Young all sprinted towards Chimaera. Marcus hit her with a few lightning bolts to gain her attention. Chimaera turned angrily towards the Demigods. Chimaera roared a deafening roar that shook the entire neighborhood.

John felt the house shake and heard the roar of Chimaera. John tried to move but couldn't. Chimaera roared again.

"God, please help me!" John yelled from within his mind. "I have to get to them to help. PLEASE GOD! HELP ME, PLEASE."

John waited but nothing happened.

Jasmine stopped running remembering that the other Demigods Chris and David were lying in wait to trap them. Marcus turned to see what Jasmine was doing.

"Keep going." Jasmine yelled and motioned with her hands. Jasmine quickly made her way towards the building that David was in. As she tried to come up with a plan, Jasmine felt the force of tons of water traveling underneath her feet. Jasmine hid to the side in a bush instead of entering either building.

Jasmine focused her power on all of the water that was underneath the ground and caused it to split. Half exploded underneath the house that Chris was in, the other half exploded underneath the house that David was hiding in. Both Chris and David were thrown very high into the air by the water that had exploded beneath them causing them both to pass out in midair.

Jasmine smiled wide as the two fell from high in the sky. The tournament would be over if they both died and they wouldn't have to fight anymore monsters. Before they hit the ground three Harpies caught them and flew the two passed out Demigods away.

"That is B.S!" Jasmine yelled angrily into the air. "That definitely has to be counted as cheating and interfering."

Jasmine looked in the direction of Marcus and Ho Young. Chimaera was sprawled on the ground all three of her heads suffocating from the lead Ho young had shot into each of her mouths.

Chimaera spent a few minutes gurgling the lead that was in her mouths before finally dying. Jasmine, Marcus and Ho Young all high fived each other on their easy Victory, but it was short lived. The Sphinx and the Nemean Lion both appeared out of thin air next to their mother, Chimaera.

The look that passed over Leo the Nemean Lion's eyes as he took in the scene looking from the Demigods to his mother back and forth. Without a second's hesitation the Nemean Lion, on his two legs, charged with un-realistic speed.

The Sphinx also began to charge but nowhere near as fast as the Nemean Lion. The Demigods were forced to split up. Jasmine ran in one direction while Ho young and Marcus ran in opposing directions.

The Sphinx followed Marcus, and the Nemean Lion focused on Jasmine. The Nemean Lion roared his fierce roar which put Chimaera's roar to shame.

John recognizing the roar as belonging to Leo the Nemean Lion tried to move again but couldn't. John tried everything but couldn't escape the darkened prison of his head that he was in.

"AAAAHHHHH!" Jasmine screamed as the Nemean Lion nearly got her as he skidded past her.

"NOOOOO!" John yelled from within his head. John screamed his hardest as he fought to get out of the state that he was in. A picture fell on the ground as John fought to free himself. Jasmine was not going to die. He would never let her see Tartarus, ever.

As Jasmine screamed again the top of the house blew apart as if a missile had just bombed the house. Sweat poured down John's face. He wasn't free yet though.

Jasmine caused a hard water shield to form between her and the Nemean Lion but he went right through it with not even a flinch. It didn't hurt him at all.

Jasmine ran into a nearby building to escape Leo. she was barely on the second floor as Leo burst through the entire front of the house causing the wall to explode inwards as he forced his way through it. Jasmine screamed as tears poured down her eyes. She did not want to die, especially at the hands of Leo the Nemean Lion. Jasmine had just climbed out of the second story window as Leo the Lion burst through the door. Jasmine felt her heart miss a beat.

Leo busted through the window being too big to fit through it. Jasmine fell backwards. She closed her eyes as she landed hard on her back, her vision was blurry. The fall hurt her really bad. Something was broken. She felt Leo move only a few feet from her. Rather than fight to see, Jasmine sat in the grass and cried, but Leo never attacked.

Jasmine opened her eyes, and Leo was suspended in mid-air. He had lunged at her but something stopped him. Jasmine turned her head to look behind her and she let out a cry of happiness, sadness and every emotion in existence. John was floating above them. His eyes were viciously focused on Leo. John flew higher up in the sky dragging Leo with him. As John reached the peak of the sky where oxygen almost was completely gone. He caused the air to lift Leo higher just above the point of the atmosphere. There was zero oxygen at the height John raised Leo too. Leo fought to free himself but John's powers were too strong.

Leo slowly suffocated above the sky. He looked down at John with sad eyes as he died. John watched as Leo's body disintegrated above him. John Teleported back to the earth to help Marcus and Ho young with the Sphinx.

The Sphinx clawed out at everyone that tried to get near him. He looked like a big cat trying to ward off a dog. Marcus was throwing cars at it.

"Ho Young!" Jasmine yelled. "Turn into something that cats are scared of."

Ho young turned into a miniature poodle. John's mouth went wide. Marcus paused with a car in his hands and considered throwing it at Ho Young. Jasmine smiled. The Sphinx had a look of confusion on its face as Ho young made miniature squeak barks at it.

"Jasmine, can you draw up hot Lava from the earth?" John asked.

"Yeah, you already know I can." Jasmine shouted back angrily. Her anger was not directed at John but more that nothing they were doing to the Sphinx was doing any damage to it.

The Sphinx stood on its hind legs rising to its full height, sixteen and a half feet tall.

"If you are done." The Sphinx began with a smile resting on an un-bruised face. "I will ask you a riddle. If you answer it correctly, I shall voluntarily go back to Tartarus, but if you lose, I shall devour you. I was dead and alive at the same time. I am like water, yet I am solid. While not being like water nor any solid form. What am I?"

Jasmine immediately went into her thinking mode. The four Demigods mobilized together away from the Sphinx as he remained smiling.

"Okay." John said. "What do we know that is dead and alive? Maybe a ghost?"

"That is tough," Jasmine replied. "Because a ghost can only be in one form."

"Yeah, but a ghost is not solid nor is it in liquid form. But is not liquid," John said to Jasmine more than to the group.

"I agree." Marcus said, giving his approval of John's answer.

"Let's not be too quick to come to any answer." Jasmine replied looking over her shoulder at the Sphinx. Jasmine already hated the Sphinx. She was ugly and conceited.

"I don't have all day." The Sphinx said mockingly.

"Shut your mouth." John yelled back. "Your mom obviously was a hoe. I can tell by looking at you that you have at least three or more dads."

Marcus tried to fight his laugh but lost and began in a low chuckle just a few here and there until he finally couldn't stop laughing. That caused Jasmine to start laughing followed by Ho Young who was laughing at everyone else laughing because he didn't yet understand the joke.

"Ha-Ha." The Sphinx roared back. "We shall see who is laughing once you get this riddle wrong.

"Yeah well, I'll bet we guess this riddle before you can guess who your three dads are," John replied back to the Sphinx laughing.

The Sphinx roared in outrage. Never had she been insulted before. Clearly this Demigod did not know who he was dealing with.

“Aww that is cute. You are practicing your whittle wroar,” John continued mocking the Sphinx.

“Okay.” Jasmine said abruptly to get John back re-focused. We have one guess for a ghost but I feel that one is too easy. This one is more of a trick question.”

“Why does it have to be a trick question?” John replied to Jasmine. ”Because I thought of it. That makes it too easy?”

“No.” Jasmine responded. ”Not at all. I was thinking ghost as well before you said it. But I remember the Sphinx always asks a question that sounds easy but is much more complex. I mean,” Jasmine continued, “a ghost is dead yet alive. It is in vapor form but is also in solid form in the body that lies in the grave. However, a ghost is not in liquid form but vapor, so it is missing one element.”

“Hmm,” John said, placing his hand on his chin as he stood thinking to himself. They made sure to keep their voices down so that the Sphinx wouldn’t hear them.

“A ghost is all I can think of.” Marcus said after a while. “Nothing else fits that description.” Marcus whispered in a low yet frustrated voice to the group.

The guesses seemed to be going nowhere, but they had to think of something.

“Well,” John finally said. “If we can’t come up with another answer, I’m going to say ghost. If we are wrong just be ready to fight. We are ready.” John said.

“Awe, perfect.” The Sphinx said as she licked her lips in a nasty yet menacing way.

“Okay, the answer is-” John started.

“God!” Ho young shouted out loud.

The Sphinx reared back till it was standing on two feet.

“Dang it, Ho young!” John shouted.

"What?" Ho Young replied. "It is the only other answer that fits those descriptions."

As John and the four Demigods prepared for the Sphinx to attack, the Sphinx disappeared from site.

As the Demigods stood all with looks of confusion on their face, the booming voice that roared like thunder sounded from heaven as it had each time a beast had been sent back to Tartarus.

Four for the creator's side, and zero for Lucifer's sons.

Chapter Twenty-One

"David," Chris said with a look of fear on his face. "Those Demigods are up on us, four beasts to our zero. We have to start attacking the monsters now before they gain too many kills for us to catch up."

"I agree." David replied. "Father's plan is not working. We need to devise our own."

"Whatever plan we come up with, I'm not going anywhere near those Demigods. They not only knew we were there but got us without even using much effort."

"I don't know how we are supposed to beat them but if it keeps us from Tartarus. We need to figure something out and soon. I would definitely rather fight them than some of these beasts." David responded to Chris.

"You both are idiots." Lucifer said as he approached his sons. Lucifer was the size of a six-foot three human being and he was wearing an overcoat to keep himself warm. Though the temperature was eighty plus degrees outside. Lucifer was accustomed to much hotter conditions and became cold very easily on earth.

"Excuse me?" David responded puffing his chest out to show he was angry.

"You heard me, dummy." Lucifer replied as he lifted his sons into the air with one swipe of his hand, and then let them fall twenty-five feet to the ground.

Both Chris and David slowly got to their feet as the fall had hurt them both very badly. David had a fractured wrist, a broken rib and a busted knee. While Chris had a concussion, a broken collar bone, a broken wrist and arm due to him using that arm to try and stop the fall. The moment he landed on it the pain began shooting down his arm.

Lucifer healed them with a quick enchantment just as fast as he had hurt them.

Both Chris and David looked between themselves wondering who the man in front of them was who had such powers that he easily over took them.

"As I stated upon arriving, you both are idiots. Neither of my sons seem to have gained any of my intellect."

"Lucifer?" David managed to ask in a shaky and unsure voice. His voice held no confidence but rather a scared to ask any questions tone.

"Ah I see you have at least a pea sized brain. Just enough to know my name."

"We got defeated rather easily," Chris angrily said. "Your plans have too many flaws."

"No, my plans are perfect. You two are just idiots."

"No, you are-" Chris was about to call Lucifer an idiot but thought better of it, as his remembrance of Tartarus swiftly made its way to the front of his mind.

"I am what?" Lucifer said, eyeing Chris daring him to be bold enough to state his thoughts out loud.

"They are just too powerful for us." Chris said redirecting the conversation away from the direction that it was headed towards.

"No, they are not. You two numb skulls just are not maximizing your powers. Yes. she without being directly in front of you, was able to attack you with her powers. But guess what? You can do the same thing. Da-dure." Lucifer said to finish his sentence quoting a favorite saying of his that he heard some of the young kids saying.

"Really?" David asked, confused and trying to figure out how what Lucifer was telling them was possible.

"You do not need to be directly in front of someone to use your powers. You just have to know where they are and focus on them and their location."

Lucifer waved his right hand across the air and suddenly Chris and Davis found themselves in the midst of a small town in Florida.

"Okay," Lucifer said to his sons. "Focus on this area and you both will take turns practicing your powers." As David was beginning to ask what exactly they were supposed to do, he never got his question out because with a wave of Lucifer's right hand, Chris and Lucifer were gone.

"Okay son, focus on that area and your brother. I want you to remember Tartarus and make him think he has been sent there."

Chris did his best to focus but failed on each attempt. Lucifer would travel back and forth and each time he came back he became more and more upset. "Maybe I need to remind you of how it feels in Tartarus." Lucifer said to his son Chris.

"No, you don't need to remind me." Chris said in an almost high-pitched tone combined with a raspy hoarse voice. Chris focused on making his brother believe he was in Tartarus. Lucifer appeared before David who was running and screaming though nothing was following him.

Lucifer watched as David fell to the ground and his arms began flailing wildly in the air. David grabbed his ribs suddenly and jolted stiff lying flat on the ground as his body was extended full length across the dead grass. It seemed as though he was dead, and then suddenly he jumped up screamed and began crying as he started running again.

"Please no! No more!" David yelled as he ran for a second time.

Lucifer was more than satisfied and without so much as any notice he teleported David to where Chris was and Chris to where David was. Once David found out it was Chris who had tormented him in such a way with an illusion of him being tortured in Tartarus, David went right to work in returning the favor. Chris knew what was about to happen and would have beat David to it, except he had no idea where Lucifer had taken him too to do what he had done to Chris. In no time Chris had monsters after him.

Chris didn't move or scream because it was an illusion. As twelve giant scorpions with tails that shot acid out of them advanced on Chris he just sat down and laughed.

"Nice try David but I know this is an illusion." As Chris sat down a scorpion shot acid at him from its tail. Chris just remained seated and attempted to yawn. "OUCH!" Chris yelled as he began to roll on the ground. The acid was real. It wasn't fake. He felt his skin burning off and then felt the teeth of the scorpions begin ripping his flesh from his body as they began to eat him whole.

If this was an illusion he thought as he woke up after being eaten alive, why can I feel everything? Did Lucifer actually place me in Tartarus?

As the thoughts swept across his mind Tartarus disappeared and his brother David and his father Lucifer appeared.

"Why could I feel everything as if it was real?" Chris asked without looking at either his father or his brother.

"Because that's what separates actual Demigod powers from your basic magician. A magician can exercise illusions to a certain and very limited extent with the help of small unnoticeable distractions. The most they can do with illusions is to deceive a person's eyes as to what they are actually seeing. While your Demigod powers can do far more than deceive the eyes. You can deceive every sense of the body, sight, smell, hearing, and even what a person feels. So, though it is not real, they feel everything as if it is."

"So, I could maybe focus on that Jasmine girl while she is in her house and torment her causing her to think she is in Tartarus or something?" Chris asked as excitement shot through his body. David stayed silent and focused on Lucifer waiting intently for him to answer as well because David was also wondering that same question.

"No, I am afraid not. That is their safe house and no monsters or Demigods are allowed or even able to attack them there. Not to worry though," Lucifer continued with a great big grin on his face. "An old enemy of the line of Athena draws near to them and she will wait patiently and there is no way that she does not at least kill one if not more of those rejects."

"I sure hope so," David said. "Is the enemy you refer to Arachnid?"

"Sure is." Lucifer replied. "Those Demigods are going to get what is coming to them." David looked at Chris and nodded his head in approval and gave Chris a thumbs up, which Chris quickly returned. Lucifer looked between the two in disapproval.

"Focus." Lucifer said before quoting Odin's words to him. "Cowards always have a backup plan because they never plan to win. You two need to not rely on the monsters to beat the Demigods but need to plan on how you will beat them. You two are by far the family disappointments but you can change that by surprising the universe with a win here in this tournament."

David became outraged within his heart at the words Lucifer his father had just said to him. David thought within himself but dared not speak the words out loud. His remembrance of Tartarus was refreshed most recently by his brother Chris who he also now secretly held a grudge against.

How could Chris, after all the time they had spent together as brothers since the tournament began, do what he did to him. Why would he use his worst fear against him? I would never have told him my worst fear had I known David thought within his mind as he still kept his eyes angrily upon his dad Lucifer.

"Is there a problem son?" Lucifer said, catching David eyeballing him.

"No sir," David responded, quickly turning away.

"Good to know. If you ever feel you want to swing on me or use your powers on me, understand one of us is going to die that day. I assure you it won't be me."

Chris listened and watched his father and his brother intently. Waiting to see what the outcome would be. He half wanted to continue the tournament alone after his brother made him relive every second of his time in Tartarus with his powers. He knew he could not trust his brother, nor his father. He also knew that his brother would kill him on command should Lucifer order him to.

"There is no problem." David said again to his father Lucifer whose nostrils were flaring and eyes were nearly popping out of his head as he heatedly stared down his son.

Lucifer pointed his finger at David and shook it in a warningly way. You could tell he wanted to say something, but instead Lucifer just disappeared without another word.

"Wow, that was close." David said turning to Chris.

"Dude, you keep pushing his buttons, you are going to regret it."

David stood awestruck. He had expected Chris to at least support him for the time being as he was prepared to joke about how scared he was that Lucifer was going to hurt him in some way, but Chris in those few words took all of the conversation out of David.

Just that quick they were no longer brothers but back to strangers. David and Chris for days did not speak to each other. Both focused solely on killing the Demigods, not even consulting one another or making any attempt to discuss what plans they were concocting in their crafty and darkened minds.

Barely less than a month had passed since Lucifer turned the brothers on each other with his little experiment. Chris had decided it was time for him to move on from David and to begin work on his own. He had already killed three monsters to

David's one. He just felt he no longer needed David around. David couldn't be trusted and when the tournament was over, he was sure Lucifer would order him to execute his brother.

David walked down the streets of Little Rock, Arkansas paranoid and drowning in depression. He was alone and now had to worry about his own brother showing up to attack him.

People walked past David making funny faces at him. Some would plug their noses and others cross the street long before they were at any cross walks. David had not showered nor changed his clothes, since the mission had started. His clothes were dirty and smelled like a skunk had a baby with some chitlins.

David noticed the looks but turned the other way and continued to walk. The looks did not bother him as much as when the camera crews began to swarm him.

"Mr. Angel can you please tell us what has happened to you?"

"No comment." David yelled at the reporters as he waved his hands back and forth signaling for the reporters to leave him alone.

The reporters continued to follow David regardless of whether he was going to answer their questions or not. David began to remember his life before the tournaments. The fame, the women, and just a good relaxing life. Now things were different and he was sure they would never return to the way they were.

David turned and focused his mind on the media following him and caused them to see pure darkness. Some screamed as they saw the sky become pitch black. While others tried to find their way to a building wall to have some sort of support to lean back against and have protection on at least one side of them. Others tried to use their phone flashlights which showed zero light. Few decided to try and do a live report of the darkness that had suddenly drowned out the daylight in the middle of the day.

To add to the darkness, David created monsters to attack the media and the large crowd of people who had been following him.

The screams of the crowd as they thought the monsters were eating them were alive were chilling but yet gave David joy.

Chris watched a giant Cyclops in the distance. The Cyclops was avidly searching for him, sniffing the air hoping the scent of a human would lead to his next meal. Chris created the illusion of a land filled with humans. The Cyclops's eyes grew wide with excitement as he saw the buffet of humans that were right in front of him walking around minding their own business not paying any attention to him.

The Cyclops reached his hand out to grab one. But for some reason he was extremely slow and the human was able to get away before he could grab them. What was happening? The Cyclops thought within his dull small pea sized brain. Normally he was very fast but he was slow for some reason. There was no way that human should have been able to get away from him.

The cyclops reached out again attempting to grab a few other humans as they passed by him and again, he was too slow. The humans easily got away from him. The Cyclops roared in anger and began to run after the humans. Chris caused the humans in the illusion to run towards his trap.

Chris had conjured an entrance to the Labyrinth that sucked in anything that flew or walked over it. And like clockwork the giant cyclops was running right towards the trap.

"NOOOO!!" The Cyclops yelled as he stepped over the entrance to the Labyrinth and began to be sucked in.

The trap entrances that Chris conjured blended with its surroundings like a lizard, making it invisible to the eye until the moment you stepped over it. At which point it turned a dark ocean blue, and whoever had stepped over it began quickly sinking in. Within seconds the cyclops was back in the Labyrinth.

The angel's voice boomed in the sky as it always did when a beast was returned to the Labyrinth whether by death or through a doorway as Chris and David had been doing.

Nine beasts for Lucifer's team. Six beasts for the Father's team.

Chapter Twenty-Two

"This is not good." Jasmine said, looking over in John's direction.

"I know, but I am not going outside. Arachnid is out there waiting for us."

"Your point is?" Jasmine replied. "Arachnid is one of the beasts we are supposed to kill. Let's look at this as an opportunity."

"We are behind on beasts and we have the deadliest one hunting us right now So what is the plan?

"I don't know." Jasmine replied. "But we need to kill Arachnid and sooner than later so that we can get back to killing the rest of these monsters."

"I have an idea." John finally said after a moment. "In that book we used to read in Mrs. Norton's class, Gemini created a shield for Hercules to use."

"Okay." Marcus said as he remembered the part John was talking about. "I think I know where you are going with this but I am not sure. Marcus said, trying to guess John's idea.

"If Gemini could create weapons for others, Ho Young should be able to as well."

Jasmine jumped up as her cheeks blushed on each side. A smile spread across her beautiful face. For the first time in a long time she was happy.

"Wow that is genius!! John, we could have Ho Young make us body armor that won't hurt us but would melt any webbing that Arachnid throws at us., The body armor could be made out of mint oil as well. That would keep Arachnid from biting us."

"Great idea." John said. "And also, Ho Young, if you could make us guns that shoot acid, that would be great."

"Well there you have it. A week trying to figure out how to get out of this house without being trapped by arachnid since we can't teleport out of the house due to the protections set up to keep beasts, monsters and Demigods from being able to attack us and just that quick we now can finally go outside again."

"A good thing too, since we are running out of food." Marcus finished.

"Yeah." Ho young agreed with Marcus. "I had more food when I was homeless than we have had in the last two days."

"Okay." John said, becoming serious again back to the matter at hand. "Ho Young we need you to create the items we requested."

"Oh yeah. Eh, uh. What were they again?" Ho young said as his facial expression became dumb founded.

"Ho Young we need body armor that won't harm us but will disintegrate any webbing that Arachnid will throw at us. The armor also needs to be designed in a way that we can fall or step on Arachnids web and not get stuck to it."

"Okay." Ho young said., "Here I go."

"No, wait." Jasmine said. "Don't forget to make the armor out of mint oil so that Arachnid won't bite us."

"Oh yeah, we definitely need that." Ho young said as he began to create body armor with his powers.

"Ho Young, why is all of the body armor pink?" Marcus asked.

"I figured we should match like real superheroes and it is breasts cancer month and-"

Before Ho Young could finish his sentence, John teleported behind him and gave him a light smack on the back of his head and then teleported back to where he was.

"Ouch!" Ho Young yelled as he turned around to see who had hit him. First Ho Young looked in John's direction to see if it was him but after seeing John innocently standing in the same spot he had been in, Ho Young's intelligent moment passed.

"Something is in here." Ho Young said very loudly as he hopped around the room on his tippy toes as if the ground were made up of hot lava rocks that burnt your feet at the touch.

"No Ho Young," Jasmine said looking disapprovingly at John. "That was John."

John put his hands out to give indication that he had no idea what Jasmine was talking about.

"John," Jasmine warningly said his name.

"Okay fine. It was me."

"Dang I thought it was bad when you used to trick me into letting you do that, but now you can do it whenever."

"But he won't." Jasmine replied. "Because that is not nice."

"Alright fine. I will do my best to stop." John replied.

"Okay." Ho Young said. still rubbing the back of his head.

"Oh please. I didn't even hit you hard." John said to Ho Young.

"You shouldn't have hit him at all." Jasmine chided John. "John you are a nice guy. You really are. Which is why I am going out with you but stuff like that almost over shadow all of your kind acts. You are constantly clowning your friends. Don't get me wrong," Jasmine continued as she saw John open his mouth to defend himself. "Most of the time it is good but at times some of the things you say go a little too far. And while your friends won't tell you, I can read their minds and the things you say sometimes either hurt or get them upset. They do their best to hide it so you won't end up calling them sensitive."

"I see." John said, not too happy about what he was hearing. But it was coming from Jasmine and he knew she was just being honest. Jasmine was the only person in the world that John would do anything for because he loved her and did not want to lose her again.

"Okay." John said after pondering in his mind for a moment. "I will stop."

"Thank you." Ho Young said to John.

"No problem," John replied." Let's get back to getting what we need to defeat Arachnid." John tried to smile but Jasmine knew John was a bit hurt. Jasmine walked over and grabbed John's hand as Ho Young created the guns that could shoot acid.

John blushed a little before reaching his arm around Jasmine's waist to just hold her close to him. When the tournaments were over John wanted to marry Jasmine. Not to own her but for her to own him.

A tear rolled down John's cheek for no reason as he thought about how much he loved Jasmine. "What is wrong?" Jasmine asked, seeing the tear.

"Nothing is wrong. I just love you and I don't care if I die a day later but I want to at least be married to you for a day before I die. That day to me will last twice as long as an eternity. Forever will fall short of how long I will love you."

Jasmine blushed but before she could kiss John Ho young yelled, "okay finished."

John and Jasmine turned towards the weapons that were on the ground. John took a step towards Jasmine and turned his body away from Ho Young and Marcus." Is it just me or do those guns look exactly like the guns off of Ghost Busters?"

Jasmine giggled before answering. "Yes," they look exactly like them."

"Ho Young." Jasmine kindly said. "Remember, we wanted guns that shoot acid. Do these guns shoot acid?"

"Yup," Ho young said as he saluted Jasmine. "They shoot laser beam acid."

"What?" Marcus said laughing out loud to himself.

"Well the laser beams are made up of lasers and acid."

"Can't complain about that." John said to everyone. "Okay let's go and kill this giant spider."

The four Demigods opened the front door and immediately Arachnid attempted to web them from the distance. Arachnid smiled as the web perfectly landed on all four Demigods. "Her smile immediately faded as the web evaporated.

Arachnid shot more webs at the Demigods to see if it would work the second time but the web evaporated again. Arachnid became furious as she lunged herself at the Demigods. John swiped his hand hard against the air causing the air to force Arachnid away from them. She did not go as far as John had intended but far enough to give him time to disappear for a second.

John reappeared and then disappeared a few more times. Each time he appeared he had another piece of what looked like amps and sound equipment.

"John what the heck are you doing?" Marcus asked, confused.

"Just set it up. I will keep Arachnid busy while you guys set up the sound system."

John flew at arachnid stopping just short of her pincers. "Dang, you're ugly. John said laughing as Arachnid's legs tried to grab John. Though she did not have fingers, the tips of Arachnids legs were sticky which worked better than fingers as far as catching prey. John dodged her first leg but her second leg hit him pretty hard on the side of his head. John fell.

Jasmine stopped working with Marcus and Ho young setting up the sound system and stepped forward with her gun ready to shoot arachnid with the acid.

"NOOOO!" John yelled to Jasmine as he caught himself in midair. John teleported to Jasmine. "Not yet." John whispered in Jasmine's ear before disappearing again.

"What the heck is he up to? And what does this stupid sound system have to do with it?" Jasmine angrily shouted.

"I don't know, but the sooner we get it set up we can help him and find out," Marcus shouted back, hoping Jasmine would pick up the hint or read his mind and understand he was needing her to help him finish.

"You realize you have no friends, right?" John asked arachnid. She went to hit John again but John had an invisible force field around him.

John landed on the ground not far from where Arachnid was.

"It is finished!" Jasmine yelled.

"About time." John replied as he teleported to where the other Demigods were by the sound system. John plugged his phone in and turned the volume up.

Jasmine cringed as she looked at John. He guiltily smiled at Jasmine. "I love you," John said to her.

"John, you made us wait and risked your life so you could blast the Ghostbusters song while we used the Ghost Buster looking guns on Arachnid?"

John nodded his head up and down as he smiled. Marcus started laughing which caused Ho Young to start laughing. "Only you John," Marcus said laughing.

The Ghost Busters song was blasting through the entire neighborhood from the loud speakers that John had brought. John, Jasmine, Ho Young, and Marcus walked towards Arachnid pointing their guns at her. Arachnid was quickly advancing on them.

"Okay on three," John said.

"Is that on three or after three?" Marcus asked, trying to imitate the movie.

"On three." John said back to Marcus as he grinned. "Okay, one.... Two.... Three." All four guns began shooting lasers out hitting Arachnid. Within seconds Arachnid had deteriorated and was no more.

"Well that was easy." Jasmine said. Excitement shot through her body. Her family's longest, deadliest, enemy was finally dead.

The four Demigods high fived each other. The angel's voice came booming through the sky.

Seven beasts for God's army and nine beasts for the Sons of Lucifer.

Chapter Twenty-Three

Thor sat in Hades' chair which was perfectly fine with Hades since he never sat in it." Have you seen this nonsense?" Thor said angrily. "These humans have turned us into fiction. They no longer worship us."

"What are you talking about." Odin asked his son, thinking Thor was ranting about nonsense.

Thor tossed his father a few fiction books about the Greek Gods. These books referred to them as the Norse Gods.

"What is this?" Odin asked, even more confused looking at a picture that had his name by it but clearly looked nothing like him.

"That is nothing." Thor said laughing. "Look at what they have here." Thor said tossing his dad a movie about Ragnarök. "That movie is so far off of what actually happened it is hilarious."

"I am not even going to watch this. What is the meaning of this? How can you Greeks, as you call yourselves or Romans as you also call yourselves. let the humans mock us as such?"

"We didn't after Ragnarök. Michael and his army came down and attacked us. They have had us in prison for a long time now. The only one who was out here and free was Lucifer. Poseidon and Hades were not in prison with us, but they were free on conditions. They had to serve the creator doing his will or they would have gotten imprisoned like the rest of us."

"I see." Thor said. "We need to teach these humans a lesson." Thor angrily yelled, obviously angry about the fictional character he had become.

"In due time." Odin said hearing the Angel announce another kill for the Creator's team. "Right now, we must focus on winning a tournament."

"This tournament is too close for comfort." Lucifer said "But my sons are doing better than I expected they would."

"Why would you put your sons in this tournament if you did not think that they had a chance at winning?" Thor asked Lucifer, quite upset at how bad of a parent Lucifer was.

"And what business is it of yours?" Lucifer responded very menacingly. Odin looked up with his eyes only at Lucifer without so much as lifting his head.

"You are a dotard." Thor said. "Just a complete moron. Don't have kids if you don't want them."

With his powers, Lucifer raised his right hand in a grabbing motion and closed it. Thor began gurgling from his throat as he looked up in pain. Not even a second could pass before a very strong power ball from Odin hit Lucifer right in his chest.

Lucifer was knocked out for three days.

Lucifer opened his eyes on the third day. The pain from the power ball still hurt his chest. Lucifer sat up to find Odin sitting at the edge of his bed.

"If you ever attack my son again, I promise you it will be the last thing you will ever do. While you may be able to beat Zeus and my son Thor, I believe you already know what happens in a battle with you facing me."

Lucifer was past angry that Odin had knocked him out. Tears rolled down his face from anger out of his right eye only.

"Penalty." Lucifer finally said. "I'll let you know how the next tournament goes." With his pride hurt Lucifer wanted to reestablish that their only chance of escaping Tartarus was through him.

"I am afraid not." Odin replied. While you were off on whatever mission you were on. I had a talk with my brother Michael. No more decisions about any tournament can be made without myself, you, Zeus and the head of all of the different sects of us angels who are all willing to come together to defend ourselves in this tournament. From this point on we all have a say in what happens in each tournament and you no longer have anything to blackmail us with."

Lucifer was angry but he knew better than to attack Odin. Odin was far too powerful for him. He had lost control of the tournament. Lucifer did not like sharing power or the fact that Odin had went behind his back and bargained his way into his deal.

"Fine." Lucifer said.

"No need to be raw about this," Odin said to Lucifer." Your vote means a lot. You are the founder of this tournament and your opinion will hold weight as far as I am concerned. Yet, what I said stands. If you ever touch my son again, I will beat the breath of life out of you. I hope you understand my words to be true?"

Odin waited for Lucifer to acknowledge that he understood his threat to be real.

"I understand." Lucifer said after a long moment. He wanted to leave but at the same time he didn't trust the others to come up with any good plan without him, so he decided to stay.

"Now that we have an understanding," Odin said, addressing the others present in the room. "Let us make a decision on the next tournament tonight before our brethren show up from the four corners of this earth and the outer realms."

"Oh God." Hades said louder than he intended too. "Please tell me that Tahiti isn't coming?"

"Oh, she is." Thor said laughing. "I thought you of all people would love Tahiti?"

"No, Tahiti is too wild and never shuts up."

The room exploded in laughter whether they liked Tahiti or disliked her, they all could agree she definitely never shut up.

"Well, what about Lucifer verses Michael in the next tournament?" Thor suggested, still upset and embarrassed about their recent altercation.

"No," Odin roughly said. "Just as I have forbidden Lucifer from committing any violent act against you, I, in this moment, am forbidding you from goading Lucifer with words or actions."

"Yes father." Thor said in respect of his father Odin.

"The next tournament I am thinking of maybe testing Gabriel. He is not as strong in battle as Michael which will give us a better edge."

"Okay you really are tripping." Lucifer laughed as he spoke. "Gabriel is more than capable of handling himself. You guys have been reforming over the years so you haven't seen his skills. Our brethren that ruled over Persia tried to defeat Gabriel twenty-three on one. Gabriel fended them off for three weeks straight by himself. Don't forget Gabriel is Michael's favorite brother." Lucifer reminded Odin.

"What happened after three weeks?" Odin asked. "Did he lose or what?"

"No," Lucifer said, no longer smiling. "Michael showed up and the two of them defeated all twenty-three of them within less than thirty minutes."

"Oh, I see." Odin said. "Well, let us do another competition. Maybe some impossible tournament where Gabriel and the Demigods will be competing against Tahiti and some Demigods of our choice to compete on our end."

"Yeah but what?" Hades said as he sat in deep thought." Whatever competition they are in would have to not only be difficult for the Demigods but also for Gabriel." Hades finished

"Yeah I see your point." Thor replied.

Aphrodites sat in silence in the meeting. She was not sure about a journey she was embarking on. If she did it, she was taking a big chance and would be an outcast among those whom she has known since the day she was brought into existence. Apollo had been talking to Aphrodites and convinced her to switch sides and work on the side of the creator.

What was being offered was not being offered to everyone. While the others thought Apollo was being held prisoner in Tartarus, which was the furthest from truth. Apollo actually was the angel who had been made the keeper and placed in charge over the bottomless pit and was free and not a prisoner anywhere.

"I have an idea." Zeus finally said after some time. "What if we send them on a quest? To recover the Ark of the Covenant. Nobody knows where it is except for God."

"Hmm... I like that idea," Athena said. "It is being guarded by the deadliest of the deadliest, Cherubims. Ooh!" Athena shouted. "And the tree of life is being guarded by the flaming sword. There is no way Gabriel can get past that."

"True, but neither can Tahiti," Ares said to everyone. "And you know Tahiti isn't going to participate in a suicide mission, because she would have to try to get the flaming sword as well."

"No, he could just let Gabriel and the Demigods try until they are all dead." Thor confidently thundered.

"And when Gabriel succeeds and gets to the tree of life?" Lucifer interjected.

"He won't." Thor roared back angrily. "This plan is perfect and will succeed."

"No, Lucifer is right," Odin said. "I grew up with Gabriel and he is the king of finding ways to do the impossible."

"Okay then what can we do?"

As Zeus finished speaking Hera appeared on Olympus in the middle of where they were all meeting at.

"Hera?" Zeus said in shock, for he had not seen his love, his wife, since Lucifer had attacked her and left her unable to speak. Hera still couldn't speak but she had an idea to help them and wanted to tell them.

Hera slowly walked up to a large table that was at the far end of the throne room. On it she created a piece of parchment and a pen. As she wrote tears poured down Hera' face from the embarrassment she felt from no longer being able to speak.

Zeus saw the tears and in anger flew at Lucifer. Poseidon and Hades appeared between the two. "This won't help brother." Hades said to Zeus. Zeus had tears in his eyes as he tried to fight past his brothers to get at Lucifer.

Lucifer stood up and prepared to attack the three brothers but sat back down upon seeing Odin stand up as well facing him. Though he did not attack, Lucifer looked at Zeus and smiled with his hands cupped together as he leaned back comfortably in his chair.

"What happened?" Odin asked.

Poseidon explained what happened to Odin as Hades took Zeus out of the throne room away from the drama.

Odin stared Lucifer down once Poseidon was finished. "So, you think because you are more powerful than some that it is okay to bully them? Let us see how you fair against me."

Lucifer stood up as if he was going to do something, but as Odin's armor appeared all over his body and his helmet on his head, sword in hand, Lucifer disappeared from the throne.

The room applauded and cheered. "I am sorry." Odin said to Hera as he held out his hand to silence the room. "I wish I could fix your voice but I cannot. I need you to remember the strong angel that you were before this and understand your voice was not what people feared or loved. It was you and the power you radiate."

Hera listened but the sadness remained in her eyes. Hera replied with a nod of her head but her demeanor showed that she was not yet ready to be strong again.

"Yeeheehehehe!" Tahiti yelled as she surfed into the throne room on an invisible wave of water. "Aloha, my brother." Tahiti said, grasping Thor into a big hug that felt like it was squeezing the life out of him.

Tahiti turned towards Hades and as she stepped closer to hug him, Hades turned to run. In one big leap Tahiti caught Hades and gave him a great big bear hug. "I am so glad to see you my brother, to see you up here with everyone tears up my heart."

"That is n-n-n- ice of you." Hades struggled to say as he slowly wriggled his way out of Tahiti's grasp.

"Oh, you are very welcome brother."

"I hate you." Hades said to Tahiti.

"And I love you brother," Tahiti replied smiling and pinching Hades cheek. Thor fell on the ground roaring with laughter. Even Odin laughed a bit to himself though he tried to fight it and hide his laughter.

"How can you not love such a joyful person?" Odin said as he gave Tahiti a hug and a kiss on both of her cheeks.

"Who knows." Hades sarcastically replied back.

Odin finally broke and fully laughed before speaking again.

"Glad you are here Tahiti but where are the rest of your brethren?"

"Oh, they will be along shortly," Tahiti replied. "I was too anxious to come and ready to see my loved ones that I could not wait. So, they sent me ahead. "

"Oh joy." Hades mumbled louder than he meant to.

Everyone laughed including Tahiti. "Oh, you know you love me, Hades." Tahiti responded, smiling from ear to ear.

"Oh God." Hades said as he pretended to throw up.

"Okay we need. . . okay we. . ." Odin could not get his sentence out because he kept laughing at Hades and Tahiti. It took time for everyone to settle down but eventually they were able to resume the meeting.

"Hera can I see what you wrote down earlier?" Odin addressed Hera. Hera nodded and shyly walked through everyone to get to Odin. She handed Odin the parchment. Odin slowly read the parchment three times before finally saying anything.

"Instead of having Gabriel in this next tournament. There are tons of demigods around. We can use in the tournament." Odin began to read the note out loud. "We can gather seven Demigods, the Demigods' lucky number, and have them not go to the tree of life which would most certainly be suicide for both teams. Instead have them find the Ark of the Covenant as was mentioned. There are so many traps and demon's guarding the Arc, not to mention there is a Cherubim guarding it as well." When he finished reading it, he pondered Hera's words. "I like this idea," said Odin. What say all of you?"

"Oh, it is wonderful and marvelous and well thought out. I cannot begin to express the greatness this idea institutes."

Hades threw his hands up into the air. "She just can't answer any question with just a short simple answer."

"Oh, there is one that I can answer with only two words." Tahiti said back to hades as she winked at him.

"Oh yeah, what question might that be?" Ares asked Tahiti.

"When Hades stops fighting his love for me, I can answer, I do."

Hades nearly choked on his drink as he began coughing up wine, barely able to breathe.

"Oh biatheladide, qwuensithstasist!" Hades shouted out two curse words in a language not known to humans.

Odin roared in laughter along with all of the other angels who were present in the room. Aphrodites forgot about her dilemma, as she to begin to bellow in laughter.

"All who agree to this tournament," Odin began but he was cut off by a sudden rush of wind. Amen –Rah the brother who was ruler over the Egyptian realm appeared in the room.

"There are traitors in your midst," he said and as he turned to point towards Poseidon and Aphrodites. They were both gone long before his finger ever made it into their direction.

"Who?" Odin shouted as he stood up ready to fight whoever the intruders were.

"Poseidon and Aphrodites." Amen-Rah said out loud. "Bring them forward," he commanded.

"They are not here." Ares said as a look of hatred and anger crossed his face. There was nothing he hated more than spies.

"Well good. If they know what is best for them, they will stay away."

"How are you doing brother?" Rah said to Odin. "It has been quite some time, hasn't it?"

"Oh yes, time it has been. Good to see you it is." Odin replied. "We were just finishing up a meeting about the next tournament. Which if I am correct, will be the third tournament."

"Yes, and what have you all decided for that tournament to be?"

Odin handed Amen-Rah the parchment with Hera's plan on it. After carefully reading it Amen-Rah found it to be quite the plan and voted in favor of it.

"Oh brother!?" Tahiti yelled as she had returned from the bathroom. "You are here."

"Holy mother of Jesus!" Amen Rah screamed as Tahiti chased him around the room three times before finally catching him and giving him a great big hug. Hades finally was able to laugh now that he wasn't on the receiving end.

"Where is Lucifer?" Amen-Rah asked everyone as he noticed his former commander, the initiator of the tournament, was not present.

"I will explain later." Odin began to say but once again was interrupted. Lucifer appeared in the courtroom with none other than Michael.

Michael's eyes went straight to his brother Odin.

"Hello Michael." Odin said as he saw his brother.

Michael nodded his head with no words to Odin. Odin had chosen his side and Michael his.

"Lucifer being the initiator of this tournament will have final say on all tournaments." The room went from quiet to great outburst as all of the Fallen Angels protested. "Secondly, any attempt to remove Lucifer from his charge over this tournament will result in a forfeit on your side and the tournaments will be over. Then your sentences to the lake of fire shall be carried out immediately."

"I hate you Lucifer!" Klione shouted over the fuss the crowd present was making.

"Start with her. She is out."

Odin paused and looked from Lucifer to Klione. "What is the meaning of this? What is going on?"

"Lucifer has complained to The Father that he started this tournament so that he could be free from the lake of fire. He added the rest of you to give you a fair chance. He didn't feel that you all should be in charge of making the decisions on what the tournaments would be. If you have an idea you can take it to Lucifer and he will approve it or not approve it."

Odin looked disgusted, "Well what about what The Father said to me? About us all having a say in what the tournaments are since our lives are on the line as well."

"He can go to." Lucifer said, smiling. Odin blasted Lucifer with his staff. Lucifer flew through the back wall of Mount Olympus. He flew off of the entire mountain and down to earth where he went unconscious as he landed.

"Where are people going that he is kicking out?" Thor asked more aggressively than he intended to.

"To the lake of fire." Michael replied.

Odin looked at Michael. "You can't. That is contradictory to what we were promised."

"Hold on." Michael said as he disappeared. Seconds later he was back. "Father will allow you to split the tournament. Those with Lucifer can go with him and those with Odin can go with him. Lucifer picked the first tournament, so this one will be decided by Asgard and those who choose to be in the tournament with Asgard."

"That sounds much better. Thank you, brother," said Odin. Michael started to leave without responding but the thought of casting his brother, who he was once so close with, was a bit heavy on him. Instead he turned and shook his brother's hand.

Lucifer returned after three days. It was too easy to see he was upset. His brows furrowed down and his mouth was scrunched up as if he was going to growl at any given minute. He had gone to The Father in an attempt to get him to change his mind but failed. Michael appeared with him to explain to all present The Father's final decision. Lucifer didn't like it much but Michael declared that The Father would not change his mind.

The Gods split up into sides. Hades had already decided to go on whichever side that Tahiti was not on. Which wound up being Lucifer's side. Once the two sides were made, they went their separate ways. Any other sects of angels would be allowed to join but would have to pick a side either Asgard or Mount Olympus, which now was being ruled by Lucifer.

Chapter Twenty-Four

"John, you need to shave," Jasmine said, examining John's face. They had now been in the second tournament for a year and three months. And a twenty-year-old John had not shaved in some time. A beard now sat upon his face. His features were more serious than when he had first started the tournaments.

Ho Young and Marcus didn't seem to age at all. While Jasmine looked younger, she was getting older. She too was now twenty years old.

"I know." John replied. "And I will but right now I am focused. Lucifer's team is up on by at least thirteen beasts. We have to get something going and fast."

***

Chris slowly crept into the hundred and thirteenth cave on the Mountains of Miseries. Leviathan's home was said to be in one of these caves and Chris had been checking caves out on the mountain for four days now. Though Chris could not see much, he could feel the presence of Leviathan in the cave.

Chris sighed deeply as he inched his way further and further into the cave. It was by far the biggest cave on the chain of mountains known as the Mountains of Misery.

Chris heard heavy breathing but his visibility was next to zero. It was pitch black in the cave and his options were between a rock and a wall. If he produced enough light for him to see, Leviathan would surely see him coming. If he didn't produce any light, he was likely to walk right into Leviathan without ever seeing him.

Chris didn't know what to do so he just continued to inch his way through the cave with zero visibility, keeping his hand on the cave wall to have some stability. Chris had stepped on something hard that seemed to crumble under the pressure of his weight.

Chris felt he should keep moving but the urge to see what he had stepped on overtook him. Chris pulled out his phone and clicked on the flashlight. To his horror, broken from where he had stepped on it, was a human skull. Chris' stomach churned and jerked. It became more wave like than the ocean as he hunched over and began loudly throwing up.

"Ooh, is it lunch time already?" A very deep and a very scary voice said through the darkness.

Chris immediately stopped throwing up. He stood up and leaned his back against the wall. He had blown his surprise attack strategy. Chris could not help but wonder if Leviathan could see in the dark or not.

"No need to panic," Leviathan continued. "I promise your death will be quick and painless. I can at least do that to repay your father for freeing me from Tartarus."

"It is you who will die." Chris yelled as he focused his powers to make Leviathan think they were somewhere else.

"Oh wow. Pretty place." Leviathan slyly said. "But not the best. Here, watch this place." Before Chris could figure out what had happened, he was in the most beautiful place he had ever seen. Stars shone all about him. Star dust floated in the distance.

"Where are we?" Chris asked while still staring at his surroundings in awe.

"Oh, we are still in the cave and I changed my mind."

"Changed your mind about what?" Chris, getting scared all over again realizing that he had no power over Leviathan.

Without even an answer a bright bluish, yellow, orange light emerged from the darkness. Chris screamed as he realized he was on fire and as his flesh began to melt off of his face and his body.

He had zero time to think as his death was approaching too fast. The thought that did cross his mind was that he could not let his brother face Leviathan.

With the last of his strength Chris yelled the spell to open the portal to the Labyrinth. He focused his mind to place it right from where the flames came from. Chris never saw the trap entrance form because he melted to ash and dust seconds after finishing the enchantment.

Leviathan tried to walk over to where Chris was dying but found it impossible to move. He realized that he was being sucked down into some kind of portal.

"NOOOO!" Leviathan yelled as he clawed and fought in an attempt to pull himself free of the portal. Within less than two minutes Leviathan had been sucked into the portal.

The Angels booming voice filled the sky. The humans only heard thunder, but both sides of Demigods heard the angel speak.

Thirty-three beasts for Lucifer's army and Nineteen beasts for the Fathers army. Four Demigods remaining on the Father's army and one remaining Demigod in Lucifer's army.

David looked up in horror. "Did he just say only one Demigod was left on his team?"

Lucifer appeared before his son David. "Your brother is dead. You are all that is left. The good news is your brother defeated Leviathan as he himself was dying, so you will not have to face Leviathan."

David sat down as reality hit him. He really could die in this tournament.

"Stand up." Lucifer replied. "For my time is short. We are fighting amongst ourselves in the heavens, and have divided into two teams. After this tournament, should you lose, Odin and Asgard will be picking the next tournament so I need you to win this tournament. Do you hear me?"

"Yes sir," David said as he stood up. The wind blew heavily against David's windbreaker jacket causing the flaps to fly out behind him. His face was pure fierceness as David stood looking like the world's greatest superhero. Rain began to sprinkle down then trickle harder until it began to pour hard.

"You got this son," Lucifer said as he disappeared into the darkness.

David believed in himself. He had been working alone up to this point and had been doing just fine. Chris' death was his own fault David told himself. Leviathan. What in the heck was he thinking going after Leviathan alone? That was just stupid.

Chapter Twenty-Five

"Whoa man did you hear that?" Ho Young came bursting into John and Jasmines room.

"Hear what?" Jasmine asked as she yawned.

"One of the other Demigods have been killed.

John sat up in his bed and instantly became wide awake. "Are you sure?" John asked watching Ho Young intently?

"Yeah, I am sure. The angel just said it."

Jasmine focused and after a moment backed up Ho Young's statement. "Yeah Chris is dead. Apparently, he went to attack Leviathan alone," Jasmine was looking at John with saddened eyes as she recalled when John had nearly been killed doing the exact same thing.

"Well one down." John said out loud. Upon seeing the sad look on Jasmines face John got a bit upset. "Jasmine they already tried to kill us once. Stop feeling sorry for them."

"I'm not." Jasmine truthfully said. "I was just thinking about when Leviathan almost killed you a few years ago."

"Oh," John said as he recounted the memory. "Yeah that definitely was not a great day for me." As John was in the middle of his sentence, Jasmine went into a trance.

"Jasmine!" John yelled. "Jasmine!"

Jasmine remained in her trance for quite some time. John actually began to get worried that she would not come out of it.

"Marcus!" John yelled. "Get some water."

"For what?" Marcus replied confused.

"So, I don't beat the mess out of you!" John angrily replied as a single tear rolled down his face.

Marcus didn't know what John wanted the water for while Jasmine was in the state she was in. In his mind she had been in the trance for twenty minutes and they needed to call the hospital or Michael or something.

Marcus brought the water for John and just as John had raised the cup to pour it on Jasmine Michael appeared with his hand holding John's arm preventing him from pouring the water on Jasmine to bring her out of the trance.

"She needs to be left alone. She is seeing a vision of far into the future and it takes time. I have seen this happen once before with Savannah. Jeffrey tried to wake her and she went into shock. She was literally brain dead until she heard Jeffrey scream. He was being attacked by the butcher and another Demigod, who's powers were to suppress other Demigod's powers. She had a vision while in her brain-dead state and broke free. She died assisting Jeffrey against the butcher and the Demigod Talca."

John stepped back and studied Jasmine. She was shaking in a way that to John signified that she was hurting.

"Can you do anything?" John asked Michael.

"No. I am afraid I cannot. All events must take place and play out as they will. Not everything is what it seems and things good don't always last." Michael said except he was looking at Ho Young and Marcus with sad eyes. "He has a right to know, friends don't keep secrets." Michael said as he disappeared.

John looked from Marcus to Ho Young as angry butterflies hit his stomach hard. Even though John did not know what they were keeping from him, he knew it wasn't good if Michael had to bring it up.

"What is he talking about?" John asked looking at the ground.

"No offence John, but it is not our place to say anything." Marcus replied looking scared. "I would have told you a long time ago but we were asked to not say anything."

"By who?" John said though he already knew deep within by who.

"Look man, I don't want to be in the middle of this," Marcus said holding his hands out as if he had power over the wind and was going to use it to hold John back.

John looked at Marcus earnestly. No anger was in his eyes. "We have been best friends almost our entire lives. I would never do this to you. What's the secret man?"

"Okay here it is," Marcus said after a moment. "You have to promise not to leave us if we tell you. That is the only reason that I kept this from you. Jasmine said we couldn't tell you because you would leave the group and get sent to Tartarus again. She, Ho Young and I did not want you to go back to Tartarus."

Ho Young stood silently to the side. For the first time he did not show any signs of ADD, or craziness. No, he understood exactly what was going on and John could tell that he was also concerned about what he would do when he found out the big secret

"I promise I will not leave the group." John finally said. "I have a feeling I know the news, but please be honest with me?"

"Okay." Marcus said. "Jasmine feels forced to be with you. She feels the love left long ago after the first tournament."

"So, the secret is she feels our relationship needs work?" John asked.

"No." Marcus answered as a gloomy and sad look compassed his eyes. John could tell it was taking all of the strength that he had to tell him the news.

"I'm just going to say it. She has been dating other guys in secret."

"When?" John asked. We are together most of the time?"

"When she asks for space and goes to the movies."

"But we have been trapped in this house the whole time."

"No just for the last few weeks. She has gone on three dates since this tournament has started."

"So that is the news huh?" John asked more hurt than anything.

"Yeah, and remember you promised that you would not leave us John. We need you man."

"I know what I promised and I won't leave the group. But I do need a moment alone if you don't mind me leaving for a bit."

"No, I understand." Marcus said, studying John to see if he was telling the truth. Ho young still remained silent. He was looking intently at the ground as if it were the most interesting thing that he had everything he had seen.

"Where are you going just so we know in case you get into trouble?"

"I'm going to go and relax at Lake Michigan."

"For how long?" Ho Young quietly whispered, wanting to make sure John was really coming back.

"I don't know man. Maybe all night. I need some time to collect myself if you can understand that. Man, I have been in love with her all of my life and I just found out she wants to give her heart to someone else." John shook his head in anger and pain as his eyes wanted to rain down on his cheeks. He was determined to change the forecast within his eyes. He was not going to cry over a girl ever again.

"Lesson learned." John said. "God hates me. I get it. I'll still fight and I'll still be a part of this group but I know now that I am what you would call un-loveable."

"Everybody has someone for them." Ho Young said trying to help.

"Yeah? So, who is for you, because I have never seen you date anyone?" John lashed out not meaning to.

Ho young looked taken back. John realized after he said it what had just came out of his mouth. "I am sorry Ho young. I did not mean that. I need to go for now. I will see you guys when I see you."

"John." Marcus began.

"I am not leaving the group." John said cutting Marcus off before disappearing.

Not even seconds after John left Jasmine came out of her trance. "Oh my goodness." Jasmine said looking scared. "Marcus?" Jasmine said looking at Marcus. "Where is John?"

"He just left." Marcus replied, not sure if he should tell her that he had just told John everything.

"We have to go get John now. If we don't, he will die tonight."

"Is that the prophecy you just got?" Marcus asked.

"No, that was just a part of it. Did you guys tell John about me dating other guys while was in the trance?"

"Yeah." Ho young said. "Michael brought it up in front of him and John pressured Marcus into telling him everything."

"I understand." Jasmine said not looking to happy but she left that subject alone.

"We have to find John quick. He was near some water and a giant squid and a giant half snake half woman are going to trap him under water. He will run out of air in his air bubble because they will exhaust his powers out."

"Dang." Marcus said. "Let's go."

"Wait. I have to find him first." jasmine said.

"No. I know where he is. He went to Lake Michigan."

"Do you think he really went there?" Ho young asked

"Yeah, I know when John is not being honest and he was telling the truth."

The three Demigods left the house in a near sprint which did not last more than a few blocks as they began to slow down as they began to tire. Only Marcus was still running at a good pace. He looked back and after he couldn't see the others, he ran back in their direction and found them out of breath and walking.

“We need a vehicle.” Marcus said more to Jasmine than to Ho Young.

“Yeah I know. Hold up, let’s call a cab.”

Jasmine grabbed her phone and called the first cab company that showed up on her phone internet.

The cab was there in fifteen minutes and they were on their way.

***

John sat in the grass. He had made a pit stop in a closed store and borrowed a sleeping bag and a few pillows. John began to get the feeling to call a cloud and sleep on it, but he didn’t. He didn’t want to do anything outside of what he had to do to remind him that he was a Demigod and on a mission with the girl who had just destroyed his heart.

For one day John just wanted to be normal and not be a Demigod. John watched as a drug deal was made in the distance between a drug dealer and some thick Hispanic girls who were riding around in a drop top convertible vehicle.

About the same distance on the other side were a few couples out to enjoy the morning. It was two in the morning so of course you had your low tide people camped out waiting for low tide which usually occurred at some point early in the morning.

John laid on top of the sleeping bag. It was a warm night so there was no point in him getting completely in the sleeping bag because it would then be too hot for him to fall asleep. John instead laid on top of the sleeping bag and covered himself with a light sheet. He needed to be covered with something in order for him to sleep well.

Somewhere in the morning John was awoken from his sleep. Something definitely was not right and he could feel it in his bones.

The air whispered into John's heart to leave but John for some reason did not.

John walked over by the water to clean some of the sand off of his feet. In an instance before John could even look up, instinct caused him to form an invisible shield upon hearing the sound of a splash.

A giant half snake and half woman had struck at him with such force that even with his air shield up, it knocked him off of his feet. John had zero time to recover. Every time he got knocked down and by the time he would get back up, the snake woman would attack again.

She had a regular shirtless woman's body with seaweed for a bra and her legs were combined together to make a large snake's body and head. The color of her legs was that of a rattle snake, brown with diamonds. At the end of her legs was another head which was a rattle snake's head.

She struck from both ends. The snake striking with its venomous teeth and the woman part with a sword but she had teeth as well. Teeth as sharp as razors perfect for tearing into human flesh.

John was getting up slower and slower. The snake woman had switched sides on him and was forcing him towards the ocean. John wanted to teleport but he didn't have a second free to focus on any place. The moment he would hit the ground he had to focus on putting another air shield up as he attempted to get up because the snake woman would be striking again.

John began to fall in the ocean water as he was knee deep in the ocean. John figured the ocean water would slow the snake down but it did not. Her attacks seemed to be even stronger in the ocean. As John found himself waist deep in the ocean another enemy surprised him. A very large tentacle which started from much farther out, reached out and grabbed John from beneath the water.

He barely was able to get an air bubble around his head before he was completely under water.

The snake woman continued to strike at John hard, fast and relentlessly. While the giant octopus continued to pull John towards it at a very fast pace through the water. He was in trouble. The more he fought off the snake woman under water and attempted to resist the octopus, the weaker he became and the less amount of air he had in his air bubble.

John became very light headed and closed his eyes. There was barely any air left in his air bubble and he knew he did not have the strength to fend off the snake's next attack. John was hoping that like in movies and in books. that he would miraculously get saved from the Octopus and the snake lady but it wasn't so.

In seconds he felt the large fangs penetrate his abdomen and his upper right shoulder. Immediately the insides of his body felt as if they were on fire as the venom spread through his body from the bite. Everything went black.

Chapter Twenty-Six

"Thank you." Jasmine said as she hurried up and paid the cab driver. The three rushed from the cab towards the Lake Michigan beach. At this point of the morning it was around 5:30AM and the beach was packed with people enjoying the low tide.

"Crap!" Marcus yelled out loud causing a few passer byers to look at him with sideways looks as if he were some dangerous animal or a hoodlum.

"I'm not getting any reading on John." Jasmine said in frustration. "I can't tell if he is using his powers to block me from reading his mind or if something has indeed already happened to him."

"John!" Marcus yelled. "JOHN! JOHN!"

No answer came. As the three Demigods ran across the beach hoping to find John, Jasmine felt the presence of the Giant Octopus and the presence of a dead snake. Jasmine focused on the giant Octopus to go back into its past to see what had conspired prior to their arrival and to see if John was okay.

As Jasmine strolled through the giant octopus's memories, she saw John get struck by the snake and then saw the giant Octopus open its mouth to eat John. Jasmine had to open her eyes as John's dead body was inches from the giant octopus's sharp razor teeth.

"Oh no!" Jasmine cried as she fell to the ground. "John is dead."

"Well I guess you can finally stop sneaking around on him!" Marcus angrily said.

Jasmine was taken back but did not reply. Deep inside she was feeling that John's death was partially her fault.

The three Demigods caught a cab back to their safe house and for three days they did not speak to each other. The only advantage that they had was that David had to take normal transportation like they did to find beasts. Without his brother also killing beasts David's pace became slow and he had only killed one monster since the death of his brother.

Jasmine cooked dinner for everyone but nobody spoke nor ate anything. John's death was very hard on everyone even though it had been nearly a month. To make matters worse, Jasmine had begun bringing her new man around. Marcus having been John's best friend gave jasmine a real hard time about it every time her boy toy, as Marcus called him, came over.

"Look I did not want to be in this tournament. John and I weren't working out. How long are you going to hold this over my head?" Jasmine yelled at Marcus through her tears. They had gotten into another argument about her boyfriend and Marcus outright told her that he felt that Jasmine was not only glad for John's death but had also maybe wanted it prior to John being killed.

"None of us asked to be in this tournament and John is not the only one who has changed Jasmine, you have changed as well."

"Okay. Fine. I have changed. Are you happy? I changed, John changed and because we changed, we were no longer good together. Why should I be forced to be with someone that I don't love?"

"Because love is not something you can just turn on and off," Marcus angrily replied.

"Oh, I'm staying out of the middle of this one." Ho young yelled out loud over Marcus and Jasmine who had continued to argue.

"Enough!" A powerful voice spoke. As the voice spoke it shook the house causing a few dishes and a lamp to fall and break. "You have argued and fought more than enough through this tournament. What happened to John is sad, but everything always works out for the best in the end."

"But." Marcus began to say but a very sharp look from Gabriel the angel cut his sentence off with a quickness.

"Focus on the tournament. For the time being forget about mistakes any of you have made and focus on what you have right here in front of you."

Marcus and Jasmine stood silently not looking at each other. John was dead and there was nothing that they could do about it. Fighting clearly was not going to be the solution, especially if they wanted to win the tournament.

Marcus slowly walked across the room towards Jasmine and gave her a big hug.

"I am sorry." Marcus said as he held on to Jasmine. Marcus still had a really big crush on Jasmine. As Marcus and Jasmine hugged the booming voice of the angel sounded through the air.

"Thirty-three beasts for team one." The angel so powerfully said. "And thirty-seven beasts for team two. As usual after giving the stats the angel's voice went silent.

Michael had a worried look on his face. "You Demigods need to get to work. You have to kill every single beast left just to tie the tournament."

"What happens if we are able to kill the rest of the beasts?" Marcus asked having never considered the possibilities of the tournament ending in a tie.

"In such a case I actually have no idea," Michael truthfully responded." I will be right back." Michael did not look happy at all as he disappeared. His look was more one of worry and weariness.

As usual Michael was back in no time. His facial expression had not changed a in the slightest bit.

"If it ends in a tie, an additional task will be added to this tournament."

"And my guess is that you don't know what the task is?" Jasmine asked

"No, I am afraid that I do not. Whatever it is, it will be the hardest task that you will face in this tournament."

"Oh, that isn't good." Ho Young said as he scratched his head. "How are we supposed to get to the beasts without John?"

"You do know that a weaponized helicopter would be considered a weapon, right?" Michael asked Ho Young hinting to him that he could turn into one.

"Oh, wow that is neat." Ho Young said. After a moment had passed when he finally caught on to what Michael was saying.

"Wait." Jasmine suddenly said before anyone could reply to Ho Young. "Lucifer sent those beasts after John. That is interfering and cheating."

"Why isn't the other team being punished like the other team was in the last tournament?"

"They are just not in a noticeable way. You will find out." Michael quickly said before Jasmine could ask him anything. Michael disappeared without another word.

"Wow," Marcus said. That sucks. They cheat to kill John and they, from what I gather, really are not being punished for it."

"No, they are." Jasmine said as Marcus finished speaking. Jasmine did not want to say the plan out loud for the same reason that Michael did not say it out loud hoping that Jasmine would finally heed his advice and read his mind.

Jasmine grabbed a piece of paper and began to write but then stopped. There literally was no way that she would be able to let Marcus and Ho young know the plan without the fallen Angels finding out.

"All I can say is that I believe Michael and that we need to get a move on."

"A move on to where?" Marcus asked with a rough tone to his voice. He hated that Jasmine always took the side of everyone but those in the group, which to him caused most of her arguments with John.

Jasmine knew Marcus's thought's but chose not to address them and cause another argument. Marcus's thoughts however, hurt Jasmine deep all the way down to her soul.

As the Demigods stepped outside it was 1:30 in the morning. Jasmine and Marcus checked to make sure that the coast was clear before telling Ho Young to turn into a military war chopper. The flight was silent for most of the trip until the chopper started singing Oh My Darling. Jasmine laughed a low laugh as Marcus also laughed but much louder.

"Ho Young." Marcus finally said. "Why?"

"Oh man." The chopper responded. "That was a hit song from back in the 1930s." Ho Young replied as he accidentally fired off a missile.

Marcus and Jasmine ran to the window to see where the missile went. It missed the statue of liberty by no less than two miles and landed in the ocean causing big waves to form. They could see sailors on fishing boats running around in attempts to keep their ships from flooding with water.

Jasmine focused her power on the ocean and calmed the raging water. "Ho Young." Jasmine very angrily said with her hands on her hips and a very sharp look in her eyes.

"Sorry." Ho young quickly said. "It was an accident."

"It's fine." Marcus quickly said, fearing that Ho Young would accidentally change from a helicopter to something else with them inside him. "Stay a chopper." Marcus added at the end of his sentence.

"Okay I will." Ho Young replied.

"Now where are we going?" Marcus finally asked after everything had settled down.

"We are going to Lockeford California," Jasmine replied to Marcus.

"Does Ho Young know?" Marcus asked Jasmine not understanding how Ho Young could know if he didn't already.

"Yup. I told you both before we left but you had turned around to do something, so I don't think you were listening."

"Oh yeah, I was looking for my earphones because I hate to travel without music."

"Oh, I can make music." Ho Young the chopper said.

"NO!" Marcus and Jasmine yelled together.

"Okay," Ho young hollered back at them. "No music."

The Demigods landed in Lockeford around 5:30AM. They were just a tad bit behind the town by a large river. The three made their way into town.

"What exactly are we looking for here?" Marcus asked. He hated not knowing what was going on.

"Well I guess I can tell you now. There is another Demigod here named Caleb and he is traveling from Manteca to Jackson to train for his job."

"Wait another Demigod?" Ho Young asked with excitement showing all over his face.

"Yup." Jasmine said smiling. "His name is Caleb and he is a descendant of Apollo." Jasmine blushed a bit as she said his name which Marcus couldn't help but notice.

The three walked through the town looking at the old buildings. They stopped in a pawn shop to ask a few questions about the town. The pawn shop owner referred them to the town information building, which the Demigods gave up looking for after close to an hour of looking with zero success.

Next, they visited the post office and a sausage restaurant that was rumored to be the best sausage in America and it definitely lived up to its reputation. They definitely made the best sausage in town.

After touring the town, the three demigods hung out by a gas station on the corner of the main street that was a part of the highway that drove through town heading towards Jackson, to wait for the Demigod.

"Oh my God." Jasmine said as she focused on Caleb to see where he was at. "He has a twin sister and she is riding with him."

"Oh, nice." Marcus said smiling from ear to ear.

"Okay here they come," Jasmine said with a little anger in her voice probably at Marcus's comment, to her it was dumb. Marcus didn't know the girl. For all he knew she could be bat crazy, yet he says nice just because it was a girl.

As a silver Toyota Corolla rounded the corner Jasmine flooded the streets with water from the sewer beneath the ground. The metal caps that acted as a doorway to get in and out of the sewers blew right off and high into the sky.

Caleb watched as the water began to pour out and flood the streets behind his sister's car and in the front of his sister's car.

"What the heck is going on?" Talitha asked her brother Caleb. Talitha Cullen was thin with blond hair that flowed half way down her back. Her eyes were blue and she was just absolutely beautiful. You would think that she was a daughter of Aphrodites rather than a daughter of Apollo.

Caleb had brown hair and stood at five foot and nine inches. Caleb was a very hard worker. He worked two jobs at the same time. Caleb had a muscular build while Talitha who looked perfect, felt she would rather lose weight. Talitha was five foot and nine inches and weighed 148. She was your typical girl who though they were skinny, wanted to get back down to their high school weight. Talitha was very beautiful. Her hair was a goldish blonde color and her eyes were blue.

"I don't know." Talitha replied. "But this can't be good." Talitha waved her hand in front of her face in a motion as if she were pulling something down. Not even seconds later, the heat coming down had become unbearable and the three demigods were on the ground struggling to survive the sudden heat that Talitha had called down to evaporate the water.

Talitha happened to see the Demigods just in time and released the heat back into the sky. "Oh my God, Caleb, look it's the three I saw in my dream."

Caleb casually looked over and immediately his eyes flared open. "Those are the three you saw in your dream?"

"That is too crazy. They are the same three I saw in my dream. When that angel guy told me that we needed to link up with them."

"Yup that is the same thing he told me." Talitha replied to her brother Caleb.

Talitha jumped out of the car at the exact same time that Caleb did. The three Demigods,

Jasmine, Ho Young, and Marcus were still lying faint on the ground from heat exhaustion. "Oh my God, I am so sorry!" Talitha cried as she ran up to them. "I didn't see you guys."

"It's okay." Marcus managed to say while still lying on the hot ground with his eyes barely open.

"Caleb, we need to find them some water," Talitha ordered her brother as she pointed at a gas station that was down the street on the corner.

"Okay I am on it," Caleb replied as he sprinted towards the gas station.

Within no time at all Caleb was back with eight thirty-two-ounce water bottles. Talitha and Caleb began pouring water on the Demigods and placing the water bottles to their mouths for them to drink. The minute the first drop of water hit Jasmine she regained her strength and recovered, water being the strength of her power.

Caleb had to make another trip to the gas station for more water bottles before Marcus and Ho Young were able to sit up with some consciousness.

"Oh man, what happened?" Ho Young said as he felt his forehead to see if he had a fever.

"It was my fault." Talitha said. "The streets were flooding with water and I pulled heat down from the sun to evaporate it. I had no idea that you guys were here I am sorry."

"Oh, it is okay." Ho Young replied. "But man, your powers are strong."

"Thank you." Talitha replied as her cheeks blushed from Ho Young's compliment.

"What exactly are your powers?" Marcus asked Talitha and Caleb.

"Well," Caleb began. "My powers aren't very cool, but I can control all of the insects on earth and in other realms."

"Other realms?" Jasmine asked eying Caleb suspiciously. "Have you been to another realm?"

"Oh yes," Talitha answered for Caleb. "We have been to two realms other than this one. We have lived in a place called Bezwindeshtyeh, and …."

Talitha looked down as if whatever place she was about to mention was the worst place that she had ever lived.

"We were forced to live with our Godly Grandpa. I guess that's what you would call him here on earth."

"Your Godly grandparent?" Ho Young answered back while scratching his chin.

"Yes," Talitha replied to Ho Young.

"You got to live with Apollo?" Jasmine asked with a bit of envy in her voice. "Who wouldn't want to live with a God? Especially if they were the descendants of the Gods or Fallen Angels, whichever you chose to call them."

"Well we didn't learn of this name, Apollo, until after we escaped. His actual name is Abaddon."

"Escaped?" Marcus asked cutting Talitha off.

"Yes," Caleb said nodding his head as he recounted the memory in his head. "We were living in the bottomless pit with Abaddon because he is the King over the bottomless pit."

"Wait." Jasmine said even though she knew what Caleb was saying was true because she had read his thoughts. "I thought Apollo was the son of Zeus and was only good for shooting arrows, and music?"

"Nope. Abaddon or Apollo, or Apallyon, or Apallon, whichever name you call him the definition of his name remains the same which is-"

"The Destroyer." Jasmine said beating Caleb to the end of his sentence.

"Yes." Caleb continued." He is the best shot with an arrow and the only God better than him at music would be his cousin Lucifer. Most on earth only know him for that but many other realms know him quite differently. He is the king of the bottomless pit and is king over plagues and giant Locust. He is known as the destroyer in both Greek Mythology and as well as in Christianity. Most in Greek mythology choose not to go that deep into his nature because they want Gods that will be what they want them to be rather than what they are."

"Oh, wow." Marcus said as shock showed all over his face. "I study all of the time but I never knew that."

"Yeah there is a lot that this planet does not know. I say that with no offence intended. It is just that The Creator keeps a lot of information back from earth because he feels that it would be too much for the human race to handle."

Jasmine felt a bit offended but held her tongue because though she felt she could handle such information. She knew that ninety-nine percent of the human race could not handle such information.

"Well what are your powers?" Ho Young asked not hiding his excitement in the least bit.

"They already answered that Ho Young," Jasmine said to Ho Young without looking at him.

"Not exactly. He told us his powers but she hasn't told us hers yet. Obviously, she has power over heat." Marcus said smiling and Talitha.

"Oh, sorry." Talitha replied to Marcus. "My powers are more in alignment with the sun. for instance, I can control heat from the sun. I can control the light from the sun in a sense. Really. I am only controlling the visual part of the light from the sun."

"I don't understand." Marcus said trying to gain an understanding of what Talitha meant.

Talitha snapped her fingers and immediately everything became dark.

"Okay can you see anything?" Talitha yelled into the darkness.

"No!" Ho Young yelled back. "AAHHH man, this is cool!" Ho Young shouted. He was having far too much fun. Talitha giggled.

Talitha snapped her finger again. "Okay now who can see light not including you, Caleb." Talitha shouted.

"I can." Ho Young replied.

"I can't." Jasmine said behind Ho Young.

"I can't either." Marcus calmly said.

Talitha snapped her fingers again.

"I can see now." Jasmine said.

"I still can't." Marcus's voice trailing behind Jasmines.

"Okay." Talitha said snapping her fingers again so that Marcus could see.

"Notice that some could see light at times while others cannot. I do not control the light of the sun one hundred percent. The light is still there when I make it dark, it just becomes non visible. Which is why I can manipulate it so that two people can be standing right next to each other and one can see light from the sun while the other can't. I can make the heat from the sun focus on one person or an entire country. Both my brother and I have a bow and all we have to do is pull back on the string and an arrow will form and shoot its target. The arrows can be regular or have a bomb on their tips depending on what we are envisioning in our minds."

"That is cool." Ho Young said as if he couldn't do the arrow part himself.

"Oh, you forgot one thing," Caleb said with the same expression that he seemed to always have on his face. It was not a mean expression, just a solemn one. Even when he laughed, he held the same solemn expression.

"We can put everything around us to sleep by playing music."

Jasmine was happy to have the new Demigods because their powers could greatly help them. She did not want them around because Marcus was definitely distracted by Talitha who seemed distracted by Ho Young.

Envy and strife were sure to be unavoidable if she liked Ho Young but Marcus liked her. Jasmine kept eyeing Talitha as the five demigods drove in Talitha's car away from Lockeford and back towards Chicago.

The drive was very long and dry. The days that they were in the car driving there was not much talking between the two groups of demigods. Even Ho Young and Marcus were surprisingly quiet.

Chapter Twenty-Seven

John opened his eyes slowly. He had been out for nearly a week. He sat up slowly and examined his surroundings. He was in a small home that was very clean and had a very nice rich design to it. The rug was as black as night and the walls were solid white. There did not seem to be a drop of dust in the apartment.

John slowly got out of bed to examine the rest of the house which is when he realized that his clothes were different.

"What the heck?" John said out loud. "Where in tarnation am I?"

"You are in my home." A beautiful woman answered walking into the room. "My name is Destiny Ridley. I am the daughter of Thor and my earthly mom was a woman named Delilah."

"Wait, a daughter of Thor? Oh, wow who were your demigod parents?"

"I don't have any. Thor is actually my dad."

"I thought only the descendants of the seven Demigods survived the flood here on earth?"

"I wasn't raised on earth. After the death of my father Thor and the Fall of Asgard, Michael, my dad's uncle and brother to Odin, took me to a place called Eden."

"You were raised in the Garden of Eden?" John asked Delilah as he took a few steps back towards the bed to sit down.

"No. The Garden is in the East end of Eden. I was not allowed to go anywhere near it. There is a certain sect of Angels who are known as Cheribums. They are not angels really but that is the best way that I can figure out to describe them to you. They are fierce and guard the garden of Eden. There is also a flaming sword that hunts down anyone that is not supposed to be in the Garden and it will not stop hunting you until you are dead."

"So, you never tried to go in there?" John asked smiling for the first time.

"No, I am afraid I didn't. That would have been suicide. Our powers are mediocre compared to many of God's other creations. For instance, Michael is the most powerful that I have seen of all of the Fathers creations."

"How many of his creations have you seen?"

"I have seen countless creations. All creations have to come back and stand before The Creator at some point even those of us who do not die."

"Wait, not all of his creations die?" John asked confused.

"No, death is only in certain places. Death is the price of sin. So whichever planets have sin will have death." Destiny replied confidently and enjoying being the smartest in the room for once.

"But if death is only on worlds that have sinned, why do you die in outer space if you fall out of a ship or you end up in space without a space suit?"

"You don't die. Without a space suit the human body which is flesh cannot function properly in space, and therefore freezes but the soul is still living within the frozen body."

"But I have seen people die on documentaries in space from losing oxygen," John replied feeling he was about to gain the upper hand.

"Again, the body. as in the flesh, is not designed to function without Oxygen. So, the body shuts down but the soul is still living inside of the body."

"I don't get it." John said after a moment of thinking to himself.

Destiny began to explain more but John realized that he still had no idea where he was except that he was in her house inside of a bedroom. He did not even know how he got there.

"Destiny." John said cutting her off. "How did I get here? What happened in the ocean?"

Destiny paused before speaking. "Lucifer cheated and sent those monsters after you. They were not a part of this tournament."

"I knew it." John said shaking his head angrily. "Did they get penalized?"

"Well not in the way that you are probably thinking, but Michael used the opportunity to add three Demigods to your team for this tournament."

"Three?", John asked with a look of confusion on his face.

"Yes, I was added and two children of Abaddon or Apollo as most of you on earth know him."

"Wow and all three of you are fighting with us or are Apollo's children fighting against us?"

"With." Destiny replied. "Now to your question about what happened. You were being attacked under water. I flew with great speed into the water. I bashed and killed the monster snake woman. Then I pulled out my sword and cut off the tentacle of the giant octopus that was pulling you. After I grabbed you, I quickly flew out of the ocean before the Octopus could recover."

"How long have I been out unconscious?" John asked earnestly wanting to know.

"You have been out for just about a week," Destiny replied with her face getting stern. Something was bothering her and John could tell but he thought it best not to ask.

"We need to get you well so we can attack the last son of Lucifer." Destiny suddenly said to John after more than a few moments of silence.

"Oh shoot!" John yelled. "I have to get back to Chicago. My friends are probably in danger."

"No, they are fine. They are with Apollo's kids preparing to attack the monsters."

"Oh." John said taken back a bit that she didn't say that they were out looking for him.

"I guess they moved on huh?" John asked doing his best to look cool and not show how he felt, which was alone. Jasmine had been cheating on him and Ho Young and Marcus had kept it from him. To John it looked like he was the odd man out.

"Alright. Well let's go kill him and get this tournament over with."

"Not yet," Destiny said in more of a commanding voice than she had intended to. "We have to wait until you get better."

"Oh, sure thing." John replied. His stomach churned inside as he recounted the memories of finding out Jasmine had been cheating on him and his best friend or so he thought, he was kept it from him and covered for her.

Now that he thought about it all of the times they argued the last year, Jasmine would start the arguments and then would walk out and leave. Now John putting two and two together realized Jasmine started those arguments on purpose so she could get out without him getting suspicious.

John began to return to a state of depression. He felt alone and un-loved.

***

"You know you are very attractive." John said to destiny one day out of the blue as Destiny walked into his room.

Destiny raised her eyebrows and curled her lip showing her discomfort in John's statement. John ignored it. "So, do you have a boyfriend or a husband since you have been around for who knows how long?"

"I know for how long. No, I do not have a boyfriend and no I am not interested." Destiny finished her sentence. She didn't say it in a rude way. She had answered John with politeness in her voice but the words did all the damage. John began to wonder what was wrong with him, and why all of a sudden were girls not attracted to him.

Two weeks went by and John was more than fully recovered physically. For some unknown reason though, Destiny refused to go and attack David, the remaining son of Lucifer. John had half of a mind to leave on more than a few occasions but something was preventing him from leaving.

All he had to do was teleport himself out, yet he did not want to leave Destiny's side. Four times they heard the Angels voice boom another beast for team one leaving only one beast that remained. The Demigods knew that the last beasts would be there tests, because in no way could David let them tie. He was sure to hide somewhere and do his bests to kill them.

Destiny woke up from her slumber with a slight yawn and her arms stretched out full length on both sides of her body. As she forced her legs off of the bed, she rubbed her eyes and headed towards her bathroom which was in her room. Her home was a three-bedroom house with two bathrooms. One was on the second floor and the other in her room.

Destiny grabbed the bar of soap and stepped into the shower after undressing. The water was too hot at first but Destiny, while avoiding the smoldering hot water, forced the shower nozzle to face the shower wall away from the curtain and began to adjust the temperature of the water in the shower until it became a comfortable temperature for her.

After showering and dressing Destiny made her way downstairs to the kitchen to begin making breakfast for John and herself.

Destiny looked up surprised as she stepped into the kitchen. John had already made breakfast and there were roses all around the kitchen against the wall's outlining the Kitchen. Just in front of Destiny roses outlined a path from her to the table. Destiny smiled and blushed.

"Aww, thank you so very much. This is very sweet of You Jonathan."

Jonathan normally would have said your welcome or anytime but he had grown and somehow knew that silence was his best answer.

John remained at the table seated in front of his own breakfast plate. He had made a grand breakfast of eggs, Bacon, sausage, slices of bananas, strawberries, and orange juice.

As Destiny drew nearer to the table, John stood to his feet and walked over to her chair and pulled it out from under the table for her.

"Thank you." Destiny said with her hands cupped together and a grin that spread from one cheek to the other.

As Destiny sat down John stepped back as she scooted her seat in to her comfort level. John returned to his seat.

"I hope you like it." John said after a moment of silence as Destiny began to eat.

"Oh, I do. It is really good."

"Wonderful." John said sounding more grown up than he ever had in his entire life. "I got the Strawberries from Alaska, the eggs from Kentucky, the bacon from California, and the sausages from Lockeford at a very famous sausage joint."

"Oh wow. You went all out I see," Destiny replied as she continued to eat, not stuffing her mouth but eating with class and refinery. Taking little bites at a time with her fork.

Destiny was amazing and from the time John saw her, Jasmine had become nothing more than a memory from his past. One that is quickly forgotten and carried off in the winds of the past and lost in the sea of forgetfulness.

John, though not used to eating so refined, took his time eating. Only taking little bites so as not to seem sloppy. Normally John would gather as much as possible on his fork but not anymore. John wanted to make a grand impression on Destiny.

As they ate and talked, Michael showed up. "It is time." As Destiny opened her mouth to speak Michael disappeared.

Destiny shook her head in anger. "I hate it when he does that."

"It is time for what?" John asked Destiny a bit confused.

"To kill David the remaining son of Lucifer."

"It is about time." John replied to Destiny with excitement etched into his facial features.

"I understand your excitement but you must understand, David has learned from your last encounter and has been trained by Lucifer since. He is far more powerful now then he was in your last encounter."

"Really?" John replied. "Well, what can he do now that he couldn't before?" John wasn't asking to be sarcastic but remembering the last tournament how Chiron had grown bigger and more powerful. John wanted to know exactly what he was about to go up against.

"Well on top of him being able to create illusions around you, he can create up to 100 of himself. He also can make any of you look like him which will make it hard for any of you to find the real him."

"I see." John replied biting his lip and nodding his head disapprovingly as he tried to figure out a way that they could beat him.

"That is not even the worst part." Michael continued. "Both teams are headed towards the final beasts right now. I have warned the others that David is on his way as well but they will need you guys there too because if they get there at the same time, the beasts and David will be too much."

"Well why don't they just not go then or fight David?" John asked confused as to why Jasmine and the others would walk right into a trap.

"Because," Destiny answered for Michael. "It is the last beasts. If David kills it the tournament is over and your team or well our team loses. Lucifer and the other Fallen Angels will have rule over earth. I am sure you can imagine what they will do to you and your families if they win."

John's eyes went wide he had not thought about the consequences of losing a tournament since Michael had mentioned it to him in the last tournament.

"We need to go." John said to Destiney. "Where is the beasts located exactly?" John asked Michael.

"Focus on Jasmine and wherever she is you will find the beasts." Destiny looked at Michael with a piercing look. John didn't see it but Michael did.

Michael without saying a word, turned his palms up, curled his lips and furrowed his brows in a questioning way. His look asked the question for him.

Destiny realized that she had been too obvious. She secretly was falling for John and she didn't want him anywhere around Jasmine.

Michael suddenly smiled and disappeared. "Okay, let's get ready to find your friend's. Try focusing on Ho young and teleport us to him."

John paused he wondered how he would act if he saw Jasmine again? Would he fall for her again? No, I can't John said within himself. I am in love with Destiny.

Yeah but she does not love you John argued with himself in his head. The argument went on for at least a moment. John knew by the end that he would not go back to Jasmine and hoped that Destiny would possibly love him too.

Chapter Twenty-Eight

"So, what do you have planned for the next tournament Father?" Thor asked Odin as their sect of fallen angels met?

"Well while I have ideas, this is not my tournament alone but ours. So therefore, I believe it only fair that everyone has a fair vote on the next tournament and their ideas heard."

"Oooh, this is already a billion times better than it was with Lucifer in charge." Tahiti shouted across the halls of Asgard.

Thor dropped his head but looked up with his eyes regretfully at Tahiti.

Odin responded to Tahiti. "Well that is good you feel that way, because that is a big reason for our separation. Okay, I need for everyone to gather around the head table. If you can get a seat great, if not then just find a place to stand because we need to get this meeting started." As Odin was speaking a loud shout sounded in the distance.

"Wahoohooohooo!!" Within seconds many of Tahiti's brethren entered into the throne room of Asgard.

"Brother!" Kanaloa the Hawaiian God of the sea yelled as he embraced Tahiti in a great bear hug. Odin smiled from cheek to cheek.

Tahiti looked around the room. "Brother where is Father Kane?"

"He could not make it," Kaou the Hawaiian God of laws and rules stated with wisdom. "If he leaves our Islands, his seat as our leader becomes vacant and anyone can challenge but as long as he remains there no other can challenge him by our laws."

"That is a good law." Odin said over the chatter of voices that had begun talking in the room.

"Brother!" Kaou yelled as he spotted Odin for the first time. Odin and Kaou had been great friends in Heaven and fought side by side in the war. They tried to tag team against Michael but Michael was just too much for them.

Odin and Kaou hugged and shook hands. Odin was more than excited to see his old friend. It took a while for everyone to get back to the meeting as Odin talked with his old friend. The other angels in the room all either reunited with old friends or were introduced to angels that they never knew since many were the offspring of the originals.

Finally, everyone was ready to meet and all either sat around the table or stood around it.

"Well, in respect to our new brethren who have now joined us, no decision has yet been made as far as the tournament that is to come, should there be one. There are four Demigods on The Creators team. Though they are only Demigods their powers are nothing short of ours."

"Four?" Loki asked appearing out of nowhere just mere feet from his father Odin's position at the head of the Table.

"You know this Loki so why ask?"

"Because unlike the rest of us, I have been keeping my eyes on the tournament."

"And what news, have you for the rest of us?" Odin asked with a look of pure concern on his face.

"Well to start things off." Loki said Laughing as he formed a chair out of thin air to sit down on. "The Demigods are only one beast from tying the tournament. With the son of Lucifer headed right for them this should be a battle worthy of tasting that human popcorn stuff while watching."

"What beasts is left?" Thor asked concerning himself with the current tournament for the first time since they divided from Lucifer's team.

"The Stone Tiger from Iraq." Loki said smiling. "Oh, this should be interesting." Loki continued. "He can turn into solid stone, turn invisible, bite through solid metal and can jump as high the sky. He is the size of giant bedrooms."

"Oh yes," Thor said. "That would be a battle I should love to see. What do you say brother, let us watch it together?"

"I will definitely watch it with you especially because of who else is involved." Loki said laughing out loud.

"Who?" Odin asked as he stood with his eyes flaring. He knew in his heart who it was and was beyond heated.

"Destiny." Loki replied not losing an inch of his smile.

"My daughter?" Thor said taken back as he sat down in shock. "I thought she was dead?"

"Oh no, not dead. I tried to kill her but Michael saved her, and raised her."

"It was you?" Thor rose to his feet and stretched out his hand for his hammer which came crashing through the throne room ceiling. Thor caught it as he flew towards Loki. Lightning flashed across his eyes as he made contact with his hammer hitting first, but instead of meeting any solid resistance the image of Loki disappeared.

The real Loki appeared in the throne room seconds afterwards. "Brother that was a long time ago when I was fighting against you and father. Besides you had abandoned her anyways."

"Yes, I did, but with the right to survive. I had no intention on killing her."

"Well than you have not failed in your intention's brother, because she lives."

"Father you must talk to The Creator, he cannot use Destiny against those Demigods-."

"Not against." Loki said. This time there was no smile on his face.

"Preposterous! The Creator cannot break the rules that he has set. They cannot add any Demigods or monsters to the tournament on either side."

"That is why he was able to. Lucifer cheated to attack one of the Demigods. He used two monsters that were not in the tournament. Michael used the opportunity to add three Demigods to the tournament.

"Three?" Odin roared. "Who are the other two?"

"That I do not know. I have never seen them before or heard of them."

"Puolghffgfsy that Lucifer." Odin said cussing.

"Okay well since The Creator wishes to strengthen those Demigods, we must weaken them again."

"Father." Thor said to Odin hoping to refrain his father's wrath.

"I am sorry son. What is done is done. The Father of all, the great and mighty Creator," Odin said sarcastically. "Will not change his mind. This is fine because I formed a spy many eons ago."

"Who is it brother?" Kaou asked Odin.

Upon hearing Kaou's voice Odin relaxed a little and his temper cooled.

"I am sorry son."

"I understand Father." Thor replied running to the throne and bowing before his father.

"The Creator gives us no choice. Either your daughter loses or we lose and spend an eternity in the lake of fire."

"I understand Father." Thor replied. Tears ran down his eyes. Odin had never seen Thor cry before. Thor's mother ran to his side.

Odin had no choice. He had to get on with the meeting. He motioned for his wife to take Thor away for the time being. Thor walked away and flew from the throne room. He was embarrassed that he shed tears in front of the other angels.

There was a looming gloom that shadowed over the throne room. Loki watched with sadness as his brother exited the throne room.

"You just can't change, can you?" Odin's voice boomed behind Loki. Odin's voice was not angry but disappointed and sad.

"I have changed." Loki said without turning around. "I knew he would attack at some point so I had my image smile to get his attack out of the way so I could gain your protection to tell the rest."

"Very well." said Odin. The same sadness was on his voice.

"You don't believe me?" Loki said more to himself than anyone in the room.

"No, I believe you." Odin responded surprisingly fast. "It is just my heart is heavy for my son Thor and my granddaughter Destiny. I swear that Michael is no brother of mine and never could have been to pull a move like this."

The room was silent no angel spoke everyone felt for Thor.

"Father." Loki said after some time. "You said you had a spy that we could use in the tournament against the Demigods but never finished. Who is the spy?"

"Oh yes," Odin said still heavy at heart. "Apollo."

"Wait I thought he was working for The Creator?" Loki asked confused.

"No. He is a spy for us. He has been playing a double agent on my orders long before the fall of the Greek kingdom and long before the fall of Asgard. He was made the king of the bottomless pit. He still is there and the creator does not know he is on our side."

Hades stood to his feet. "So, my nephew is not a traitor?"

"No, he is not." Odin patiently said. "We will use him in the next tournament. Apollo is very powerful and is the destroyer. We will set the next tournament up so that he will be set to destroy earth and the Demigods will have to save the planet. That is if everyone can agree to that?" Odin asked as he surveyed the room.

"Oh, that is a very good tournament." Poseidon said to the group of angels. Hades and Tahiti both nodded their heads yes and raised their hands to show they supported Odin's idea for the next tournament.

One by one everyone in the room showed their support for Odin's idea.

"Okay, it is settled then. Meeting adjourned." Odin said to his brethren. Immediately they all began conversing with each other again. Odin approached Aphrodites who had been quiet during the entire meeting.

"Is everything alright?" He sternly asked as he looked into her eyes as if he could see right through her.

"I just don't want to burn in any lake of fire," Aphrodites honestly replied.

"Neither do I." Odin told Aphrodite's. "We shall win our freedom. If this tournament and the next shall fail than we will still have more chances, four more chances to be exact.

Chapter Twenty-Nine

"Ho Young, he is coming!" Jasmine yelled.

"Where?" Ho young replied. The great Tiger had turned invisible again. Jasmine caused water to fly in all directions. The water hit the great tiger giving away his location. Jasmine used her powers to keep the water on the tiger so that they would be able to see it. Since that was the most that she could do because hitting the tiger with water did zero damage.

Marcus launched a light pole at the Giant Tiger. The pole broke into pieces and the Tiger sprinted towards Marcus. Jasmine caused the water to go into the Tiger's eyes as she had done with Leviathan but it did nothing to the Tiger. He had turned into stone again and was nearly upon Marcus.

Caleb sprinted just fast enough to get in front of the Tiger to distract it from Marcus. The tiger took the bait and Caleb kept his speed up just enough to stay out of reach of the Tiger.

As Caleb ran all of a sudden, he couldn't see anything. Everything was pitch black.

"What is happening? I can't see!" Caleb yelled.

Marcus realized Caleb was in danger and launched another Metal light pole right into the Tiger's eye. After he gained the Tigers attention by throwing a different light pole in front of it in between him and Marcus.

The tiger again ran towards Marcus. Caleb began screaming and running. Jasmine was watching the scene in frustration. They were losing control. Ho Young was flying above the tiger in the form of a giant flying dolphin. Jasmine did not have time figure out what Ho Young was doing.

She knew the Demigod David was there and in Caleb's head. Talitha had stayed back. She was supposed to be searching for

David but the battle and her brother had her distracted. They were in downtown Nashville and she knew nothing about Nashville.

John appeared in the sky next to Ho Young, which was not a problem since he and Destiny could both fly, but the sight of the Flying Dolphin completely caught John off guard. John and Destiny both started to fall but quickly caught themselves.

"Ho young what the heck are you doing?" John asked Ho Young.

"Hey John. Oh, what the heck man!? Are you alive?"

John raised his hand in the air and caused the wind to slap the dolphin Ho Young in the face?

"Ouch." Ho Young yelled as he flew in circles.

Jasmine looked up into the sky and tears nearly burst into her eyes. John was alive. She saw him flying next to a flying dolphin and some girl who she had never seen before. Whoever the girl was she was pretty and she could fly like John.

"Ho Young!" John yelled after catching a glance at the tiger. "Why are you a dolphin?"

Destiny was flying next to John wanting to hear the answer herself. "Oh man, that is simple. Dolphins are the smartest creatures alive." Ho young replied.

John shook his head in disappointment at Ho Young. "Ho Young turn into something that can hurt the Tiger."

"I don't know what to turn into because this tiger is different. It can turn invisible, into stone and can jump as high as the sky can go. He is very fast and strong." As Ho Young spoke the Tiger slashed at Marcus, but Marcus was too fast and caught its paw. Marcus slammed the Tiger over and over again about eight times before throwing it out to sea.

The Tiger was not affected at all and began to swim back towards them at an alarmingly fast pace. All of a sudden, the scene in front of John changed. He was back in Tartarus.

Michael had trained John for this. John formed a shield made out of air similar to the one that he used to block Jasmine from reading his thoughts. The visions of Tartarus immediately disappeared but John could tell that David's power was still working on everyone else. John focused his powers on all seven Demigods who were present. John paused for a second as he got a good look at the new Demigods that Destiny had told him about. John created the same shield of air around their heads as he had around his. Immediately he could tell that they were no longer seeing visions.

Things began to get out of hand quick for the Demigods. A hundred Davids appeared out of nowhere just as the Tiger reached the shore. John was flustered he did not know what to do. John turned invisible to give himself a second to think without being attacked. He surveyed the scene below. His friends were doing good and the tiger was attacking both the Demigods and all of the Davids.

As John watched the Tiger it hit him like a ton of bricks. He knew how to beat the tiger. John appeared next to Ho Young and teleported him away from the fight.

"Ho young, I want you to kill every David around the Tiger and the Tiger at the same time."

"How do I do that?" Ho young asked confused.

"Simple my slow friend. Turn into Hot Lava. Hot lava melts anything in its path including a stone tiger and nothing can hurt Hot Lava because it melts on contact."

"Okay." Ho Young excitedly replied.

"I am going to teleport you and after I teleport out immediately turn into Hot Lava."

"I understand." Ho Young replied. Next John Teleported next to Destiny.

"Destiny can you focus your lightning bolts on all of the Davids?"

"Yes, I can." Destiny replied with as much excitement as she could. John could see she was getting worn out from the battle.

Next John teleported to Jasmine. "Okay Jasmine, we need to find the real David who is nowhere near here if I am correct. Can you focus on the real one?"

"It will be hard because there are so many." Jasmine cried in almost a whimper.

As John was speaking the Tiger and all of the Davids by it became focused on running from the Hot Lava. As they ran, they began to fall one by one as they were electrocuted from lightning bolts raining down from the sky.

Others were passing out from heat exhaustion around Talitha as she pulled the heat down from the sun. Caleb was moving at light speed and his hands were no longer hands but very small hand sized miniature suns. They went right through whatever he touched. One minute a David would be standing there whole and the next half of their face was melted away, or a fist size whole would be in the middle of their chest.

Jasmine focused. She ignored all of the Davids screaming and focused past the minds of all of the Davids focused on running.

"I found him." Jasmine finally said after what seemed like ten minutes. "He is just beyond the cliff in an old abandoned cottage that sits alone on the hillside."

"I need to delay Ho young killing this beast until David is dead. Fly with Destiny. Dang I forgot, I have to go to in order to keep him from getting into the both of your mind's."

"Actually, we all can just go after David because the Tiger is gone. Ho Young scared it off." Jasmine said staring at John as if she had never seen him before. Destiny saw this and with all of the fake David's dead she quickly flew down to interrupt Jasmines conversation with John.

The six Demigods gathered around John as John teleported them to where David was hiding in the cottage. John made sure that they were all invisible before he teleported them, so that David would be caught off guard.

As the seven Demigods appeared at the cottage David was walking out of the door as he looked around. He had no idea that the Demigods were only mere feet in front of him. As David took one step forward, Marcus grabbed him by his bottom pant leg, and violently slammed David into the ground head first. David's brain scattered all over the ground.

"What the heck man?" John said jumping back with the other Demigods to keep brain juice and chunks from getting on their clothes.

Marcus did not answer. His face contorted in pure hatred and anger. John had never seen Marcus look the way that he was looking.

Team One wins. The Angel voice sounded.

"Dang, no fireworks?" John sarcastically said. John looked up towards the sky and yelled Lucifer's name and flicked him off.

Destiny stood next to John close enough to be a part of his body Jasmine noticed it. She read Destiny's mind and took a step back.

"You like him huh?"

Destiny looked at Jasmine with cross eyes, "Excuse me? What was that?"

"I didn't stutter." Jasmine said laughing. "You like him. I just read your mind."

Jasmine jumped back as a lightning bolt struck inches in front of her feet.

"What the heck?" Jasmine yelled as water burst out of the ground and blasted Destiny back. Destiny flew back at Jasmine with great speed as she flew a hammer appeared in her hand.

Fear showed on Jasmine' face. John jumped in between the two. And used his powers to separate them.

"Destiny you are better than this." John yelled hoping she would hear him. John barely saw it but he saw Caleb shoot a sun ball at Destiny. John used the wind to change its path away from Destiny.

With one swoosh of his hand John had Caleb in the air. John disappeared so his sister could not focus on him. John slammed Caleb hard on the ground. John appeared in front of Talitha and blinked three times quickly to use the power that he least liked and never used.

Talitha immediately fell under John's control. When John blinked three times at anything looking into his eyes, he gained mind control over them. A power he gained from his Demigod great, great, many greats, grandma Vanessa.

John turned towards the group his facial expression was even more fierce than the one that had just been on Marcus's face as he killed David.

"I know everybody better chill out right now. Don't you never let me see you sneak attack anyone in my group. You better understand me homie," John said as his blood boiled. "That is on my dead homies and my mom. You feel me?"

"But dude she was attacking Jasmine," Caleb earnestly replied.

"I know but after Jasmine used her power on her first."

Jasmine ran from the scene crying. All kinds of thoughts raced through her mind. Does he love her? Why did he defend her over me? Tears poured down Jasmines eyes.

Caleb ran after her to comfort her. "Are you okay?"

"No," Jasmine honestly replied.

"Why do you even like that dude? He obviously is a butt head."

"No, there is more to the story. I wish I could tell you, but..." Jasmine couldn't finish her sentence as she began to cry as hard as she could.

John released Talitha from his control by blinking three times again while looking into her eyes.

"Listen," John yelled to the group. "Number one rule in this group is we do not use our powers on each other."

"That is a little hypocritical, don't you think? I mean after you just used your powers on my brother?"

"I used it on you as well." John said looking fiercely at Talitha. "Your brother attacked Destiny while I was holding her back and that is not even a bit cool."

"Okay but she was attacking your girlfriend. That is pretty messed up on your part to defend another girl over your girlfriend."

"Ex-girlfriend." John replied. "I see you have not been informed on how Jasmine has been cheating on me for the last, who knows how long."

Talitha's eyes went wide. She had not heard about that. They never really talked about it and every time Jasmine or one of the others mentioned John's death, they mentioned him as Jasmine's boyfriend.

"Oh," was all Talitha was able to get out.

Marcus ran forward and embraced John. "Bro we thought you were dead."

"I know. I heard. I was badly injured and would have been killed. I was ambushed by two beasts not in the tournament sent by Lucifer. They caught me off guard and as I was dying. Destiny showed up and saved me. She is the daughter of Thor, as you probably noticed." John said relaxing his face finally and smiling for the first time.

"Wait. A descendant of a Demigod daughter of Thor, or an actual daughter of Thor?"

"Actual daughter." Destiny said feeling out the group to see if they if she was allowed to speak. "I was raised by Michael in a place in the sky called Eden."

“I thought Eden was on earth?” Marcus asked falling into more confusion.

“No, it’s not; it is a long story that we can explain some other time.” Talitha said as she saw Caleb and Jasmine walking up together.

“Is everyone ready to go home and wait for the next tournament?” John asked tired and worn from the battle. His eyes were heavy and he just wanted to go home and sleep.

Jasmine looked at John for a while, but John avoided looking in her direction. Jasmine wished with all of her heart that she had not cheated on John. Jasmine felt that John had not given Destiny his heart yet, so maybe there was still a chance.

“Really glad to have you back man.” Ho young said to John. “Oh wow, this is cool. If you die again, I can get a second chance to do my speech, because I messed up on it at your funeral.”

“Yeah, that is why I came back.” John jokingly said to Ho young while giving him a funny look out of the side of his face, and shaking with laughter. “I came back so you can get a chance to get your speech right at my eulogy.”

The group all except for Caleb and Jasmine laughed.

“No, no, no!” Ho Young yelled running in a circle and waving his finger no. “I didn’t mean it like that.”

“And if you mess up again, I’ll just come back from the dead and keep doing until you get it right.” Marcus had to turn around from the group because he was laughing so hard and couldn’t stop. Even Caleb chuckled a bit against his will.

The Demigods all joined together and John teleported them back to their home in Chicago. John opened the front door shortly after arriving. A homeless person was pushing an old abandoned store cart full of his possessions down the side walk. There were two kids playing each other in basketball.

A gang was hanging out on the driveway. John looked at them for a while. He had hung out with them a bit before finding out that he was a Demigod. John left the gang after they jumped his friend Tyrell who was also a member of the gang at the time. In a strange way he missed those times. They seemed simpler. Now instead of patrolling street corners he is part of a team that saves the world. It's amazing how quick things change. John thought to himself as he walked in the house.

The other Demigods were getting comfortable. Jasmine and Caleb were sitting on the stairs talking to each other and giggling about something. John wasn't sure how he felt about Caleb, but John did not like how Caleb tried to defend Jasmine especially if he thought that they were going out.

John found Destiny sitting down talking to Marcus. They were engaged in a deep conversation about her dad Thor and about Eden where she grew up. John didn't want to interrupt so he moved on.

As John rounded the corner and walked in the kitchen, Ho young had Talitha in tears as she was laughing at the things he was doing. Ho Young was doing impressions of movie stars.

John was happy that everybody was getting along. This was a completely different scene than just two hours prior. John couldn't believe that this tournament had taken so long. It had been two years. Which meant that they had been doing these tournaments for over four years already.

There was nothing to do but sit and wait for Michael to randomly show up one day and tell them about the next tournament, when it started, what it was, and whatever else he had to tell them.

About the Author

My literary passion began in fifth grade, thanks to my teachers, Mrs. Norton from Nordale Elementary, and Mrs. Dolan from Hunter Elementary. I remember being introduced to so many great books in both of their classes such as, *Sign of the Beaver, Sing Down the Moon, Johnny Tremain, Time Enough for Drums, My Side of the Mountain, Indian in the Cupboard, The Witch of Blackbird Pond* and many more.

That year, I began to read on my own. I found my passion in reading had greatly grown, and I sought out great books at the Noel Wein Library. *The Boxcar Children, The Hardy Boys,* and *The Goosebumps Series* were some of my favorite reads.

I later discovered the Harry Potter books when I was seventeen years old, and it was then that I began my writing career. Reading was my escape from reality. I thought to myself, if I can at least partially escape the hardships of life through reading, how much more in creating my own reality through writing.

www.ingramcontent.com/pod-product-compliance
Lightning Source LLC
Chambersburg PA
CBHW070610310726
48982CB00001B/36

* 9 7 8 0 5 7 8 7 6 1 9 8 5 *